CHOICES

CHOICES

Buck Young

Eggman Publishing, Inc.

Cover design and production: Susan McGlohon, The Pure Idea Workshop,
Nashville, Tennessee

ISBN: 1-886371-00-8

Eggman Publishing
2909 Poston Avenue
Suite 203
Nashville, TN 37203

DEDICATION

To Emily Brooke Young who lives 487 miles inside my heart.

CHAPTER 1

"Kerr, Stuart Kerr," he corrected the mailman who could have cared less. He went to the front porch and sat down. Now it was official. He was actually getting bills in the singular, and only from places like Georgia Power, and the telephone and the cable television people. No more ladies' ready-to-wear shops with pastel names. It was little consolation for the failed three-year marriage that now had him living apart from his wife and three-month-old daughter. He sat looking in the small fifty-year-old, frame house that wore the same address as his bills and tried not to remember the house on Lake Lanier that he could no longer call home. How had it all happened?

Life as a fraternity boy at the University of Georgia was something Stuart had anxiously awaited since the second grade. That's how old he was when his older brother had decided, among several options, to play football between the hedges. Those years of traveling with his parents from Columbia, Tennessee to Athens, Georgia that brought growing friendships and tailgate lunches, left little room in his mind for any other college alternatives. The ideology increased a few years later when his only sister enrolled in UGA and the trips to the classic city were now enhanced by his own puberty and the notice of campus assets that complimented tradition and spirit. No question, this was the life.

His decision was made by age eight, confirmed at thirteen and implemented at eighteen as a college freshman. The same week of registration, it was "Hotty Toddy" down the steps of the SAE house with his primary concern being that four years might not be sufficient time to embrace all of this new challenge. With more beer and belles than the average imagination could conjure, he vowed not to let academics interfere with his college experience. He quickly adopted an attitude that when a diploma is the simple goal, anything above a C is wasted, and that regardless of the situation, an individual must choose to elevate it to problem status by worry. So therefore, nothing was a problem to those who refused to worry; for worry free was problem free.

As a result, Stuart, whose brothers and sister had all pursued graduate degrees after finishing Cum Laude or Summa Cum Laude, would graduate.......Thank the "Lawdie."

But what about the girl? They had begun to date as sophomores, and that, too,

1

had followed a natural progression. The socials, football games and crowded road trips had placed them in a public relationship that allowed little time for one-on-one examination. They were having so much fun that the next step seemed obvious. Married only six months after graduation, the honeymoon lacked luster. A return to Gainesville moved them immediately into a house on the lake, two new cars and a small private plane, all paid for with parental cash. With the house fully decorated, the yard work maintained by hire, and average work hours for both, they were free to pursue their increasingly different interests. Too free, in fact. The marriage lacked glue. There was nothing in place to enforce compromise or require personal sacrifice. With nothing to work together for, they did not stand together well. By the time Brooke was born, the marriage had died a slow, peaceful death. Even the uncontested layout of the divorce was simple. So why did he now feel so empty?

It was not the loss of this person. He and his wife had never really lived as though they were married. She did her thing and he did his. That oversight had been allowed to become the rule rather than the exception while they were dating. The fact that it had gone on unchecked, now insulated him from what should have been a painful void. The once present love, infatuation or whatever it had actually been, was gone and he did not find room in this examination to cite that as the problem.

Family and friends had taken sides when the problems first appeared. He and his wife had lived on independent tracks so long, they actually had different friends, so that area was clear.

Stuart's job involved her father, therefore it had to be abandoned. But Stuart had replaced his former job with one of similar salary and duties. That consideration was now more in the asset column than the liability. He had begun to look forward to the new challenges these past two weeks had presented.

The material considerations were not tough to handle. The house and plane were gone, but he had his car. And, he was only twenty-five years old, therefore time was on his side. He decided to try to remain in Gainesville.

Brooke was a big part of his decision to stay. The mere thought of her was painful. Maybe he had not wanted anything above a C in school. Perhaps he had done a poor job of being a husband. However, he felt with intensity that he had wanted the role of father to be different from his other endeavors. His father was the only role model he had ever had and he was flanked by an angel.

Stuart wondered if maybe it would be better for Brooke if he just disappeared, especially if Brooke's mother remarried. He decided against that option. Selfishly, if not by any other logic, he decided that no one could ever answer the call of "Daddy" like he could. That was an unimpeachable office to which he had not been elected, but appointed, and he would do everything in his power to fulfill the privilege.

He walked inside to have a private moment. He felt awkward and closed the curtains in the small rectangular den. He wanted to pledge to God to be a good father, but he couldn't bring himself to do it. He felt he could not be trusted since he had broken his oath to God to stay married for life. He identified a second reason for his empty feeling. Not only had he let Brooke down, but he had backed out on a deal he had cut with his Creator. He was not able to ignore it or talk to God like it never happened.

The phone rang, waking him from his personal reverie.

"Hello." he answered.

"Hey, Darling."

"Hi, Mom. What's going on?"

"Well, we're just coming in from an adventure. Your daddy and I have been down to Pulaski to see the new colt. You know the mare that was so crazy with the last one she had, no one could get near her?"

"I remember. The colt nearly died."

"That's right. Anyway, when the time got close this year, Daddy asked that the Shaw twins take her down to their place and put her in a stall. He felt like it would be better for everybody."

"How's the colt?"

"Doing fine. But I called to see how your are doing."

"I'm fine, thanks," he lied. "I'm enjoying work and might even have a chance to be in your area in the next couple of weeks."

"Great. How?"

"My boss asked me to look at finishing up a project in Huntsville. I don't know much about it, but the foreman has had a heart attack and the job lacks a month or so being complete. I'll know more about it in a few days."

"That sounds good. Huntsville is not but a few minutes from here."

"About an hour and a half, I think," he smiled.

"No time at all. You should just move in with us and commute."

"I would like that very much."

"Wait just a minute, Daddy is trying to snatch the phone out of my hand."

"Hello."

"Hi, Daddy."

"Is your Mother trying to schedule your life as well as mine?" he asked, the sarcasm dripping from his voice.

"I don't see you fighting it," Stuart observed.

"It's easier to divide the decision-making up. Your mother makes all the little decisions like where we are going to live and whether or not we need a new car. I make the big ones, like when summer is going to be this year and whether or not to change the sunrise from the east to the north."

Stuart broke out in his first laugh in three days. "Keep me posted on any changes that might affect me in your decisions," Stuart laughed.

"Your mother wants to speak to you again. Is everything going alright?"

"Yes, sir."

"Do you need anything?"

"No, sir."

"Come home when you can. We love you."

"Love you, Daddy."

"Well, tell me what you're doing in your free time," his mother began.

"Not a whole lot," he admitted. "I don't have much free time, but what time I do have, I spend hiking. I've done a lot of camping, too."

"I sure hope this thing in Huntsville works out so we can get to see more of you."

"That would be nice.....excuse me, Mom, someone is at the door."

"We love you and will be talking to you soon," she completed.

"Thanks for the call. I love you too."

He hung up and walked to the front door. Instead of a visitor, he found his two-year-old black Labrador Retriever, Maggie. She was chasing a metal bowl around the porch with her muzzle in an attempt to get the last morsel of leftover pizza which Stuart had tossed out earlier that morning.

His mind returned to the phone call as he dropped himself down on the couch and picked up the remote control. He was thinking of his parents for the first time as being married people. He never had considered before that they were husband and wife. The reason may have been their success story in itself. He had always thought of them as a unit. And they had always been committed to that ideal. Had they not both said "we love you" and "we hope to see you soon."?

Not only that, he now realized that they had referred to him and his own wife in the same plural sense. They had truly become one entity and he could not imagine them apart. Fifty years as a "we" and not a pair of "I's." They had endured so much and somehow remained faithful to their promise. He, on the other hand, had failed and there was no other word for it. He could call it any justifiably elegant term he wanted, but it was a "shot at and missed" objective that would affect several people from now on. Especially Brooke, who would have a paragraph of explanation to follow her introductions for years to come. He had to admit that this situation had been elevated to problem status. Because, try as he would, he could not help worrying about it.

CHAPTER 2

It was Thursday night and Stuart went back to his motel room after an early dinner by himself. He sat down on the bed and picked up the phone and dialed the same number he had dialed when he had a stomach ache in school.

"Hello," the same voice answered. He was almost tempted to say, "Mom, I'm sick. Come get me."

"Hi, Mom," he said as he disguised his loneliness.

"Where are you?"

"I'm in Huntsville," he stated. "I start work on this interchange project tomorrow."

"Great. What time will you be home for dinner tomorrow night?"

He knew she cared about all the details, but she was one to cut through the fog if the sun wasn't doing it fast enough. He had learned somewhere in adolescence that his mother was no airheaded, Pollyanna blonde, but a woman of deep character who had earned the nickname "Sunshine" in spite of her share of storms. "I'll be there around 6:00," he conceded.

"Good. I'll tell Daddy to get a prime rib," she said. "Now, tell me what this project is going to be like."

"It's similar to the type work I was doing a couple of years ago. We are tying in the four access ramps of a road that wasn't previously an interstate exit."

"Is that on I-65?"

"Yes, ma'am."

"Well, that should be fun," she said reassuringly.

"It depends on how you define fun, I guess, but it will be nice to be out of the office this time of year. I'll see you tomorrow," he said and hung up.

Friday was typical and even without having been on this particular job site, Stuart knew what to expect. He spent the first hour getting to know the three equipment operators that had been left to do the finishing work. The subcontractor list had been provided him at the office. He met the engineer who represented the Alabama Department of Transportation.

He was told they would be on the job until 2:00 that afternoon. Fifty-hour work weeks were not uncommon and if a deadline was approaching the hours were even longer.

Lunch was freshly-made sandwiches from a small concrete-floor grocery that had opened a deli counter shortly after the project began. A bag of pork rinds complimented the sandwiches and both were washed down by either Nehi Grape or Coke. Stuart opted for the Coke.

"What time are we knocking off, boss man?" The question came from a truck driver who was hired as a subcontractor to haul topsoil.

"What's your hurry?" Stuart smiled.

"My ole lady says there's going to be something special going on at my house tonight, and if I want to get in on it, I'd better be there."

"Will 2:00 be soon enough?" Stuart laughed.

"Just right."

He finished lunch and asked the engineer to drive him to the D.O.T. office so he could review the drawings and get an idea of the drainage design.

They drove the small, winding road that led to the office and parked in front of the one-story, previously residential, building. After looking through the entire set of plans, Stuart thanked him and got back in his truck. It was after 1:00 and he stopped on the way to get a six-pack of beer and iced it in a flimsy styrofoam cooler. He drove to the loader operator first and slashed his index finger across his throat. He held up one finger which signified that the next load would be the last. He pulled over in the shade of a big sugar maple knowing that the word would spread automatically. Soon, the two working pieces of equipment had formed a tight line with the parked backhoe, and the operators were locking the cabs. He opened the tailgate and presented the rewards to the thirsty group. They drained the cans in a matter of minutes. He went back by the motel to get a receipt he had forgotten and started up I-65 North.

The late afternoon thunderheads caused him to think of what it would be like to be flying and riding the invisible roller coaster of thermals between the mountainous pillars of turbulence.

He drove his graduation present, a three-year old Cutlass, into the chert driveway and turned off the air conditioner as he lowered the windows on either side. It was that special hour of the day when the heat of a spring sunset does not have the intensity to hold its grip. The sunlight hit the old homeplace square in the face as it had countless times since a collection of slaves under the direction of master builder Nathan Vaught had completed their project in 1833.

The boxwoods on either side stood at ease in their sentry posture of welcome. The classic Colonial, three-story house that had been built and stood for nearly a century and a half had burned a few years earlier while the family was away at the time. The current structure was a two-story reconstruction of the original, using the actual original walls that survived the fire. They were eighteen inches of true masonry, consisting of two grades of brick that were manufactured on the site. If not as elegant, it was certainly more sound in its testimony that houses burn, but homes are fireproof.

He parked his car in the spot where he had first taken the wheel of a car and walked up the familiar brick sidewalk to the back door. He knocked and simultaneously opened the door into the large kitchen, whose warm brick walls and delicious smells were inviting and relaxing.

"Anybody home?"

"You bet we are," came the voice from around the door. "Get in this house!" The tall, blonde smiled with every feature of her face.

"Hi, Mom. You look great," Stuart returned.

Just then, Stuart's father came through the arched brick opening and into the kitchen.

"Welcome home, son," he said, thrusting out his hand.

"Thank you, sir." Stuart shook his hand. "The place looks like nice folks live here."

"Scotch?" came the rhetorical question.

"Yes, sir. Water, please."

They took their respective glasses and walked across the den to find a seat at opposite ends of the same couch.

"How's work?"

"The Huntsville project is new to me, but seems to be pretty straight-forward. I've done a number of similar jobs and the worst part of them all is the final stage which is where we are with this one. But I'm looking forward to being away from the office a few weeks."

"How are things otherwise?"

"I guess that's one reason I look forward to being away from the office. Maybe I won't notice the radical change in my life."

"How's Brooke?"

"She's great, thanks."

"It's amazing how much she looks like your mother already...funny how certain traits skip a generation and resurface."

"I hope she has Mother's attitude. She'll need her courage and positive outlook to cope with some of the things she'll face now."

"You've lost weight," he observed.

"I can't help but feel silly in a restaurant by myself. And cooking is something that I used to enjoy but I'm beginning to think I was doing that just to show off." Stuart responded.

"The transition is a day-to-day process. Some things you'll have to do for a while whether you want to or not. Let us know if there is anything we can do."

The plural was so natural to his parents, he couldn't believe he had never noticed it before.

"Thank you, sir."

"Why don't we have one more drink out by the pool?" his father offered.

They walked out the door Stuart had come in by and sat in the wrought iron chairs that overlooked the pool and garden.

"What are you going to raise this year?" Stuart asked, referring to the garden.

"I'm probably going to cut back quite a bit."

His mother laughed. "No sense in having to put up with those nasty letters from Green Giant about flooding the market with beans. Since there's just two of us, I think we ought to be able to get by on a couple of thousand bushels."

"I like to watch things grow," Stuart's father explained.

"I understand you have a new colt," Stuart mentioned.

"Yes, a real beauty. This one is made right from top to bottom. I hope we can get a break and get the attention of some of the right people early."

"Okay....what's this?" Stuart asked as he noticed a newspaper on the chair.

"What's what?" his mother said innocently.

"Helen...her picture's in the paper." Stuart replied as he looked down at the picture of his high school sweetheart.

"What does it say?" she asked.

"Shows her pictured with a small group. Some of them are kids. The caption says 'Big Sisters'." Stuart remarked.

"Yes, that's a volunteer organization that I've heard about."

"I didn't even know she was in town," he pondered.

"I heard from someone that she had moved back here when her mother died and sometime later, when her father remarried, she moved into her stepmother's house over on Nelson Street." "I'm going to get into some clean clothes." Stuart stated lightly.

He folded the paper under his arm then went downstairs to the bedroom that had been his since the fire. He had entertained most of his high school friends at one time or another in the twenty by forty subterrian bullpen. He tossed the folded paper onto one of the double beds and proceeded to pull things from his overnight bag directly onto his body as he changed clothes.

Dinner was a standing rib roast with the ribs in and enough trimmings to gain five pounds by merely discussing the meal. They sat at the rectangular table that occupied most of the kitchen from the stove to the hearth of a functional fireplace that had at one time been the only source of heat in a room originally designed to be something other than a kitchen. Homes of the era always placed the wood-fueled cooking operations in a separate building outside "the main house."

"What a meal. I won't have to eat again for a week," Stuart said as he pushed back from the table.

"You need that twice a day for a month to be able to stand up in a windstorm again," his mother said as she made her first comment about his appearance.

He ignored the comment. "I think I'm going to dig up something to read and fall asleep on purpose."

"Sleep as long as you want. Breakfast will be late in the morning."

"I need to get you..." his father began and was cut off abruptly.

"You need him to relax, period," scolded his mother.

Stuart gave his father an 'I'll see you in the morning and we can proceed' look and said his goodnights.

He propped up in bed and thumbed the "Outdoorsman" catalog while his mind wandered. His first thought was, in general, about dating. He wondered if, at his age, they were still called girls. And where could they be found now that they didn't travel in flocks called sororities? He allowed himself to picture one of those meat market bars with plastic smiles and hyper-extended hormones. The mental picture caused him to wince. He then thought of how nice it would be to talk to someone familiar. He looked without reaching to the folded paper on the other bed and back again to his catalog.

He was not in the mood to wrestle the sandman. Sleep was upon him in no time.

Stuart finished the tamping and checked the fence post for stability before reaching for the oak plank. Holding the plank against the post with the heel of his left hand, and pinching a sixteen-penny nail between his thumb and index finger, he struck three sharp blows with the hammer.

By sliding it up and down a couple of times he confirmed that the plank was not fastened to the post. "Like it?" he asked his father.

"Down a little.....okay, nail it,". "Better put three in it, son." his father advised.

Stuart repeated the process for the remaining three planks.

"That does it. I sure want to thank you, son."

"My pleasure," replied Stuart, as he put the tools in the truck.

"Momma should have us one of those 'prodigal son' brunches by now."

"Suits me just fine. Let's go," Stuart replied heartily.

They drove to the stable and parked the truck. Maybe it was imagination, but the aromas were evident before they opened the door.

"Nice light brunch, Mom," Stuart observed with delighted sarcasm.

They washed their hands and sat down to bagels, cream cheese, bacon, cheese grits, and quail along with a pitcher of homemade tomato juice.

"This is the last of the juice," she announced.

"Worked out nearly perfect. We'll have some tomatoes in a month or so," assured Stuart's father.

"I think I'll go to the grocery and think about putting something together for..."

"Mother, please, there's a law against child abuse. I think I'm going to sit and think, or sit and stare, or maybe just sit."

They half-heartedly cleared the dishes. Then his parents left in the truck together to run their errands. Stuart decided to go downstairs to change from the clothes he had been working in that morning. The paper on the bed once again caught his eye and he picked it up and took it to the kitchen. He looked at the phone and then at the picture.

If he gave her a call, he thought, she would be nice and it would probably turn out that she was seeing someone anyway. He dialed the number he had found in the phone book, confirming the initial of her first name and the Nelson Street address.

"Helen?"

"Stuart?"

"Yeah, uh, uh....." the recognition threw him. "How are you doing?"

"I'm fine. How are you?" responded the voice of his high school sweetheart.

"I'm fine...." he answered too quickly. He was beginning to wish he had calculated a purpose for the call. He could not believe he had dropped his guard in the second complete sentence.

"Bob told me about your problem. I'm sorry," she consoled.

He was glad she had not used the "D" word. "Yeah, well, it's been less than peachy for a while," he confessed. "Listen, I'm in town visiting my folks and I thought it would be nice to see you."

"That'd be great. When did you have in mind?"

"Well, I'm leaving fairly early tomorrow. How about this afternoon...say around four."

"I'll be right here," she encouraged.

"Good. I'll see you then," he confirmed.

"My house is on the right at the end of the first block coming from Trotwood."

"Okay, see you in a little while."

He went back outside and walked slowly around the yard. The pasture of grazing cattle, a clear picture in his boyhood memory, was now a neighborhood in the distance. His father's retirement plan had worked well. The large, once demanding farm now provided a good enough income so that his father enjoyed a gentleman's life. This was the only home Stuart had ever known. They had moved when he was five months old and had raised everything from cows and corn to four children, not to mention a little Cain in the past twenty-five years.

The stroll was soothing and the day was not as hot as the day before. He made the circle and found himself back where he had started at the pool. He went in and poured a glass of tea and decided to go for a drive since he had an hour before time to meet Helen. He wrote a simple note that he would be home around six and made no mention of where he was going.

The drive past his old high school and football stadium proved the adage that the only thing certain is change. The new fencing and reworked concession stand were much needed improvements, but they were testament to the fact that being indispensable is just an illusion of inexperience or even ignorance. Maybe that was one of the benefits to coming to the old antebellum homeplace on Sunnyside Lane. The core really had not changed much in the years he had known it as home, but changes were all around it. Some of the land was developed and the tractor was not run as often, but what it had instilled within the soul of young Kerr remained.

He passed the expanded hospital and turned left toward town. The two-story duplex was situated on the corner to which Helen had directed him, and he parked by the curb. The walk led to the small cottage-size porch and invited one into the arched doorway.

He knocked three times on the storm door. "Come in," she greeted and pushed the door with her entire arm. "Sit down. Would you like something to drink?"

"Yes. How about some tea? I worked outside with Daddy this morning and I never have gotten enough to drink."

"I bet you have had enough to eat....for what appears to be a change. How are your parents, anyway?"

"Fine, thanks," he said, ignoring the remark about his weight, and enjoying the casual feeling at being with someone who knew his family and him. "How's your dad doing?"

"He's fine and seems to be adjusting to his new wife." She returned from the small kitchen and presented Stuart with the tea then sat in a chair that faced the couch where he was sitting. "It's funny you called. Bob and I had just run into each other yesterday. It was the first I had heard of your divorce."

There it was and it made him squirm. "It has not been a bad situation as far as terms go, but I'll admit I've enjoyed plenty of things more."

"Change is rarely easy and this kind of pain will take time to heal."

She might have meant it as encouragement, but she had just brought his worst enemy into the picture.....TIME. He did not have a lot of strengths, but anyone who had known him long knew he was short on patience.

"Actually, it gets better every day," he told himself outloud. "And it will all be over in a few weeks," he said conclusively.

"What?" she perked up. "Is your divorce not final?"

"Semantics," he said, now looking directly at her. "We've been separated for months and the procedure should go quickly. We've agreed on the particulars and everything is so clearly defined that we don't have to physically do anything at this point."

"But there is still time to save your marriage," Helen said with excitement.

"Yeah, and there's still a way to raise the Titanic, and make it sail again," he said. "But, you can't bring back those people who died anymore than you can bring back the feelings two people must have for each other to make a marriage work."

She could tell that they were not completely parallel in their thinking and that this was too deep for the first ten minutes of a casual visit. "Well," she said lightly, "it wouldn't take that much effort to restore those twenty-five pounds you've lost."

"Is it that noticeable?" he asked.

"Only when there is a bright light directly behind you," she laughed.

Laughter. How nice, he thought. It had been infrequent and now, coming from someone who knew him and was a caring person, somehow gave him the same feeling one gets when the doctor prepares to convey test results, starting with a smile. He admitted to himself that the information she had was not complete and she was not an analyst, but he couldn't help feeling as if he was going to be okay. The next two hours were spent catching up. Helen was teaching now. Her mother had died three years earlier and she talked openly about it. They were able to talk fondly of her, for Stuart had held her in high esteem during his three year courtship with Helen.

They finished the visit and Stuart went home to enjoy another pleasant evening similar to the first.

Returning to work was somehow harder the next day. Perhaps it was the lack of definition in his life. Maybe it was that unpleasant stage of a project that winds down to the details. Details were not his first love even though attention to detail had been required of him from time to time.

He missed Helen, he thought. He missed something, so he decided to call Helen. After all, it had been twenty-four hours since they last spoke.

"I just...." he began his justification "wanted to talk to someone."

"I'm glad that you felt comfortable to call."

"I guess I'm not in the mood for solitude," he laughed.

"That's understandable. I've not known you to be alone since puberty," she reminded.

"Is there anything wrong with that?"

"Nothing wrong with having green eyes, until you try to deceive yourself and act like the unchangeable is changed. You're going to gravitate toward someone if you don't take charge of your emotions. That's why I think you should redirect your attention toward your wife."

Bang! Where had that come from?

"I don't understand," he stumbled....then recovered quickly. "Actually, Helen, *you* don't understand."

"I'm not trying to make it complicated. But, you're not divorced yet and therefore, have time to save your marriage."

"I don't think you realize how ridiculous that is."

"Stuart, do you remember your story of the Titanic? How you said it could be raised, but the people who were killed could not be brought back."

"Sure, I haven't been asked to bid on the project of raising it, but if we can send a man to the moon and a peanut farmer to the White House...."

"I'm glad I have your attention," she began by letting him know that his old tactic of covering the important with humor only served to illustrate that he considered this issue important.

"The analogy was inaccurate in a very critical area. You said your marriage was like a shipwreck on the bottom. In fact, it would be more accurate to say it is in the process of sinking."

"The only thing wrong with my analogy is that the design was off to begin with to the degree that the ship would have never been allowed to leave port if the proper inspections had been performed."

"Whatever. My point is, that in following this metaphor, it is undeniable that most captains begin to shift energies to abandon ship rather than save the ship. Marriage, in my opinion, is a ship that should not carry such easily accessible lifeboats."

"Why do I feel that this conversation is sinking?"

"You know..." she concluded, "no matter how platonic these type contacts are, I'm not comfortable with them. I don't want to be any type of lifeboat that invites you to abandon ship. You need to go and try to stop your ship from going down."

"Does that mean I shouldn't call you again?" he asked.

"Anytime you want to talk about how to keep it afloat."

"Thanks a bunch! I really didn't have anything else in mind, believe it or not."

"I'm not flattering myself enough to suggest otherwise. I just think this is about focus and options, and the fewer options, the sharper the focus," Helen clarified.

CHAPTER 3

It was suddenly Thursday night and Stuart flipped past the Atlanta Braves baseball game as he watched the television in his hotel room. He muted the sound and kicked the shoes off of his feet. Without rehearsing, he picked up the phone and dialed a number he had given out as his own for almost the past three years.

"Hello."

"Kathy?"

"Uh, yes." The voice indicated a questioning of the call.

"How is everything?" he awkwardly began.

"The court date is set, so all that's left is to be pronounced divorced," she reported kindly.

"I know all that. I was just wondering if we have done everything we could do."

The voice seemed to appreciate the question, but was confident in the answer. "We have been through counseling and everybody is in agreement that the marriage was a mistake from the beginning. You're probably just having second thoughts about the change."

"I guess. I just wonder if what we're doing is wrong."

"Wrong for who?"

"I don't know. It's not wrong for you to be able to pursue your interests which happen to be light years from mine. Maybe it's not so wrong for me to be me as opposed to trying to be someone else who neither of us likes," he stumbled.

"I know, but it's time we moved on," she stated simply.

"I suppose so." His voice picked up, "Is Brooke there?"

"Yes, you want to say hello?"

"Before I hang up, I do, but is it alright if I take her to do something a little different this weekend?" he asked.

"Like what?" she wanted to know.

"Outdoor stuff," he laughed.

"Sure, she would love it. But you're not going to do something like hang-gliding or repelling, are you?" Kathy checked.

"She's almost a year old. She could use a rush," he teased.

"The biggest rush she better get is from wetting her pants. Take plenty of diapers and let me know where you'll be."

"Chattahoochie National Forest," he answered.

"What time do you want to pick her up tomorrow?"

"About four. I'll call you if there's a change," he confirmed.

"Okay, here she is."

"Hey, Poco Pie," he spoke up cheerfully into a silent phone. He could only hope that she was recognizing his voice and smiling.

"I'm going to take you camping tomorrow," he continued. "I'll be...." he hesitated at the potential measure of the word 'home'. "I'll be back tomorrow afternoon. I can't wait to see you. I love you, Darling."

He hung up the phone and a tear dropped onto the receiver. The only comfort he had was the unsettling 'second-best' realization that Brooke had never known any different, since he had moved out when she was three months old.

****

"Where are you?" the familiar voice called out.

"I'm in my bedroom, Ruth. Come on in." Helen beckoned.

"I'm in," she pointed out.

"I can see that," Helen acknowledged. "Welcome."

"What are you doing?"

"Going through some old stuff," Helen accounted.

"I'm not surprised. I heard who was in this very house a few heartbeats ago." The know-it-all look was obvious.

"What do you know?" Helen asked without really smiling.

"I know that it was a guy and he was your old 'main squeeze' and my sources indicate he's available."

"Look," she stopped what she was doing and sat back on the bed. "Stuart is going through something tough and, frankly, I'm glad he felt comfortable enough to come by. But, believe me, there's nothing for you to get any ideas about."

"So, when are you going to see him again?"

"You either don't get it or you're carrying this thing too far." Helen argued.

"Okay, okay. But at least tell me the story."

"He was in town visiting his parents. He called and asked if it would be alright to come by. Of course, I said 'fine' and he did. End of story."

"How did he look?"

"Thin, actually, and a bit pale," Helen remembered.

"See, you noticed," Ruth said sassily.

"Oh, stop. I do remember what he looked like before."

"Tell the truth, Helen. Did you feel anything?"

"No. Not like you think, at least. I did feel for him. It was pretty obvious that this thing is hurting him. He was always so full of himself, not obnoxious, but a little cocky. It was....I mean, he was different somehow."

"What happened when you two stopped dating?" Ruth probed.

"We were being 'mature'," she mocked the operative word. "He's a year older and when he went to Georgia, I still had a year left in high school. We decided to date other people and when the year was over, I went to Ole Miss. That put us ten hours apart and pretty much cinched the split."

"Kind of off the subject, but I just happened to think that I never knew what you did right after school," Ruth wondered.

"I moved to Jackson, Tennessee, and did speech therapy. It was my major in school, so I took a job that involved two grammar schools and did pretty much what I'm doing now."

"What about guys? Why didn't you ever get married?" Ruth asked.

"There were a couple. In fact, one in particular. He was a great person, but it wasn't a fit, somehow. I don't think I was ever going to be ready to move to the Delta and talk politics," Helen recalled.

"You know I always felt particulars need to be in place, but the bottom line is the guy ought to cause you to lose yourself without losing your identity," Ruth rationalized.

"What have you been reading?" helen raised her eyebrows.

"Never mind, go on." Ruth ordered.

"After a couple of years, Mother died and I moved back here. I'm not sure if it was for Daddy's sake or mine, but I think it was good for both of us. I'll always be thankful for that time."

******

"Let's see, Poco Pie, have we got everything? Flashlight, fishing pole, grill, mattress, stove, hammock, tent and groceries. This stuff is as much fun to have as it is to use."

Stuart had not been camping in a month, and had never camped with Brooke. He had been awaiting the expedition with eager anticipation. He buckled Brooke into the car seat and left one diaper out just in case the drive and her regularity were out of sync.

They drove north on Route 60 to Cleveland, Georgia, and beyond the sign that welcomed his soul to the Chattahoochie National Forest. He parked in an area that contained spots for RVs and pads for tents including tables and lantern hooks. He unlocked the trunk and took out the backpack and brought it around to the passenger side door. He slipped into the pack as easily as a fireman pulls on a jacket. Next he hefted his precious cargo onto the top of the pack, which was now at the same level as his shoulders. This enabled Brooke's feet to come just around his neck. He took a bandana from his hip pocket, twirled it into a loose roll, and tied each end to a foot, forming a safety chain around his neck. The pressure of her ankles, plus her fistful of his hair, made it purely precautionary. He took a quick look and noticed only a few cars, which suggested a good possibility that the trail he was traveling today would be private.

They crossed the timber bridge and turned upstream toward the upper Desota Falls. The hike was one he knew well and the early summer evening promised comfort now. Later the temperature would drop enough for the appreciation of a fire. The awaited sights, smells, sounds, and feelings of the park did not disappoint Stuart. He was not sure if it was the mountains or just him, but the combination had a peaceful stimulating effect that he hoped Brooke would inherit so they would be able to share this, if not the ordinary, father/daughter things.

Stuart and his load approached the campsite that was as vacant as the trail had been. He popped the tent up in no time and decided to try the water.

"Come on, Darling," he beckoned with his outstretched hands. "Let's see how you like white water." He picked her up and removed her shirt and Barbie-sized jeans. The water was at its greatest contrast, in terms of temperature, at the beginning of warm weather, and it was bracing as he stepped in up to his knees. He looked across the small stream to a spot that had a smooth pocket in the shelf rock that would just accommodate a one-year-old bottom. He placed her in it as if it was a car seat and her eyes and entire face lit up. At first, she appeared anxious but soon sent signals of sheer delight.

The diaper anchored her as the stream immediately saturated it, and she splashed up and down, flailing her arms like naked wings. Stuart later placed her upon a large nylon ground cloth and threw a sweat shirt of his own around her after changing the seven-pound diaper. In a matter of a few minutes, he had a fire going. He pumped the small fuel stove and set a blue speckled pot on its lighted burner. He then emptied powdered hot chocolate into a single cup and sat back on the tarp. Brooke reached for him and he responded by propping himself against his pack in a lounging position, placing her on one thigh, nestled into his chest and arm. The sweat shirt warmed her and the radiant heat of the fire made their faces tingle.

"You know, Darling, when you stare into a TV set, your mind goes into neutral, and you see only with your eyes. On the other hand, when you stare into a camp fire, you see with your mind and sometimes, if you're lucky, you can get a glimpse of your soul."

She sat motionless and brought her eyes to half-mast. The water was showing some steam at the pot's spout and he shifted himself in order to be able to pour. The metal cup of the same pattern had cooled slightly, which made the drink safe for Brooke. They resumed their position and the fire stayed on duty.

"I hope you won't be offended if I don't join you in the strained peas we brought. I rather had my mind set on the T-bone."

He raked an indention in the fire and dropped the small rectangular grill level on two preset stones. The coals he had pulled underneath with his poker were silver and gave the appearance of velvet as the tiny air currents brushed their surface in alternating directions. He spread the coals evenly and tossed the inch and a half cut on the grill. It responded with instant sounds and smells. He pulled the tongs he had brought out of the lower compartment of the pack and slipped a glove onto his left hand.

"I prefer my steak without the seasoning of singled knuckle hair," he explained as he flipped it to confirm the progress it was making. Brooke watched with a bright look in her eyes.

"I guess that makes you hungry just looking at it," he observed. He reached into the side pocket of the pack and produced a jar of baby food, whose contents were the color and texture of freshly mown grass.

"Doesn't this look wonderful?" He rolled his eyes and stabbed her spoon into the jar.

Brooke stiff-armed the attempt to get it into her mouth.

He scratched his jaw and flipped his steak. Another attempt was met with more objections than the first.

"I don't blame you, Poco, but this is all we have."

She reached for the hot chocolate and he obliged. "You need to hurry up so I can eat my T-bone when it gets ready."

The next thrust of a full green spoon landed closer to her ear than mouth. He put the jar down and took his steak from the grill and cut into it. Her crystal blue eyes danced and she reached out.

"I don't learn so fast, do I? This is going to have to be our secret." He cut a tiny portion and mashed it with his fork before giving it to her.

There was no objection or hesitation. She fell back against the pack in the flannel pajama one-piece he had dressed her in and ate a fourth of the steak.

"Time for bed. We've got a big day planned tomorrow. Can you say 'free climb'?" he laughed.

CHAPTER 4

Stuart walked into the small, brick office building and into his personal office with a simple wooden desk, purchased for practicality rather than aesthetics. He sat down and pulled out a business card holder file and turned to a new addition.

The door opened and he guessed, "Ken?"

"Morning, Stuart. How did your weekend go?"

"Great, thanks. I took my little girl to the mountains and we went camping."

"Listen, my wife and I had some time to talk Saturday and we came up with something I want to talk to you about when you have time."

"Sure, let me make one call to catch this guy in Alabama before he gets out of pocket. That job is ready for grassing on the slopes and I want to get it hydroseeded before it gets too hot this year."

"Go ahead." Ken sat in one of the two chairs in Stuart's office and crossed his legs while Stuart made the call.

"How is the Huntsville project going?" Ken asked.

"It should be finished in a few weeks."

"How about the airport job?"

"That's why I'm hanging around here for a couple of days; plus, there's a small job in Dawson County that I was going to pick up the drawings on when I went through."

"Where did you get that information?"

"They advertised for bids in the Gainesville paper."

"Well, this all fits with what I wanted to talk to you about. I started this company twenty years ago on a shoestring budget when I didn't have enough money to pay attention. I lease–purchased a motorgrader and had to drive it from job to job because I didn't have a truck to haul it. Now things are going well and I'm tired of eighteen hour days with seven day weeks. My point is, you had some good experience before you came here and I think I can offer you something you'll find interesting. Have you ever wanted to own a piece of the action?"

"Sure. But there's something you need to know about me. I have, as you know, had a change of address and marital status lately. I would fit more into your first year category of being independently poor, so I wouldn't be in a position to buy much of anything I couldn't eat in the same day."

"I know, I know. I've been married three times. You'll come out of it okay. I really didn't necessarily mean a cash purchase. Have you ever heard of 'sweat equity'?"

"In theory." Stuart nodded.

"Well, I guess you can always tell a college boy but you can't tell him much." The twinkle in Ken's eye prevented any resentment Stuart might have otherwise felt.

"I feel that we can come to terms without any problem so long as the rest of the necessary items are a fit. When I was coming along, we did anything we could to stay out of debt. That would probably go against the things you learned in school about leveraged buyouts, ESOPS and zerodown acquisitions."

Stuart sat up more attentively. He could not believe this jean and boot, eighth-grade education was fanning this verbal six-shooter at him. "What?" he asked.

"I remember your resume saying you had a degree in economics, so I thought you'd know what I was talking about."

"I, uh, do...it's just that I thought..." he hesitated.

"That I didn't have much use for school?" Ken asked.

"That's what you've said." Stuart answered.

"Well, I never said I didn't believe in reading. I learned to read when I was four and count before then. Anyway, I was saying that those things can be worked out. I wanted to talk about who all rows this boat. Gary has been with me for ten years and I don't know where I'd be without him, so I want him in the loop. He has shown me that there is nobody better at melting red clay hills on a grading job than he is and you know how important production is to a job."

"You don't have to sell me on Gary."

"Stuart. The two of you would make a great team."

"Put me in Coach, I'm for it. But, let's talk more about the mechanics, if that's okay."

"Typical bidder's response, everything has to balance," Ken's eyes smiled. "This business is unique in that every project has its own profit and loss results. I own the equipment these jobs now use, or what I should say is, the corporation owns it and we could set a rate that each job would pay for each piece of equipment. The money would be paid to me personally, and I would transfer stock on a preset value basis. Meanwhile, you and Gary would be expensed to the job at your current salary."

"So, the advantage for you is you get to be hard to find, so long as things are going well, and you've developed a retirement plan that will take several years to complete." Stuart surmised.

"You catch on pretty good. I'm glad to see they didn't siphon your brains out and put just book-learning back."

****

"You've improved more than just a little, Helen," argued Ruth.

"Thanks. I used to play a good bit several years ago," Helen explained, as she wiped her brow and put her tennis racket in its case.

They shouldered their rackets and began walking past the old home that was now at the north entrance to Woodland Park.

"You know, Helen, I was thinking how you would be a natural at leading the next topic in our Bible study. We've been meeting at your house for a long time and I'm not the only one who thinks you ought to be the next leader."

"I've done it before. It was in Jackson, but they were younger and it was a part of being a volunteer leader for Young Life."

"What do you think?" Ruth asked.

They crossed the wooden bridge over the railroad and turned down a cottage-lined street with old trees and neatly mown lawns. They walked past a young family in their front yard sitting in the grass and playing some kind of make-believe game with the tiny cones of an old hemlock tree. Ruth's stride broke to a slower pace and she did not disguise her prolonged look. "Do you ever picture yourself as a wife and mother?" Ruth continued without mentioning the obvious scene.

"Yes, I have to say I do. Why?" replied Helen.

"I don't know," Ruth answered lightly. "I just wonder where we will all be in five years."

"I think it's wonderful that we don't know. I'd probably spend so much time in dread that I'd forget to live life."

"What kind of life do you want to live, Helen?"

"Just the one that's mine, and I don't know if I can find it all by myself."

CHAPTER 5

The following day Stuart picked up Brooke and started the five-hour drive, choosing what he thought to be the scenic route on Highway 53 across Lake Lanier and into Dawson County. The midsummer day was hot and he hoped there would be an improvement as he moved into the higher elevation of Tate, where he pointed out the marble quarry to Brooke. She acknowledged with a passive stare. They finally joined I-75 south of Dalton and WFOX began to fade. Stuart punched the scan button. The variety of rock-and-roll to deep country cycled through completely and his attention drifted while the melody continued. A talk show was concluding and he pushed the button that would hold the station.

"We've been talking with teacher and author, Larry Burkette, about his series called 'Business by the Book'. Is there anything you would like to add before we say goodbye?"

"Just that the important thing in all of this is that God is not departmentalized out of our businesses even though we don't sing hymns as part of our daily routine. The purpose of business should be to glorify Him and only cite profit as something we must pay close attention to, rather than live for."

"Thank you, Larry. This is WMBW, Chattanooga. Up next is the continuation from yesterday's Dr. James Dobson interview, 'What Wives Wish Their Husbands Knew About Women'."

Stuart's mind took him back to his freshman year at Georgia. It was spring and the last real date he and Helen had had. Being three-hundred miles apart, they had agreed to see other people he recalled, and both had done so. The date was a big spring weekend with a band and parade and costumes. Magnolia was the party of the year and it lasted three days, officially. Some got a headstart and went academic AWOL as early as Monday. He now remembered their conversation in detail:

"Stuart, you've changed," she had complained. "I don't know exactly how, but you seem consumed with all this."

"I think it's just that you are still in high school and have not had a chance to go through a situation where you are not at the dinner table with your parents every night," he had excused.

"I mean your mind is constantly on things I don't understand," she tried to explain. "You have a stock broker and watch the Market like some Wall Street nerd.

You told me a few weeks ago that you spent all day in the basement of the library going through microfilm of the 1929 newspapers for some crazy reason."

"I was trying to see what it would have been like to live the six-month period prior to the Crash. I wondered, if I had been there during that time, could I have predicted it," he had defended himself.

"You used to be so....free and lighthearted except on the Friday night games you lost. Now, I don't really know you."

Brooke brought him back to the present with her voiced opinion for a change.

"We'll stop in a minute," he appeared.

She seemed to understand. At least she calmed down at his touch.

"You can look right through a guy, Poco. Heaven help the poor guy that falls for you, if he has anything to hide."

The grin was hidden by the passy but nothing could disguise the dimples on either side that caved in when her eyes lit up.

Two and a half hours later, they parked under the limbs of the old locust that extended over the boxwoods defining the driveway. He carried Brooke with one hand and opened the door simultaneously with the other.

"Look who's here!" came the cheerful voice of Stuart's mother. "Come here and see your Mommy Ann, you precious girl."

Brooke lit up instantly and lurched to be gathered into the arms that had trumped a hundred stormy nights.

"How do you do that?" realizing he might as well have asked a bird to teach him to fly.

"Do what?" his mother asked innocently.

"Nothing. Where's the old man?"

"He's in his chair reading. Let's go tell him you're here." She reached automatically into the designated drawer and produced a treat that suited Brooke as though she had phoned ahead for it.

★★★★★★★

"Thanks, again, Helen."

"Thanks for coming, Debbie. I'll see you next week if not before."

"You did a great job, Helen."

"Thanks, Beth, I just sort of followed the material."

"I will definitely be back next week."

"You did great, Helen," the final comment came from someone seated. "I might even say I told you so."

"Thanks, Ruth."

"I can't imagine you in five years. I think God is preparing you for something else."

"Don't let it consume your thought life. Besides, I think God is preparing us all for something else," she said lightly.

"But I can see it in you. You are so....together. You are not swayed by the stuff that causes others to question and compromise. You're special alright, and not just to me. You're respected by a lot of people and I can't help thinking that there's something out there with your name on it."

"I appreciate the complement, but you need to know I am very content with things the way they are."

The phone rang and Helen excused herself to answer it.

"Hello."

"Hi, Helen."

"Stuart, where are you? You sound like you're next door."

"I'm in town and I've got Brooke with me. Do you think it would be okay for me to come by tomorrow for a minute?"

"Sure. How about late morning?" she narrowed.

"Okay. I'll see you around 11:00."

"Well?" demanded Ruth.

"That was Stuart and....," Helen attempted.

"He's coming by in the morning at 11:00. I can't wait to meet him. Listen, Helen, how do you expect me to advise with you unless I meet this guy? Here's the deal." She scrambled to hold the floor as she picked up Helen's tennis racket. "I'll come by around 11:15 to return this racket and I won't stay."

"Whatever," Helen softened with some ineffective disgust.

****

Stuart laid the sleeping Brooke in bed. He covered her and reflected upon the many nights in her life that he would not be able to kiss her goodnight. This was not the way the privilege of parenting was supposed to be played out. He walked away from the crib and had a second thought. He picked her up and placed her instead in his bed and climbed in. He propped himself up on his elbow and watched her sleep until he could not hold his eyes open either.

The next morning a drizzling rain fell, and he turned to find Brooke was gone, but realized his mother had taken her. He took a quick shower and went upstairs to see that he had slept through the first shift of breakfast and Brooke was sitting with both legs crossed on the counter with her whole fist in a jar of strawberry preserves. The evidence on her face from ear to ear and chin to eyebrow testified that the process had set fun as its objective.

"Good morning," he greeted his mother and daughter. "If we could get a little larger jar, we might get her whole head to go in," he laughed.

"She has had a good breakfast of...."

"Crepes de la Mommy Ann," he interrupted with a smile.

He grabbed a bagel and a piece of bacon and took a swallow out of the milk carton.

"Don't you want some cream cheese?"

"No, ma'am, thanks. I think I'll have some strawberry face paste." He kissed Brooke and smacked his lips before disappearing in the direction of the master bedroom.

He and his father walked through the kitchen and offered their explanations about how critical their mission was to the farm and maybe even to the country, and pledged to be back in an hour.

"I'm glad we have a chance to talk," Stuart began. "Ken has offered to transfer forty-nine percent of his business to two of us. There's a guy named Gary that has been his general superintendent for several years. The idea is that Ken would retire and I would do the bidding and purchasing, while Gary would oversee the building of all the work."

"How are you going to pay for the stock?"

"Sweat."

"Unusual, but legal tender, I suppose. How does it work?"

"We set a value on the stock and a value on the equipment. As we complete a project, we tabulate its profit or loss after making an allocation for the equipment, which Ken owns."

"Sounds reasonable, so long as the values which are set are fair."

They backed up to the dock and went to the front door of the dog pen.

They went through the ritualistic process of discussing the options available for killing fleas on dogs, fleas in kennels, and fleas on folks.

The rain had stopped as they left the building and they climbed into the truck and resumed their conversation on the way home about the best way to squeeze profit out of a grading project. They walked back into a different scene of a clean kitchen and Brooke sitting in the same spot on the counter, this time cutting out thimble biscuits.

"Mom, I'm going to change her into one of those little lolly jumpers. We're going visiting."

He drove to the same spot along the curb in which he had parked before and carried Brooke to the door. "Is anybody home?" he called through the screen door.

"Stuart, she's a doll." Helen exclaimed as she examined the child. "Look at those blonde curls."

"Thanks. How have you been doing?' Stuart asked.

"Fine. Work starts back soon and I've been putting materials together for that."

"That's speech therapy?" He refreshed his memory.

"Yes, for a couple of elementary schools."

"Excuse me, I think I need to make arrangements for her to lie down." He gestured at Brooke who was sitting propped against the base of the secretary in the hall. "She's on Eastern Time still, and has been in "Mommy Ann Land" all morning without a nap."

"Come on into the front bedroom." She got up and opened the door. "I can put some pillows on either side of her on this bed. She ought to be fine."

They walked back into the den and sat down.

"So, how about you? You seem to have found your way back to the table," she smiled.

"Well, I'm not having to work out of town as much and I'm slowly remembering how to cook."

"Knock, knock," called the voice from the storm door.

"Who is it?" asked Helen.

"Ruth," was the response of the person now standing inside.

"Ruth, meet Stuart Kerr, an old friend."

"Hello, Stuart."

"It's nice to meet you," he smiled.

"Nice meeting you." She turned toward Helen. "Let me show you one thing, Helen. I can go out the back door."

They walked into the kitchen together and Ruth let the swinging door close silently. Ruth's eyes sparked and her mouth smirked. "Why is my Bible teacher a filthy liar?" she asked through clinched teeth.

"What do you mean?" Helen whispered.

"You said 'weak, gaunt, and pale'."

"I said thin. But he's regained some weight."

"So now that you have him off the critical list, are you okay?"

"What do you mean?" Helen challenged.

"I'll spell it out. He's six feet four, bronze and cut like a marble statue with a knee buckling dimple."

"He's okay," Helen conceded.

"Okay? Camaros are okay. Mustangs are okay. There is a Dino Ferrari in your den!"

"Shhh.... His heart is what concerns me. It's broken."

"Then get some glue for him and have your hormones checked."

"You have to be going." Helen pointed to the back door at the end of the kitchen.

"Pluck your eyebrows, you look like a wolf. And put on some cologne. If you can't think like a woman, you can at least smell like one."

"Bye." Helen pushed her to the door. She stopped in the bathroom on the way to the den and leaned over the sink to inspect her eyebrows. She picked up the cologne and put the bottle down without using it and let out a sigh.

She walked in and found an empty chair where Stuart had been seated. She turned to see him as he stepped out of the front bedroom and carefully closed the door behind him.

"I was just checking on my Poco Pie," he explained in a low voice.

"Who? What did you call her?" Helen asked.

"Oh, it's a silly thing, really. Poco means 'little' and pie is the Greek symbol in economic equations for profit. I guess she is the first thing that's happened to me that's pure profit."

"That's nice."

He and Helen talked of their careers and Stuart had begun to explain his new business deal when a cry from the bedroom interrupted him.

"That didn't last long," he observed by looking at the clock.

He rose and retrieved Brooke off the bed.

"She is kind of fouled up, I guess. It's time for her to eat something and I need to take her home. I could leave her at Mother and Daddy's for her afternoon nap, if you want to ride down to the Trace and hike for an hour or so later."

"Stuart," her eyes broke contact. "I want to be up front about this. I think you should be working toward restoring your marriage and...."

"Wait a minute! Wait a minute!" he demanded holding up his finger. "My divorce became final this past week."

"I had no idea," she said emptily.

"I don't think you're willing to accept this, but the lines are down," Stuart explained.

"It's your job as the husband to put them back up," she argued.

Brooke started arching her back and crying.

"I guess I'd better get her home," he said calmly.

"Thanks for coming by and bringing her."

"Sure, see you later."

"Bye, bye."

CHAPTER 6

Stuart stared blankly at the Saturday morning choices as he sped through the cable channels with the remote control. He had just run three miles and was bored at the day's prospects. He picked up the phone and quickly punched the numbers.

"Joe?" he said after the hello.

"Hey, Stud."

"Let's bust out to the mountains."

"Can't. I'm out to dinner with the hag and two more couples." Stuart could hear Linda's background objection to the label of "hag." He was also able to hear more conversation mentioning his name.

"Look, Stu, Linda had an idea. You remember a girl named Elise who finished at Brenau last year and stayed in the admissions office?"

"Not really. Well, maybe," Stuart said half-heartedly.

"I can tell we're not talking about the same girl. Elise is a traffic-stopping piece of work."

"Where are you going with this?" he asked, still melancholy.

"What if Elise were able to join us tonight at Rudolf's?"

"I don't know, Joe..."

"Fox," Joe protested.

Stuart stopped to think of the evidence of Joe's taste in women and how it was quite trustworthy.

"Come on, Buddy," Joe broke the silence. "It has been a month since your divorce and I don't know of a single date you've had."

"There haven't been any," Stuart said flatly.

"I'll confirm with her and get back to you."

"Okay."

****

Stuart drove up at 6:00 and pulled to one side of the driveway.

"Hey, man," came the greeting from the deck in the back yard.

Stuart walked around the end of the house and into the backyard.

"What's the news?" Joe asked.

"Nothing special," Stuart replied, stepping onto the low deck. "I appreciate what you're doing tonight, in spite of my attitude."

"It's not like you have a disease." He turned his head toward the door leading into the kitchen. "A beer for our honored guest, Hag."

Joe took a couple of steps toward the door to get the beer himself and was stopped short by Linda coming out with a beer in her hand. She handed it out to him.

"Who's going tonight?" Stuart asked casually.

"The Fredricks and us and, of course, you, and Elise is going to meet us there," Joe answered.

"I thought you said two other couples this morning," questioned Stuart.

"The Burtons cancelled at the last minute," said Joe.

Stuart took a swallow of his beer and held the dark bottle up to the evening's faded light. "Linda?" was his one word request for an explanation.

Her answer was non-verbal, but clear as she looked into his eyes.

"I don't blame them, Linda. It's probably tough on everybody to know what to do. We were couple friends and now one of the couples is a pair of singles. I hope this is not uncomfortable for you." He continued to look at his beer bottle until the final word when he sincerely looked at Linda.

"It's your business," She assured him. "Besides, I'd do the same if it were Cathy over here to be 'fixed up' with someone."

"Let's go," Joe interrupted. "The Fredricks will be waiting and they're not getting along so great these days either."

The threesome got into Stuart's car and drove toward town across Thompson Bridge. Stuart listened as Linda reminded Joe that he was teaching children's church tomorrow, and inquired as to his preparation. The drive down Green Street was impressive. Either side offered stately old homes that were now converted professional offices with manicured lawns and walkways. The evening lighting was complimentary to the beautiful front elevations of the homes. About halfway between the civic center and the post office was the newly renovated two story Victorian that now housed a fine dining establishment of Atlanta influence, complete with male servers, linens and escargot. Stuart drove into the driveway and they surrendered the car to a waiting valet. The short, but wide, rock steps led to a heavy door on wrought iron hardware.

They gave their name to the hostess and were told that no one else in their party had arrived. They then climbed the old stairway that led to the lounge. The authentic multipane windows along the wall coupled with the walnut stained wainscoting gave the room a light elegance. The twilight delegated its responsibility steadily to the single bulb table lamps. They seated themselves and Stuart chose the window chair with its back to the wall. The waitress seemed to appear from nowhere.

"Can I get anyone anything from the bar?"

The two men looked at Linda to order first. "Blush, please," she nodded.

"It's still white whiskey weather," began Joe. "I'll have a Vodka tonic."

"And you, sir?" the waitress asked of Stuart.

"Scotch. Water, thanks,"

"Nervous, Stu?" teased Joe.

"No, I guess I really haven't thought of this as an official date. I mean I didn't call her and I didn't pick her up." He changed the subject with his shift of position toward Linda but a figure in the doorway caught his attention.

Stopped just inside the large, cased opening was the tall, brunette with Malibu skin tone that was to be Stuart's companion for the evening. Her long, and most likely shapely, legs were covered by navy tailored, slacks. The full cut, lightweight, cable cotton sweater was broadstripe navy on white and softened her confident chin. Her full mane of shining hair was pulled to one side and clasped in place with a large brass barrette. Joe had turned to get her attention. She half smiled and began to make her way through the obstructing tables with a walk that would have taken three choreographers to analyze.

Before she was close enough to hear, Joe turned back to Stuart and said, "I've reserved this portion of the program for questions." Then more articulately, "Close your mouth, Stuart."

She approached the table and Stuart stood, "Elise?"

"Yes," she stuck out her hand and gave him a full grip handshake.

"I'm Stuart Kerr."

"Nice to meet you. I hope I haven't kept everyone waiting."

"No, the others aren't here yet. How about a drink?"

"Sure. Dewars and water, please."

Stuart excused himself and made the round trip to the bar. He returned with her order and sat down beside her. "I understand you are in the Admissions Office at Brenau."

"That's right. At least, for the time being. I'm interviewing in Atlanta with some marketing firms. That was my major and what I want to get into. How about you?"

"I'm a poet," he stated flatly, remembering the old days of making ridiculous the mundane small talk of college socials.

"Just my luck," she sighed. "I understand they are less than masculine."

"Typical of the iambic pentameter guys. I lean more to the sonnets."

"Intellectual, I suppose." she chuckled.

"No, actually, I was raised on a farm, so they are a nuisance in our art. I call them country sonnets," he was now enjoying this little sparing match.

She was suddenly distracted. "Excuse me, there is someone I need to speak to," she explained as she stood.

Stuart stood instinctively.

"Are you going somewhere?" she asked.

"No, I, uh....need to stretch my legs. Writer's cramp, you know."

"Good. I'll be right back."

****

"Hello?"

"Helen?"

"Yes?"

"You'll never guess who this is."

"Yes, I will," she stalled and thought of how she disliked this game.

"I'll give you a hint," the voice volunteered.

She thought without speaking that a name would be a nice start.

"You can call me Reverend, now," the voice said.

"Andrew?!"

"That's right."

"Where are you?"

"I'm in town for an interview."

"What kind of interview?"

"I'd like to tell you all about it. Would it be okay if I brought a pizza over?"

"Sounds great. How about seven?"

"See you then."

CHAPTER 7

Helen hung up the phone and showered quickly. She grabbed a pair of jeans and a tee shirt from the closet. Andrew was ten minutes early and she was not surprised. She greeted him with a one-armed hug and ushered him into the house.

"I've finished seminary and I sent out several resumes. There is a church here that seems interested and I'm going down tomorrow morning to sit in the congregation and see what happens."

"So, if you took the job, you'd be living here in town?" she caught herself in the silly situation.

"That's right. It's been a long time since I was here." His voice indicated memories they had in common. "By the way, Mom told me to send you her best."

"That's sweet. I'll never forget the weekend I spent with you a couple of years ago. She cooked all that Cajun food and I ended up getting as sick as a goat. I stayed in the bathroom more than the living room. I can't remember ever being so embarrassed."

"You could do no wrong in her eyes," Andrew reminded Helen.

****

Sundays just didn't seem like Sundays anymore. The late afternoon was a lonely time for a single man. It was not that Stuart minded being alone....it was just that a balance would be nice. He heard the noise of a car engine over the Atlanta Falcon's game on television and convinced himself he was mistaken.

"Is anybody in there?" the voice called from the front porch.

"Come in, Elise," he offered, combing his hair with his fingers.

"I was on my way to Atlanta and thought it would be nice to have some company. Want to ride?"

"Why not?" he accepted. "Let me grab a shower...Would you like a Coke or something? I'm afraid I don't have much to offer."

"That's a matter of opinion," she said with her eyes cut in his direction.

He walked through the door joining the den and bedroom and closed it behind him. He continued through the bathroom door and closed it. He unzipped his pants and hesitated, then reached and locked the door. He sped through the shower, but did not shave. Bluejeans, white golf shirt, no socks and topsiders. His hair was combed only with his fingers and the cologne was waived.

"Ready?" he asked as he walked back out to the den.

"Let's roll." She opened the front door and led the way to the red convertible. She situated herself in the driver's seat and with one motion, slid a pair of sunglasses from the dash to her nose. One glance in the rearview mirror of her own reflection and they were on their way down Dixon and past the rock to the junction of Highway 53. They crossed the lake a second time at the county line.

"If it's still warm tonight when we get back, we ought to take a swim off that point." She indicated the promontory at the end of the park to their left.

Stuart glanced at his jeans and started to point out that he had not brought his swimming suit, but he thought better of it. He checked his watch and the speedometer and prepared to see her set a record for the drive to Atlanta.

"You know," she pondered, "if you consider the whole outlying greater Atlanta area, there are four million people here. Of course, that would include almost to Gainesville. But let's face it, Atlanta will soon swallow Gainesville whole anyway."

Stuart thought that Atlanta might swallow a lot, but it would probably spit him out.

"Will there be anything open on Sunday night?' he inquired.

"This town never sleeps."

****

"Will you please move it? I honestly think it would take you an hour and a half to watch sixty minutes."

"The courts will be there when we get there. It's not as though we have to reserve them for a specific time," calmed Helen.

"Good grief, your phone is ringing," sighed Ruth.

"Hello."

"Helen, it's me."

"Hi, Andrew," she greeted cheerfully.

"I just wanted to let you know how everything went. The committee was further along than I thought and they called a meeting of the session and decided to offer me the job and I took it."

"Great. Congratulations! When do you start?"

"One of the elders has an apartment building and I'm going to move in next week, sight unseen."

"This is unbelievable. Well, I know you'll have a church family, but I still want to have some people over and give you a chance to meet them."

"That's awfully nice, Helen. I'll look forward to it."

"Call me when you get back to town."

She hung up and started for the door.

"Well?" demanded Ruth, now seated on the couch.

"I thought you were in a hurry," Helen smiled authoritatively.

"Tennis can wait when there's grit to be gathered. Wait up, I'm not kidding," she called to Helen as she went through the door.

They began the three block walk to the park that they did a couple of times a week.

"Tell me how you know this guy," Ruth pumped.

"We dated some the year after I left Ole Miss. I met him that summer at a friend's house in Memphis. I went to Jackson, Tennessee, and he went to Jackson, Mississippi, to seminary. He still went to visit his folks regularly in Memphis and I would meet him there."

"When did you stop seeing him?" Ruth pursued.

"I don't know, really. We wrote and talked on the phone less and less and then one day it had been a couple of years. Who knows how those things go?"

"Sounds like you're going to have a chance to find out."

"He's probably gone back to Jackson to get his wife, 1.7 kids, station wagon and cocker spaniel," Helen sighed with exaggerated humor.

They walked the long way around to the courts past civic shelters, playground equipment and grassy spaces. "Somehow, I don't expect that to be his personal profile," Ruth speculated.

CHAPTER 8

Helen stopped at the small converted residence a couple of blocks off the square. The gift shop had a variety of speciality items and she was confident she could pick something up there that would do nicely. She made her selection then went to the grocery. When she got home, she went to her carport and removed the plant from the plastic pot and shifted and fluted until it looked as though it had grown in the ceramic pot from the gift shop. She set the new assembly on the steps and bounced into the house to freshen up. Then, she drove up to the apartment only three blocks away which Andrew had described.

"Hello?" she called as she walked up the brick steps. "Is there a minister in the house?"

"Come in," greeted the invisible host. Andrew emerged from the kitchen. "To what do I owe this privilege?"

"Your need of taste," Helen teased as she stepped through the door he was holding. In one scan, she could see the militant alignment of the furniture.

"Is there something out of order?" he asked anxiously.

"No chance of that," she smiled.

"What could be more practical?" he defended his taste for order. "The books are within reach of my favorite chair and the lamp is on the left. The couch is a safe distance from the window to avoid sun damage and I don't find anything on television entertaining whose copyright is later than 1960 anyway, so I didn't even figure on getting one. Why?"

"Well, it looks practical and.....well engineered. Anyway," she extended the plant. "Here, welcome to Middle Tennessee."

"Thanks. Can you sit down for a minute?" he invited.

"No, thank you. I'm afraid the excitement of my laundry just won't wait." she declined.

"That reminds me. Where is the nearest laundromat?" he asked.

"I'm not sure. Is there not a washer in the building?"

"There soon will be. The man that owns the building is going to install an industrial-size setup to service all four apartments. But for the moment, I need to catch up."

"Why don't you let me do the first load?" Helen offered.

"I couldn't think of it. I didn't mean to....."

"Nonsense. I'm going to be washing anyway and I'd be glad to do it."

★★★★★★★

Saturday morning TV was not what it was when Stuart was a boy. At least his memory was more pleasant than this reality.

"Maggie," he said to his four-legged companion, "let's pick up Brooke and take a drive or a hike or something."

The perked ears confirmed enthusiasm if not understanding.

Stuart picked up the phone and called Brooke's mother. The day was not one that had been scheduled but that had proven flexible before. However, today was not convenient, they had plans that conflicted.

"I guess it's as good as it can be under the circumstances," he said aloud. "It's just the consequences of a less-than-ideal situation."

He put the old green bedspread into the back seat of his car and invited the anxious labrador in. They drove to a secluded, small park on the north side of Lake Lanier and walked down to an old seldom-used boat ramp. He had a tennis ball in the kangaroo pocket of his sweatshirt and he threw it into the lake. Maggie was wet before the ball was and unaffected by the chilled water.

Stuart looked at a boat working its way around the point. The medium size, walk-through windshield model displayed a classic scene of a young couple and two children. The father had his ecstatic daughter in his lap pretending to be in full command of the helm. Her life jacket made her look like an advertisement for tires in the way it swallowed her three foot high frame. It could do nothing to obscure her dimples or muffle her shrieks of delight, however. The mother cautioned the speed by pumping her hand palm down.

Maggie was the only one around when the tear trickled down Stuart's cheek.

CHAPTER 9

Stuart jumped from the bathtub in step with The Four Tops and went to the mirror to complete the shave he had done blindly in the shower. Afterwards, it was a comb, then fingers to break the wet-head sheen, a toothbrushing, gargle and a liberal splash of after-shave.

The freshly starched, heavyweight oxford was a white button-down. The slacks were gray and actually creased for the occasion, held in place by an alligator belt complete with monogram buckle. Black tassel loafers and a blue blazer accented by alma mater buttons to complete the ensemble. He left precisely on time to cover the five minutes to Elise's apartment.

The door was elevated above the parking lot with four concrete steps and he stood on the small porch as he knocked. The door was opened by an attractive girl he did not know.

"You're not Elise," he observed.

"I'm her close friend Rene and I have some good news and bad news for you," her eyes sparkled.

"The bad news first, please," he played along.

"Elise was hit by a train today," she smiled.

"What could be good on such a day?"

"As she died in my arms, her last request was that I take her place tonight."

"I hope I can be of comfort to you in this terrible time of loss," he took her hand and held it with both of his and looked somberly into her eyes.

"Elise!" she called, "Come quick." She gestured him in with the other hand. "I have to be going. Make yourself at home."

"Nice to meet you, Rene."

"Come in," came the soft voice now in the small hallway. "I see you had a chance to meet my roommate. I'll be ready in just a minute. In fact, it would be faster if you could lend a hand."

He turned to see better as Elise stepped into a more lighted spot in the den. Her heels were dark and styled her long, hosed legs to the negotiable limits of a split, wool skirt that hugged her hips and struck a sharp contrast at the slim waist to a loose, silk blouse.

"Can you get this?" she asked more directly as she stood a quarter turn from square with the mirror.

"Sure." He took the necklace from her outstretched hand and took his adorning position directly behind her as she now faced the mirror.

She leaned her head forward and slightly to the left, allowing her hair to slide away from most of the back of her neck. He held the ends of the necklace in each hand and lifted it over her head from behind. The clasp was small and the end to be linked was improvised so that it had to be angled precariously or it would not fasten. He had to bend his head down for a lighted view and as he did, she barely straightened her neck enough for the back of her head to gently touch his forehead. At the same moment, the link was secured and he dropped his hands.

"That's it," he said.

"Thanks. It's old and almost impossible to do by yourself."

"Shall we?" He offered her his arm in escort style which she accepted in perfect posture.

"By all means."

He took her to the passenger side of the freshly washed Cutlass and opened the door. She slid into the front seat like a shadow and he walked around behind the car and got under the wheel. She was seated closer to the middle than he remembered leaving her and her fragrance was apparent.

He pushed in the tape and adjusted the sound. The back windows were slightly open as they slowly went toward Green Street.

"So what did you do today?" she asked casually.

"I took my dog and went to a place on the lake for a while and then drove up to Trey Mountain."

"Where's that?"

"Up above Helen....Georgia," he stammered and wondered what he would say if she questioned his need to clarify a town 25 miles away.

"You know I've heard about Helen a lot, but I've never been there. What's it like?"

"I haven't spent much time in the village. The story is it was modeled from a Bavarian village. They have an Octoberfest with knockwurst and bratworst and what's the worst is the crowd of yokels in the way of the mountain."

"You know, that's a concept that's foreign to the first Native Americans. They had no exchange of real property."

"Sounds dreadfully uncapitalistic and non-competitive," he laughed.

"I guess their competitive needs were met by bouts with hunger and cold."

"Maybe, but I can't imagine having a desire for something and not wanting to possess it."

It was completely dark when they reached I-85 and I-285. He followed some refreshed directions through a couple of junctions and turns into what looked like a shopping center parking lot.

"Ever been here before?" he asked as he assisted her in getting out of the car.

"No, I haven't."

They stepped through the front door and she hesitated. "I feel like I've fallen through the looking glass," she remarked as she took in the view of Victorian decor and waiters in livery.

"Kerr," Stuart answered the unspoken request of the host.

"Very good, sir. Your table is ready."

They followed his beckon past tables set with fine china and heavy silverware.

"How is this, sir?" he asked for Stuart's approval of the table.

"Fine, thank you."

The booth was semi-circular and the host pulled the table out for both to be seated and then slid it to them like some elaborate ride at a theme park.

"Did you bring an appetite?" Stuart asked Elise as a team began to serve them bread, water, menus and lighted oil lamps that looked more like candles.

"I doubt if my discriminating palate will find fault with anything here."

"Good evening, ma'am, sir. My name is Phillipe and my speciality is wine. Are you friends of the grape?" He extended the wine list. "I will be available for any questions you might have in a moment."

Later, the waiter whose specialty was wine, returned for their orders.

"Madame?"

"Mamselle," corrected Stuart "will begin with escargot, then lobster bisque and a Caesar salad." He turned to Elise for consent and continued, "And the stuffed flounder."

"Very good, sir," he said without making a written note.

"I would like a shrimp cocktail, hearts of palm and prime rib....medium rare."

The waiter simply nodded like a genie and vanished.

"Oh, don't you just love this place?" Elise exclaimed, looking further than the restaurant.

"You mean our table," he teased.

"That too," she re-entered orbit for a second and then gazed. "I mean this town. Atlanta.....you can just feel the power pulsating here."

"What kind of power?"

"The power of business, of entertainment and night life, the power of people." Her eyes were wishful. "It makes you want to be in the whirlwind and makes you feel so....so significant."

The wine steward appeared with a recommendation. He displayed the label to Stuart as though it were a cape taunting a bull. "Might I be so bold as to make a recommendation?" He allowed for a tasteful cross reference of label to list and then to price so Stuart could see it would not require a co-signature.

"Certainly," he consented.

With a band conductor's flare, the medallion around his neck was filled and drained to his own satisfaction and then the routine of Stuart swirling and tossing his tester portion to the back of his throat was played out before Elise got the first full glass.

"I'm curious," Elise took the chance to dialogue. "I'm relatively sure from my sources that you are not a poet and I'm to believe that you more than casually enjoy the outdoors, yet you carry off this Sir Walter Raleigh bit, too. Which are you?"

"Why do we have to choose?"

"I'm not saying we even have a choice." She swallowed half of the contents of her glass. "I think we are products of some debated ration of heredity and environment."

"Therein lies the quandary." He refilled her glass and turned the bottle with his wrist to avoid a misplaced drip.

"Go on," she prompted.

"My mother was a Memphis debutante. They lost several notches in the depression, but were not exactly reduced to poverty. She was exposed to the finer things in life. My daddy, on the other hand, was the son of a pastor and raised with little material emphasis. He was not a hard luck story by any means, but felt that opportunities were scarce and should be seized with the frugality of a Scotsman. He became a doctor but continued to be more country boy than blue blood. He earned a comfortable living and Mother thought it did no harm to expose us to some of life's fineries. Daddy maintained that most of what a man needed could be found outside. They came to terms in mutual support of both priorities and Jack-Spratted us to a combination of influence. How about you?"

"Savannah," she began. "My mother and father were divorced when I was four. My Mother either developed or succumbed to a drinking problem. She was treated formally more than once and labeled an outcast when it was decided she was not fit to rear a child. She moved to Columbus where she lived with an older sister and I was not to see her. Meanwhile, my father, an investment banker, raised me as the son he never had. He never even dated, let alone remarried, and I spent my childhood in private schools trying to be what I thought he wanted me to be. I don't remember him participating in any recreational activity with me at all. In fact, I don't remember him ever taking a vacation."

"Were you a tomboy when you were young?"

"No, the way to earn his approval was academics and particularly those courses with a business direction. So I worked on my grades and tried to make decisions that would allow him to identify with me. I guess part of choosing a girl's school was some kind of display that I could actually be female. Frankly, I still struggle with trying to do that simple thing."

"You have a lot of raw material to work with."

She smiled as she showed a rare hint of shyness.

CHAPTER 10

He walked to the door and was smothered by more hugs.

"Hi, Mom." He put down half his load and returned the hug.

"Hello, son. Can I take something for you?" his father offered as he sidestepped around the bags and people. "Maybe we should have retained the services of a traffic cop," he muttered as he made his way to the kitchen. "Seems like everybody came to Rome at once."

Stuart took his cargo downstairs and put it up before grabbing a diaper out of Brooke's duffel bag and rejoining the group on the screened-in porch that overlooked the valley.

Upon his return, Brooke began to voice her opinion on the matters at hand.

"I think she's hungry," declared Stuart's mother.

"Let me get her something...." Stuart said and started to rise.

"You sit right there and visit with your daddy. I've done this enough to conduct seminars," Stuart's mother volunteered.

She carried Brooke so naturally, the crying stopped instantly. They went into the kitchen where Maury was washing lettuce. Stuart's sister turned from the sink. She craned her neck to be sure Stuart had not followed. "OK, give me the grit."

"Well, when your brother told us he was going to be close to home, I did some checking around. I knew Helen was still in town and I knew I wanted him to know it...without me telling him. I remembered she had been written up in the paper for an involvement with some kind of volunteer work. So, I found a copy of the paper and put it on the table out by the pool, you know under a magazine cover partially.

"You should be..." Maury began.

"Decorated. I think it was ingenious. He took the bait in less than five minutes and my sources tell me he went by to visit her the next afternoon."

"Sources?" Maury smiled.

"Sure, you can only leave so much to chance. Pauline drove by Helen's house a dozen times before she finally spotted a black Cutlass with a Georgia tag."

"You baited him," Maury teased.

"The paper was less than a month old. Besides, all's fair in love...and that other tacky thing men do."

"What's the story now?"

"I don't dare ask. Pauline has seen his car there one more time."

"Well, be careful. Don't let him know you're interested."

"Don't worry. I was matchmaking when you were in Brownies."

"Do you have a Coke or something?" asked Ruth.

"Help yourself," offered Helen. And then, "Bring me one, too, please."

"Sure thing. Do you want it over ice?"

"That would be nice if you are going to, anyway."

Helen finished pulling the load out of the dryer and carried the basket into the den. Ruth brought in the glasses and sat down.

"Friday night and I'm watching you fold clothes. I hope this comes out if I ever go to counseling."

Helen smiled but did not stop folding, except to take a sip from the glass next to her.

"I've been thinking," began Ruth, "what we need in this town is a place.......Hey!" she stopped short. "Those jeans look a bit large for you," she pointed with the index finger of the hand holding the glass.

"They're Andrew's," she said simply.

"I beg your pardon," demanded Ruth as she stood up.

"They have had some problem with the plumbing in his building and haven't been able to put a washer in yet. They hope to have it fixed in a couple of days. Anyway, he is still trying to get settled and..."

"Don't you think it's time we got a few things settled?" Ruth butted in and pulled the basket out of Helen's reach.

The phone rang and interrupted their friendly argument.

"Want me to get that while I'm up, Helen?"

"Please."

"Hello?"

"Is Helen there?" The uncanny timing and familiar voice were more opportunity than Ruth could resist.

"Andrew?" she asked with fake innocence.

Stuart hesitated on his end for a minute. "Yes, who's this?"

Ruth swallowed hard. Now what? "Uh, hold on just a minute, please." She avoided putting her hand over the phone. "Helen, it's Andrew," she called into the den.

Helen took the phone and thanked her. "Hi, Reverend. What's new with the flock?"

"I'm afraid there's been some mistake."

"Stuart? I'm sorry, Ruth thought you were someone else."

"That's fine. How have you been?"

"Doing good. I haven't talked to you in a while. Is everything still going okay?"

"Fine, fine. What's new with school?" he asked.

"I'm just trying to keep all the plates spinning on the little sticks. The first part of a school year is usually over by now, but for some reason, this week has had four Mondays in it."

"I guess with new kids, it's not just a matter of picking up where you left off," he commiserated.

"Not exactly. And this year it has been made definite that I will only work at two schools."

"That ought to make things more simple," Stuart surmised.

44

CHOICES

"At least I feel the quality of what can be done will improve with the smaller case load. How about your work?" Helen asked.

"Thankfully, one project seems to end about the same time another one is ready to start up."

"I'll bet you're glad the summer heat is over."

"Yes, but unfortunately, when it rains this time of year, it takes longer to dry enough to work, so the work time suffers somewhat." He sensed the strain this small talk was placing on the call. "Listen," he changed the subject. "Speaking of fall, I was wondering if you would like to see some of the colors along with the gazillion other people I rode behind on my way to Rome?"

"You're in Rome?"

"Yes, it's Maury's birthday and we try to get together when it falls on a home game for Georgia. Most of the time, it's Ole Miss weekend. Anyway, several of us are at her house and I thought about maybe next weekend taking a drive."

"How is she doing? I haven't talked to her since Mother died. Please tell her hello for me."

"I will," he committed without elaborating on her deliberate sidetrack.

"About getting together..." she began. "I think we need to talk some more about that."

"Sounds like you want to talk and want me to listen."

"You know that I feel you should still be working on your marriage."

"I don't think you call it that at this stage. You know the divorce is final."

"Yes, in the eyes of the law, but I'm not sure about anything else."

"So, talk. I'll listen," he invited.

"I don't know what to say except thank you for the invitation and I won't be able to make it."

"So, you don't date divorcees?"

"In a manner of speaking....no."

"That seems a bit legalistic, don't you think?" he accused kindly.

"What does that term mean to you?" she asked, surprised.

"Well, what am I supposed to do for the rest of my life, just accept the fact that I have an indelible mark on my record that makes me unfit for human companionship?" He showed some disgust in his voice. "If I had known this, I'd..." he stopped himself.

"You'd what?" she asked calmly.

"Nothing."

"Tried harder, maybe?" she filled in.

"You don't understand," he accused.

"What I do understand is the simple truth that marriage is taken too lightly and divorce is thought to be a solution without consequences. Those consequences are not discovered until it's...." she stopped.

"Until it's what?" he asked.

"Nevermind," she asked more than stated.

"'Until it's too late,' was what you meant. Look Helen. I know something about consequences, but the fact is, I can't do much about that now."

"I don't want to punish you or judge you for something that I don't have any business forcing," she consented.

"I won't push you, Helen."

"For what it's worth, I'd like to see you if...." she hesitated, "if I could."

"Me, too."

"I'd better run."

"Bye, bye."

Helen hung up the phone on the kitchen wall and turned to find Ruth standing there with her arms folded. "You really think you're doing the right thing?"

"I don't know, Ruth."

"I hate to see you go through life constantly denying yourself what you want." Ruth offered.

"Don't you think that's a little general?" Helen wondered. "Besides, I know what I want is what is right."

"You are not something that should be just....to yourself. You should be sharing yourself with someone," her friend explained.

"Thanks. I think I hear a complement in there somewhere and I appreciate it."

"Anyway, how are *you* going to resolve *his* marriage?"

"I don't intend to resolve it. I just don't want to be one of the reasons it's not resolved."

"What does he say?" Ruth continued.

"He thinks that the marriage is broken beyond repair and it's too late to change it."

"He may be in a better position than you to make that call," Ruth pointed out.

"That's okay for a dating relationship, but not good enough for marriage. Scripture is clear on the subject and we are either getting together and studying the Bible for fun or for life-changing effect. I can't act like I don't understand what I'm learning, regardless of how I feel."

"How do you feel?"

She walked into the den. "Like folding clothes."

CHAPTER 11

Stuart took the book he had started to read off of the end table. His mind moved more quickly across the page than his eyes and he was soon separated from the plot by his own preoccupation. Maybe it was his conversation with Helen that had him feeling instead of thinking, but he didn't feel good, that was certain. The past was haunting him and he didn't know what to do about it. His thoughts were interrupted by another phone ring.

"Hello."

"Well, you are still alive after all," the voice chided.

"Had you heard something to the contrary?" he asked.

"No, that's just it. I hadn't heard anything at all," she scolded.

"Hold on a second, Elise. I need to take something out of the oven."

"I may still be here when you get back."

He was back almost immediately. "Okay, I'm here."

"That was fast."

"It's a small house," he explained.

"I know. I was there some time back. So, how have you been?"

"Fine. Work's fair and I got to see some of my family in Rome this weekend. How about you?"

"I've been missing you." Her voice stopped at the end of the statement.

He found the boldness somewhat intriguing. "Let's do something, then," he suggested. "How about....I know, let's do some rock climbing this Saturday."

"It's Tuesday. Is Saturday the best we can do?"

"Yes. I've got to go to Savannah to look at a job that's going to bid and I know I'll be gone at least overnight, maybe even two."

"Okay," she said simply.

"Good. I'll see you about eight."

"As in A.M.?"

"That's right. You wouldn't want to do what we'll be doing at night."

"That's a matter of....well, whatever you say. I'll see you then."

"How do you like the new arrangements, Helen?"

"It will take some getting used to, Mr. Richardson, but I think you and the other principals were right. Dealing with only two schools is going to add quality to the program."

"Let me know if there is anything you need," he offered as he started to walk away.

She stopped picking up the materials that had been left from the final session of the day and said, "Now that you mention it....this room is....well..."

He interrupted by snapping his fingers. "I've lost my mind. I knew there was some reason I came down here. Do you have a minute to walk up to my office?"

"Certainly."

They walked the single length of hallway to the main office and on into his office. He had a set of plans on his desk and he unrolled them to the sheet that showed the floor plan of the existing building in broken lines and the proposed addition in solid lines.

"This will be your new room," he indicated with the end of a ruler he had picked up in the process.

"Actually," he qualified, "it will be shared, since you are not here every day, but we will have a permanent desk for you in it."

"That will be great. Any idea as to when it will be ready?"

"I hope in three or four months. They plan to get started right away. Meanwhile, in the new setup, I want to see your rotation schedule so we can keep a control on the number of students you see during a specific time."

"I will put one together this week, if that's soon enough."

"That's fine. No need to rush." He rose concluding the meeting. She thanked him and then walked out into the main office where an unexpected voice startled her.

"Hello, Helen."

"Hi," she said trying to connect the familiar face.

"Pauline Wilson," the lady pleasantly assisted.

"Of course, Mrs. Wilson. It's good to see you. It has been a while."

"Probably since high school," she smiled. "We used to get to see a lot of you at the Kerr's house."

"How are you?"

"I'm fine. I'm here to pick up my niece's daughter. I'm getting her out a little early to go down to the river. By the way, how is Stuart doing?"

The question was certainly simple enough. Why did it momentarily lock her jaw? She felt compelled to explain why she would be able to answer it at all.

"Fine," she decided, "I talked to him just a couple of days ago and..."

"I'm so glad," she broke in, smiling.

Glad of what, thought Helen? Glad I talked to him? Glad he's fine? What does she think she knows anyway?

"Yes, ma'am, he's fine," this time more conclusively.

"Well, you tell him we asked about him when you see him. I'll be seeing you, dear."

"Bye," Helen said, thinking to herself that out of nowhere suddenly had come this responsibility to explain to the world why she was not going to see Stuart again.

She walked to her room and spent a few minutes gathering enough information to design a rotation schedule for her cases. She stopped on the way out at a pay phone in the lobby.

"Hey, Ruth, what time do you get off today?"

"Hello, and sometime in the next hour if I need to. Why?"

"Let's go get a beer." replied Helen.

"I'm sorry, I thought this was Helen." joked Ruth.

"So, now I'm a prude?" she challenged. "I drink beer."

"No, I've just never known you to set it as a target for an outing. Anyway, what's wrong?"

"I don't know, I just need to talk to somebody."

"Glad you picked a professional. Where and when?"

"Your house in one hour."

"See ya there. Bye."

She continued out of the building and on to the car. Her drive home was from patterned habit and required no thought. Fortunately so, because it got none. A quick stop home for a Coke and change of clothes and she was almost to the door when the phone rang. It was Andrew.

"I was hoping to do something to thank you for helping with my laundry a couple of times."

"That's not at all necessary. It was my pleasure."

"Anyway, how about dinner Saturday night? I'll pick you up at six?"

"Sounds good. See you then." Helen hurriedly accepted.

As she walked down the street toward Ruth's house Helen realized she had no real purpose in mind for the conversation she was about to have. Ruth was just driving up when she walked into the yard.

"Hi, come help me take some of these groceries in."

"Sure," Helen said, reaching for and taking one of the sacks. "What is all this?"

"Well, I'm sure you didn't bring any beer."

"No, in fact, I forgot all about it."

"No shock to me. So I stopped by and got some. Come on in."

They walked in and put most of the articles on the counter and took out a beer each and poured them into glasses, then continued into the den and sat down.

"So, what's the scoop?" began Ruth.

"I'm not sure this is the emergency I may have led you to believe on the phone."

"Don't back out on me now. I left work early for this."

"I don't know where I stand on something that may not be important anyway."

"So, it's your confusion about a principle that has you uncomfortable."

"Say, Ruth, that's pretty good stuff," Helen said sincerely of Ruth's ability to summarize the situation so precisely.

"Would you like me to get you a pad and pencil? As long as I'm hot, you may want to take notes," Ruth said, laughing.

"No, there's still a chance you were just lucky. Anyway, this thing with Stuart has me bothered."

"Are you bothered by the fact that you think you have hurt him by making him feel untouchable for something he can no longer control?"

"I may take you up on the pencil and paper offer," Helen said smiling. She set the beer down with one sip missing from the glass and sat back in the corner of the sofa. "Let's talk about that aspect of it for a second."

"Specifically?" asked Ruth.

"You said 'he could no longer control'," she reminded.

"I mean simply, his divorce is final."

"In the eyes of the law, you're right. But marriage is a holy state and what God brings together, no man should put asunder."

"So you are saying that they are still married, even though the law says otherwise. That's ridiculous! Is this 'The Word according to Helen'? So, he's open game for every woman in the world, except you?"

"No, not exactly. But what I am trying to say is that I don't feel I can be a part of Stuart's escape from his marriage."

"He doesn't have a marriage. He doesn't have a wife. He has an ex-wife. It's over! Kaput! Gone! It is no more!" she raved.

"I think he still has the responsibility to reconcile his marriage, no matter how I feel about him."

"Are you deaf? Have you heard a word I've said? Anyway, how do you feel about him?"

"That's not appropriate to discuss," Helen answered flatly.

"Oh, my gosh. You're the one that brought it up."

"Still, the other must be resolved first."

"It's resolved. What is wrong with you?"

"I think I'll talk to his former wife this weekend."

"You know, it's really sad to see your closest friend lose her mind right in front of you." Ruth shook her head.

"That's what I'm going to do alright," resolved Helen. "I'm going to tell her she should reconcile her marriage."

"Because Stuart is warm, compassionate and a hunk?" Ruth mocked.

"No. Because they promised 'until death do us part'. And I want to hear her side."

"So what day do you plan to do this?" asked Ruth.

"The sooner, the better. I think I'll drive down this weekend. Maybe Sunday. I would go Saturday but I just accepted a date for Saturday."

"Andrew?"

"Yes, but not a 'date' date. It's more of a 'thank you note date' for helping him get settled."

"What's the deal with him, Helen?"

"He's a nice guy and fun to be with."

Helen was walking toward the door. "I've got to get home. Thanks for the beer."

Ruth looked at the half-empty glass. "You sure you can get home okay?" she teased.

CHAPTER 12

Stuart was up at 6:00. The trip to Savannah had gone fairly well and the challenge of the job appealed to him. He took some time to roll out the drawings on his table and make some notes as to the location of the dirt to be hauled and distance to the dyke being proposed. The distance was not exactly ideal for the plan he had in mind, but the site was so smooth and flat that he was confident he would not have to use trucks.

He left the plans out, pulled on his tennis shoes and went for a quick run around the block to loosen up. After he was finished, he took a shower and put on hiking shorts, a long-sleeve T-shirt and hiking boots. He stuffed a small day pack with a light sweater and a few snack packs of trail mix and dried fruit, checked his watch and decided to drive on over to Elise's place. He knocked on the door and waited. No answer. He waited about two minutes and knocked again, this time louder. He waited again and checked his watch. Ten minutes till 8:00 and *still* no answer. He walked around the side of the building and picked up a rock and tossed it at a window whose location and curtains made it reasonable to assume it could be a bedroom. The light came on and Stuart darted back around to the front and knocked again.

"Stuart?" came the raspy voice through the door.

"That's me," he declared.

She opened the door and half hid herself behind it. "I seem to have overslept just a bit," she admitted. "Come in while I change."

"Thank you," he accepted, surprised to see the definite difference the lack of makeup revealed.

"I'll just be a minute," she said, shuffling to the bedroom and not bothering to close the door. "What should I wear?"

"Heels and a leather skirt," Stuart said dryly.

"What did you say we are doing? Rock climbing?"

"That's right. You're not having second thoughts, are you?"

"Not a chance," she said confidently.

She finally emerged, dressed appropriately, and they left. They drove in Stuart's car up to Helen and then out a couple of miles and eventually took Richard Russell Highway. He knew of a couple of spots that provided pretty views without a high level of climbing difficulty. After parking the car, they walked up a steep grade along a trail to some visible blue-speckled granite.

"This is what we climb?" she asked skeptically.

"For starters," Stuart smiled.

"Are you going to give me any pointers like 'don't look down'?"

****

The evening air was cool and Helen was enjoying the thought of a dinner date. She did not know if the idea appealed to her more in concept than in particular, but she knew she felt peaceful about it.

Andrew's car rolled up to the curb and stopped. She ran to the car, flung the door open and jumped in before Andrew even had a chance to get out of the car.

They drove in a comfortable silence to a Chinese restaurant. After they had ordered, Helen handed her menu to the waitress and asked Andrew, "Tell me how things are going with work."

"I like it a lot. The people are great and I love working with young people."

"You know I have never asked you specifically what your job is."

"More youth pastor than anything else, with some other duties shaken in. But I have the freedom to spend a lot of time with the youth."

"I'm sure that's rewarding."

"Well, you take this one girl, for example. She is dealing with the typical 15-year-old stuff. Her teachers are too demanding, her boyfriend is lying to her and her mother doesn't understand her."

"What about her father?"

"Her folks are divorced."

"Oh, I see. How long?"

"Just a couple of months, and after eighteen years of marriage."

"Have you ever thought, Andrew, about what you'll be doing in the ministry 10 or 15 years from now?"

"I just started this. Why?"

"I just wondered, if you were a senior pastor someday and you had to deal with someone going through a divorce, how you would handle it?"

"I'm not capable of doing it now, but I certainly know how I feel about divorce."

"Yes, I do too," she said hesitantly.

"Here's your dinner," he gestured as the waitress arrived.

Helen was polite but distracted the remainder of the evening. They said "goodbye" with a handshake at the door and she went in to throw a few things into a travel bag for the trip the next day. She had no plans to spend the night, but wanted to be safe if she was delayed or met with trouble. She arose the next morning at 5:30 and was on her way at a little after 6:00 with a map highlighting the route. The road to Chattanooga was vaguely familiar to her and went faster than she had anticipated. She had been on the road a couple of times years earlier when she visited Stuart in Athens during his freshman year. But she had never been to Gainesville.

****

"Because it's Sunday, Maggie," he laughed in response to the big dog's almost inquisitive face. "I always sleep till seven on Sunday morning and that means your breakfast is late." He shook his head in disbelief as he realized he was indeed talking to a dog with no one else around to benefit. He looked out and weighed the options of this free day. He decided to skip church and go for a drive, better yet, a night away too. There was a project he remembered that would be bid in this month's letting somewhere around Chatsworth. He could meet some of the local Department of Transportation people Monday and pick up the drawings. As for today, he could drive through the mountains and maybe find some new camping spots.

"Come on, Maggie, let's bust out of here."

With the tank full of gas and no stops for food or facilities, he had wound his way into Chatsworth in no time. He looked at his watch. Not even lunchtime yet. "Well, girl, what do you want to do? If I hadn't spent the whole day yesterday crawling across rock outcroppings with Cover Girl, I'd say we could tackle that one," looking up at an impressive grade with a rock face showing. "But, the Chattahoochie National Forest comes into this county somewhere around here and I'm not sure of property lines and all that, so I'm not that gung ho." Another look at the watch. "You know, I don't need to see the DOT people till 10:00 or 11:00 in the morning. I know where everything is now.....let's go see the folks. It can't be more than 3 1/2 hours.

He stopped and asked the teenager running a convenience store to direct him to I-75. To his surprise, the mile marker where the ramp brought him in indicated he was only a few miles south of Chattanooga. Sunday night, he thought; Welsh rabbit on toasted saltines....easily worth the drive. What a pity "Bonanza" wasn't on television anymore.

****

Helen looked at her watch. 11:30 but she had made a mental note and not changed it to Eastern Time. She was surprised that she had actually made it to Gainesville without stopping for directions. She now pulled into a shopping center parking lot with a pay phone in one corner. She was able to drive up close enough to stay in the car and reach everything. She dialed directory assistance on the touchtone and was given Kathy Kerr's telephone by the operator. She dialed the number and waited.

"Hello?" someone answered on the third ring. "Yes?"

"My name is Helen Allbright," she began. "I don't know if you have any idea who I am...."

"Yes, I remember your name. Stuart dated you in highschool, didn't he?"

"That's right," Helen said, relieved that she was not a stranger. "I have an unusual request. I wanted to meet you and talk with you about something. I know this is without notice, but I am in town now. Do you think you could give me a few minutes?"

"Uh, I don't see why not. Where are you?"

"I see a sign that says 'Lakeshore Mall'."

"You can get here without any trouble," she said, proceeding to give Helen the simple step-by-step directions. In only a matter of a few minutes, Helen was pulling into the driveway, not knowing what she was going to say or how it would be taken.

"Come in," was the greeting at the door before Helen was all the way onto the front porch.

"Hi, thank you," she responded smiling.

"Would you like a Coke or something?"

"No, thanks," Helen said, sitting in the seat offered her in the den. "This is nice," she complimented, looking around. "Is this the house you and Stuart lived in?"

"No, that was sold and I bought this right about the time of the divorce."

"I see....Well," Helen said, looking at her now, "I'm sure you wonder what I could possibly want to say."

"Yes, I am curious," she said pleasantly.

Helen cleared her throat. "Stuart tells me that the marriage is over; I know the divorce is final, I just need to know that there is no chance of a reconciliation."

"Stuart and I have not loved each other for some time. We did try to have a marriage but it didn't work."

"I've just come to understand that love isn't always something two people feel. It's just something you have to do sometimes."

"I appreciate you wanting to deal with that. You need to know that many months have passed since our marriage died. We were separated and now divorced. That is pretty much that," Kathy concluded.

"I guess I just wanted to hear everybody's side of it."

****

Stuart rolled into Columbia well before dinner time, and stopped by Giant Foods on the way in.

"What are you taking home?" the clerk asked.

"Fixings for a Welsh Rabbit," Stuart said, with his eyes selling the idea.

"Your mother was in here right after church and picked up some chicken, but it was fresh and I'm sure she was going to broil it and hasn't started by now, so it will keep."

"Hope so. I've been tasting this since Chattanooga."

"You'd better take some 'Woster', too," she said, turning to the teenager sacking at the end of the counter. "Randy, look on aisle one and get Stuart a bottle."

"Thanks, Jo Ann."

He put the single sack in the front seat and hesitated before pulling into the traffic at the parking lot exit. "Why not" he thought without speaking and turned left toward Helen's house. He made the one necessary turn less than four miles later and noticed her car was not in the carport. He got out at the slim possibility she was home and walked toward the door when a car stopped beside the yard.

"Hey, you're on private property," came the cheerful female voice.

"I'm kind of a private guy," he smiled, walking to the passenger side open window and looking at Helen's friend, Ruth.

"Let me pull over."

"Are you the watch dog as well as the gatekeeper?" he asked as she joined him standing in the yard.

"I didn't know you were coming. How are you, Stuart?"

"Fine, Ruth. I was just going to see my parents and thought I'd drop by."

Another car slowed to a stop and the driver got out and walked toward the two now almost at the small front porch. He was carrying something in a plastic sack.

"Hi, Andrew," welcomed Ruth. "Helen is out of town and we decided to have a party at her house. Do you know Stuart?"

"No, I don't think we've met. I'm Andrew Melvin."

"Hello. Stuart Kerr," Stuart replied, shaking the offered hand.

"Stuart Kerr," thought Andrew out loud. "I think I've heard Helen mention you, but it seems like it was some time ago....maybe in Memphis."

"Possibly. Do you live in Memphis?"

"Not anymore. I'm a bonafide resident of 'Mule Town' now."

"Andrew is..." began Ruth.

"A pastor at Zion," finished Stuart, remembering the conversation with his mother.

"That's right, partly at least. I assist in those duties where the youth are concerned. Anyway.." making his bag visible, "I had hoped to drop this by to Helen but I guess she's out for a while?" he said looking at Ruth.

"She's out of town, but I think she will be back later tonight." Ruth gestured to receive the bag.

"No, that's okay," he answered. "I'll be seeing her in a day or two anyway. Nice meeting you, Stuart," Andrew said walking toward his car.

"My pleasure," said Stuart, nodding and sitting down on the porch behind him. "Where is Helen, Ruth?"

She looked at her watch and thought of how she could quibble with the truth. "I don't know, exactly." She hoped she had not over-emphasized her last word.

"Wonder why Andrew was so confident he would be seeing Helen in a day or two?"

"Who knows?" Ruth said casually.

"I'm sorry, Ruth. I don't have any right to know any of this, let alone interrogate you about her whereabouts and social life. The next thing you know, I'll be off on some tangent about how this Memphis dork is no good for her just because he has a dishrag handshake and poor posture...."

"You'd be right....I mean, if you had said it," she said smiling a little less cheerfully.

****

Helen sat in her car waiting to turn into traffic and looked at her watch. She would be home late evening but not much after dark. "This is ridiculous," she said out loud. She turned back toward town and drove less than a mile and into a convenience store.

"Do you know where Longview is?" she asked, looking at an envelope she had retrieved from her purse which had a handwritten return address.

"Yes, my aunt lives on Longview," the girl answered with a smile.

The directions were simple and she pulled into the short, gravel, empty driveway five minutes later. She walked up the front porch steps and bent over to pick up the Sunday paper. Knowing now that she was probably alone, she haphazardly knocked on the door and to her surprise, it creaked open.

"Anybody home?" she called.

Hearing nothing she leaned in and saw no sign that would indicate recent activity. She thought for a minute of leaving a note and then, if she did, what would it say? She tossed the newspaper onto the end table and saw the rolled end strike the answering machine. The mechanical clicks and single beep caused her to go to it quickly and search for a button to turn it off without disengaging it altogether.

"Hey man...this is Joe...I hate this thing of yours....anyway, I've got two tickets to the Auburn game in a few weeks....call me."

Beep.

"Stuart, it's Elise. I just wanted to thank you for yesterday. I know I was awkward, but I didn't think I'd ever get my heart to slow down. I've never done that before, but I hope you'll give me another chance. Call me, bye."

Beep, beep, beep, then the mechanical rewind.

Helen gritted her teeth. "Never done that before," she mocked outloud. "What is he getting into?" she continued to herself.

Her mind was no longer on deciding whether to write a note and she briskly walked through the front door and to her car.

CHAPTER 13

Stuart sat staring at the column of numbers in front of him. The desk in his office was close to a drawing table that he used to roll out blueprints. The set of plans that was now rolled out was the project he had visited a week earlier in Chatsworth.

"Hi, Stuart. Everything going to suit you?"

"Yeah, Ken. How about you?"

"Fine, fine. Didn't I hear that your ex got married this past weekend?"

"That's right, she did."

"So, what does that mean? Do you have a new husband-in-law?" he said laughing.

"I guess so," Stuart replied, being a good sport. "Listen," he changed the subject with his voice, "I've been thinking about how to bid the job in Savannah. It will be in this next letting and you may remember that I drove down to see it a few weeks ago."

"I remember. What did you think of it?"

"I don't know, but I never try to second guess how much my competition will bid. I just want my price and if I get it, fine, if I don't, fine."

"It's your job." Ken assured.

"By the way, I've finished the numbers on the job in Habersham County. It turned out a lot better than we had hoped." Stuart volunteered.

"Good. Was the production that much faster?"

"Yes, we made several changes in the storm drain line and it cut down on the ditch depth a good bit. We were able to finish two weeks early."

"Nothing like pocketing ten days of payroll and equipment," Ken smiled.

"Speaking of pocketing the money...."

"You know," Ken interrupted, "I've been thinking and it probably would be best if we did our settling at one time each year say, after Christmas break. That way, if one job is a winner and the next a loser, we don't have to swap money back and forth."

"Okay....Habersham goes in the win column."

"Suits me....Who's that?" Ken asked, looking out the window.

"Looks like Joe's car....yeah, that's Joe. I wonder what's on his mind?"

Joe came in and shook hands with Ken at their introduction, and propped himself on the stool by the drafting table.

"I'll see you later," said Ken, excusing himself to the shop where a mechanic was working on his pickup.

"Okay," acknowledged Stuart, and turned to Joe. "To what do I owe this privilege?"

"Just wanted to see if you were hungry."

"It's 11:00."

"Well, I didn't eat much last night and I rarely eat breakfast, so I thought I'd have some brunch."

"Sure, why not?"

They walked out and Stuart nodded to Dee and said he'd be back when he was full.

"Where were you last weekend?" Joe asked.

"Home, mostly."

"I tried to call you Sunday morning before church." Joe told him.

"What Sunday are you talking about?" Stuart asked, perplexed.

"Last Sunday, ten days ago."

"Oh, I was out of town. Why?"

"Did you get my message about the tickets?"

"No. What tickets?"

"I left a message on that thing of yours that I had found a couple of tickets to the Auburn game."

"This is my first news of it."

"That's funny. Where did you say you were?"

"Actually, I spent the night with my folks. Why?"

"I don't know. I made a mental note to say something to you a few days ago, but it slipped my mind. I was on my way home from lunch after church and pulled into a gas station. I remember it was Sunday because I was pumping gas with a tie on. Anyway, this fine looking 'she-male' came out of the store and got into her car. When she drove off, I saw a Tennessee tag."

"Is that terribly strange?" Stuart asked, unimpressed.

"No, but I noticed the tag had the county name on it and for some reason, it reminded me of you, too. Don't you have a sister named Maury?"

"Yes, I do and my parents live in the county with the same name. It's my mother's maiden name. What did she look like?"

"Your sister?" Joe asked, laughing as he parked in front of the Cake Box.

"The girl, Dufus, the girl."

"Lighten up. She was quite a number."

"Could we do some things like hair color, size or something?"

"Is there someone in Columbia I don't know about?" asked Joe.

"No....maybe....I don't know."

"Why don't we go inside, get a table and you can tell me all about it," Joe controled.

They walked through the glass door and halfway through the restaurant and seated themselves in a booth against the plate glass window that made up the building's front.

"Hazel!" Stuart said, greeting her with a gleeful half-shout.

"Don't even start on me today," she said gruffly, but with her eyes twinkling.

"I'll begin with potatoes," he said, ignoring her. "Deep fried to a golden brown, lightly salted, with some of your homemade sauce on the side."

She put the pencil behind her ear in protest and shoved the ketchup bottle at him so he had to stop it from going in his lap.

"To drink?" she asked, still not writing.

"Sweet tea, shaken....not stirred."

"Joe?" she asked, now removing the pencil from her ear.

"Make it two, Baby." Turning to Stuart, Joe asked, "What's the deal with this hometown honey?"

"I don't know," Stuart replied, somewhat exasperated. "We dated all through high school and part of my freshman year. She was a year younger and by the time I was a sophomore, she was a freshman at Ole Miss. Somehow we just stopped seeing each other, and I wound up married a few months after my graduation. I have now learned that she never married."

"The girl I saw last Sunday was nobody's old maid."

"I can't imagine it really being her. Why would she come to Gainesville without contacting me?" His voice trailed, "Why would she come to Gainesville at all?"

"Have you been seeing her?" Joe asked.

"Not really. I don't know, sort of....no."

"Now we're getting somewhere," he laughed.

Stuart took a swallow of water and shifted in his seat. "It's not a conventional situation. I stopped by to see her a few months ago for....I don't know why." He tried to start over mentally. "You don't know how to act when you get divorced. You divvy up furniture and visitation time, but you don't know what to do about friends. It's awkward on them and everybody. I wanted to spend some time in a place that did not grow out of my marriage; a place that was there before I was married that wouldn't see me as a recent amputee. Helen was that kind of platonic link to a time when it was just me, alone, that people knew. She not only knew and accepted me as single, she knows things that are a part of me that are never going to be learnable by anyone else. I guess it was a return to a foundation of some sort. And among other things, she's solid."

"Do you have feelings for her again?"

"Okay, boys, and I do mean boys. Here it is. If you don't like it, tough. You ordered it so live with it," Hazel shoved the plates in a strong gesture to force their reaction.

"Hazel, you're a rainbow in my day. Let's fly away together and pontificate the realms of the universe." Stuart took her hand in his and looked into her eyes.

She stepped back and slyly cut her eyes downward at him. "If I were twenty years younger, I'd take the starch out of those khakis for you," she said and strutted off.

"So," began Joe, "have you seen Elise lately?"

"We went hiking and did some climbing the Saturday before I went to Tennessee."

"That sounds more like you than anything you've done together yet."

"Like me, maybe."

"She didn't take to it?" Joe asked.

"About like I would take to violin lessons."

"Look, Stuart, I'm not supposed to tell you but Elise talked to me yesterday. She wonders why she has to call you all the time. I think she kind of has a thing for you."

Stuart felt affected by the news and did not say anything.

"Does that make you nervous?" Joe continued.

"I'm not sure what that makes me. One of the things this divorce has done is make me find it hard to consider myself as attractive to the opposite sex."

"Well, you've got her fooled."

"I guess I should accept the fact that there is not exactly a line forming at my door."

****

"Helen, we need to talk," announced Ruth, as she barged in the door.

"I've already told you about my meeting in Gainesville. I've told you everything that was said. It doesn't matter now, anyway. I was probably out of line to even go down there."

"When I told you that Stuart came by here, I really thought the two of you would have been in touch by now. I guess you haven't?"

"No, not since before then," Helen said sadly. "There's something else about my trip to Gainesville that I never told you."

Ruth sat silently, almost patient.

"I went by Stuart's house on the way back to see if I could catch him at home. I didn't, of course, because I later learned from you that he was here. Anyway, I knocked on the door and it was apparently not closed all the way, because it swung open. I had picked up the paper and stepped inside to make sure he wasn't there. When I put the paper on the table, I accidently turned on his answering machine and I overheard a message from someone he is obviously seeing."

"What did she say?" Ruth's patience was long gone.

"I don't know what it meant, but the thing that gripes me is that he will not take a minute to get his head clear about the big picture. Since I've known him, he has been 'attached' to someone. I don't see how he can be in a position to know what's best for himself. This is just an unexpected slant that this wench is sliding in."

"What makes you think she's a wench?"

"She put on some wounded puppy routine. You know the type that set out to make men feel protective and all that junk."

"I hate it when women stoop to such levels," ridiculed Ruth.

"Oh no! I forgot the time," Helen said, looking at her watch. "Andrew is picking me up. Stall him while I put on my face."

"Hi, Ruth."

"Come in, Andrew. Helen will be out in a minute."

He walked in and sat on the couch and began to stare about the room. Ruth decided to try to make conversation.

"How do you like Columbia?"

"It has some very attractive features," he said, his voice hiding meaning and his eyes drifting toward Helen's closed door.

"That's, uh....that's certainly true," she responded nervously. "So, where are you two going on a Wednesday night?" she asked lightly.

"Church."

"Of course, I was thinking of going myself but just had not gotten around to it. I mean, getting ready and everything."

"We'd love for you to come with us. I'm going to be teaching tonight, and the dress is come as you are."

"Teaching? On what? Not that it matters in my decision."

"First Corinthians 13."

"Yes, as a matter of fact, I think I'll take you up on your generous offer. I sure hope Helen won't mind."

"I'll bet she'll be glad to have someone to sit with."

Helen came in and expressed her approval that Ruth would be joining them. They drove the six miles down to Zion Church and parked on the grass beside the driveway. The old scene of evergreens and century-old boxwoods was beautifully soothing. A graveyard in front paid tribute to the families whose involvement over the past one hundred and seventy-five years had shaped each other's lives and influenced this community's seed bed.

"This place is so rich in history," said Helen, looking all around.

"Hello, Helen Dear. How in the world are you?"

"Hi, Mrs. Armstrong," Helen said, hugging her. "I haven't seen you..."

"Since the funeral," she consoled. "We were talking about you just the other day and remembering what a tragedy it was for you losing your mother at such an early age. We sure are glad to have you visiting with us tonight, especially on the arm of this saintly young man," she said, putting her hand affectionately on Andrew's shoulder. "You know we just think the world of him down here."

"I'm sure he feels the same way," Helen assured her, with her eyes on Andrew more than Mrs. Armstrong.

"Come on over here, Darling, and see some of your parents' old, dear friends." She pulled Helen's hand as she led her through the wrought iron gate to a small group standing on the sidewalk talking.

They all greeted Helen and ushered themselves inside.

CHAPTER 14

"What time do you think we ought to get there?" asked Stuart, looking at his watch.

"I think thirty minutes early will be fine," smiled Elise.

He sat on the couch and tried to determine if she was making any move to stand. He was embarrassed to admit that he had forgotten the time she had said the concert started. She called him and said she had tickets for the concert and wanted him to go with her. She had told him to be at her apartment for a drink around six. He had arrived at ten after and now looked into his empty scotch glass and wondered what to do.

She stood, but did not make an offer to get him another drink. He took the cue to stand and began to shuffle toward the door. She stopped and stood in front of a framed mirror in the entry foyer. She set a jewelry case that he had not noticed on the small table under the mirror and opened it, took out first one string of pearls, then another and finally decided on a third, shorter, multi-stran set. She moved her hair aside by tilting her head to the left and forward while turning her face to the right.

"May I?" he asked, reaching for the necklace.

"Please," she said, holding each end and making the exchange occur on each side of her neck, slightly below the ears.

As he manipulated the clasp, her perfume began to live up to what the advertising campaign had said it would. She held her hair to the side and the view included her low cut front at an irresistable angle. She was no more than five or six inches shorter than he, and this procedure put his nose and mouth close to her right ear.

"Thank you," she said, looking into his reflected eyes as he took his hands away from the completed task.

"It was truly a pleasure." Then he stepped back a couple of steps and quietly exhaled through his nose the breath he had been holding for longer than he realized.

They walked out the front door and down the steps to the driveway and on beyond the car to the sidewalk. She reached for his hand as they walked onto the small campus and toward Brenau's Pierce Auditorium.

"I think you will enjoy this," she said confidently.

"It's not often I find myself in a suit on Friday night."

"You look really good." she said.

"Thanks, I mean I...."

"Have you ever been to a concert like this?"

"You mean with just a few instruments and no singer?"

"Yes." Elise replied with amusement.

"Once in college, on a Sunday afternoon while everybody else was at the SAE House watching the Falcons."

"Did you like it?"

"It was okay," he lied.

They walked up the wide steps to the columned entrance and through the door. The floor sloped toward the front and the seats were older, curved-back and wooden. He could tell the minute he trusted his seat with his full weight, that they were not designed to accommodate the length of his legs. His knees pressed against the seat in front of him.

****

"You did realize that we are going to be coming back Sunday?" Andrew was laughing as he put Helen's third piece of luggage into the car.

"Well, you said that my day Saturday would be free and I don't know what options I have in Atlanta," she justified.

They got in the car and he sat for a moment. "I filled up with gas, turned everything off in the house and went to the bank. I keep thinking there is something missing."

"Conference materials?" Helen asked.

"No, they said in the mailer that they would provide all that."

"How about a map?" she tried.

"I don't have one, I'll..."

"Here." She offered no explanation and hoped none would be required. "That's, of course, a Georgia map. We ought to be able to get to Chattanooga without much trouble."

He handed it back to her and started the car. "I was hoping to get to talk to you one more time after we made plans to go, but we missed each other. Is there anything that I might not have told you that you would like to know about the weekend?"

"What is tonight?" she asked.

"Registration. I've never been to one, but I would assume they will have a reception room with some type of hors d'oeuvres. Then I'd guess there will be some type of welcome given and we will be told where the various workshops can be found. The times and speakers are all scheduled in the information they mailed. Dinner will be 'on our own' but I would imagine we'll end up with some people and go with a group."

"Who all will it be?"

"Mainly pastors and their wives and maybe some children."

"And tomorrow?"

"You can do whatever you like. There will most likely be some people who will go shopping or to some other sites in the city."

She thought that it would probably work out alright, but the thought of spending the day with strangers was not exactly what she had in mind when she had accepted his invitation. "Or, I guess I could go to some of the workshops," she said.

"I don't see why not. I just don't want you to be bored. The real reason I brought you is for the speaker tomorrow night at dinner. I think you'll really enjoy it."

They rode on for a few miles and didn't say much. They were on I-24 when Helen noticed a Camaro rapidly pass them on the left. The paint was faded metallic gold and the bumper sticker said 'Just Divorced', with broken, black wedding bells on the corner of the layout.

She let the car get out of sight and asked "How are things with the girl you were working with that has the divorced parents?"

"Doing much better. She has made friends with one of the girls in the youth group and her grades have improved, along with her attitude."

"That's good. Divorce is tough on so many aspects of a person's life."

"That's why it is just simply not God's will," he stated matter-of-factly.

"Do you think there is any room for grace?" she asked.

"I'm not sure what you're asking."

"If someone looks up and finds himself in a situation of divorce and can't change the past, should he be penalized for the rest of his life?"

"You mean should he remarry?" the pastor rephrased.

"That's pretty much the bottom line of what I mean, I guess," she admitted.

"Divorce and remarriage are two separate issues in the minds of some people. Personally, I feel that a marriage should be saved at any cost. Even in the event of Biblical grounds, I think the parties should forgive and repair the damage. The vows say for better or worse...until death do us part."

"What if, after the divorce, one of the previous parties marries someone else?"

"I'm not really prepared for all of this. You might be better advised to talk with someone else," he declined.

They walked into the lobby of the Waverly Hotel and she waited while Andrew checked in at the front desk. He returned with a key in his hand. "This is your room. Mine is a few doors down on the same floor."

When both of them were moved into their rooms, and Helen was about to freshen up for the evening, she was interrupted by Andrew's knock at the door.

"Can you meet me in the lobby at about 5:30?" He said.

"Sure," she said, glancing at her watch and mentally calculating the time change.

She fell back on the bed and kicked her shoes off. It felt good to stretch her back and enjoy a moment of silence. The hour passed all too quickly and she wondered about the reception as she rode the elevator down. Andrew saw her from his position in the lobby and walked over to meet her. They turned and went to the large room set up with refreshments and hosts standing by a table with name tags and schedules.

"Hello," nodded Helen to the closest host. "I'm Helen Allbright."

"Hi, my name is Judy Lovell. I'm from Gainesville," she responded.

"I'm from Columbia, Tennessee," Helen said, now stopping and turning to face the new acquaintance.

"Are you here with your husband?"

"No, I'm with a friend."

"Well, we are certainly glad to have you," she said, looking over her shoulder to the small group approaching the table.

"Let me clear the door. I'll talk to you later," Helen said, walking on in to the hospitality suite.

Andrew appeared beside her and they walked to a group of people that looked like none of them really knew each other, either. They stood and chatted casually for a few minutes, then Helen noticed the two ladies at the reception tables were apparently finished with their duties.

Judy came up to her and smiled, "I felt like I interrupted you a minute ago. I'm sorry. What are you planning to do tomorrow?"

"No plans," she said acceptingly.

"Would you like to drive up to the mountains with a couple of us?"

"That sounds great, thank you," Helen accepted.

"I have a friend from Mississippi that I haven't seen in a while and we've been talking the last few days about meeting here this weekend and spending the day sightseeing up around Helen."

"Around what?"

"Helen. It's a town in the mountains modeled from an actual existing Bavarian village in Europe," Judy explained.

"I hope I'm not intruding."

"No, it's not like we are long lost twin sisters. We haven't seen each other in a while and when she was trying to decide if she ought to come to this thing, we just talked ourselves into it. I think you'll really like tomorrow and we'll be back in plenty of time for tomorrow night's activities."

"Thank you, I'm looking forward to it. What time should we leave?"

"It won't take long. I think if we leave by 8:30, we'll be fine. Meet me in the lobby at 8:30."

"Sounds fun. See you then," Helen said, walking back to the group and telling Andrew her plans.

"So, you get to sleep in. I have to be in my first meeting at 7:00," he said, pointing to his schedule. "In the Bulldog Room," he read aloud.

****

The concert ended about the time Stuart's muscles went from sleep to full rigor mortis. He unfolded himself from his chair and stretched for a minute before turning and ushering Elise out with his hand.

"Wasn't that wonderful?" she asked as she squeezed his hand.

"I enjoyed it," he assured her as he tried to convince himself. They continued up the inside slope to the doors and stepped out into the cool night air. She reached and pulled his arm around her and snuggled in close to him as they walked down the steps.

"Cold?" he asked.

"Not for long," she said looking into his eyes from very close range.

She tilted her head slightly, touching his right jaw and put her arm around his waist under his coat as they walked along. When they reached the door, she opened her handbag and presented the key to him. He turned the lock and pushed the door open, allowing her to step in front.

She turned on the light in the hallway and hooked the index finger of her right hand into his left hand and led him in to the den where she steered him to sit on the couch.

"Would you like anything?" she asked, still standing.

"No, I'm fine, thanks."

She sat down facing him with her knee touching his thigh. She took both of his hands and slipped them around her neck and onto her necklace clasp.

"Do you do as good of a job taking it off as you do of putting it on?"

He smiled and answered with a single motion that unfastened it and then presented the pearls to her. She took them and leaned across him to set them on the end table. She stopped halfway and tilted her head. He responded and she slowly closed her eyes as their mouths met.

"Mmmm...'" she said with her eyes opening very slowly. "More, please."

He obliged by holding the back of her head with his left hand and pulling slightly as they kissed again.

"How are you with zippers?" she asked with her eyes at half-mast.

He wanted to object to the forwardness. He was not sure whether it was an unclean feeling or if he was getting enough of her pulling him along.

He kissed her lightly and drew his head back a little further than normal. "You know, it's getting late and I guess I ought to think about turning in."

"What a wonderful idea," she said and stood up, still holding his hand.

"Elise, what I meant was that...uh...I should be going."

"Oh, I see," she said shortly.

"Listen, I really..."

"Goodnight. You won't mind if I don't walk you to the door, I hope?"

CHAPTER 15

"So, what are you going to do?" Joe asked.

"I'm going into the hills and not come out, at least until tomorrow." replied Stuart.

"You're going to miss a great game."

"I know you've been looking forward to this and I really appreciate your understanding. I'm sure you can get anybody to go without a problem. All I want to do is take my dog and go where I don't have to think, talk or refrain from breaking wind out loud."

"It still sounds like a spec sheet for a guy's trip to Sanford Stadium," objected Joe.

"Have fun, and bring me back a dead War Eagle."

Stuart hung up the phone and walked into the extra bedroom where the closet was filled with equipment. He pulled out his backpack with the divided cooler bottom compartment, the two-man tent and the sleeping bag. He pulled the 12" grill from the shelf and the side saddle dogpack from the corner of the closet floor.

He took everything into his room and tossed it onto the bed. He opened the top drawer of his bedside table and retrieved the pistol lying against the side closest to the bed, and included it among the equipment.

He stuffed the soft items such as the tent, ground cloth and sleeping bag, into the dog's pack. The utensils and food container went into the pack he would carry.

"Come on, girl," he called to Maggie.

He loaded her in the back, onto the old green bedspread, and they backed out of the driveway and into a perfectly beautiful day.

****

"I hope this doesn't mess up your day, Helen. I would go on and go, but Cathy and I had talked about seeing each other and just because she is sick doesn't mean we can't get a visit in."

"I understand perfectly. Tell her I hope she feels better, even though I didn't get a chance to meet her."

Helen looked at her watch. It was 8:20 and she was more disappointed than she had indicated to Judy. The lobby was not very active and she flagged a bellman down to get directions to the Bulldog Room.

A few minutes later, she found herself walking toward the labeled door, wondering if she should interrupt the meeting inside. As she approached the door, it popped open and gave her a start. She stepped back and saw the setup of tables with water glasses and notepads facing a podium and overhead projector.

Andrew was the fifth or sixth one from the door and she caught his eye from her position in the hall. "Well, I thought you'd be gone by now," he said looking at his watch.

"The trip was called off due to illness," she explained sadly.

"I'm sorry to hear that. I know you were really looking forward to a drive in the mountains."

"Andrew, do you think I could possibly borrow your car and go on by myself?"

"By yourself?" he asked.

"Sure, that's how I live," she reminded.

"It's fine with me," he said reaching into his pocket. "I guess the keys are with the valet out front. Here, take this ticket and have at it."

"Thanks. I'll be back this afternoon about 5:00."

"Have fun and be careful."

She walked lightly through the lobby and out to the valet's side office. Soon she was in the car and on her way with advice to take I-285 to Georgia 400 to Dahlonega.

Georgia 400 was like an interstate in every way except traffic. She rolled the windows down and breathed the soul-cleansing air that accompanied the Blue Ridge Mountains which had emerged on either side of her.

She came to the big bridge that ended 400 and followed the road toward Dahlonega. The town square was unique in as much as a small road circled the central courthouse while an additional divided area gave access to the small shops and restaurants. She made a mental note of the Christmas Shop and followed the sign to Cleveland. Once in Cleveland, it was an easy matter to be directed to Helen. Driving with a continued glance back and forth at an impressive mountain, she finally stopped in the gravel drive of a craft shop where a woman was draping a quilt over the front rail.

"That's beautiful. Did you make it?" Helen asked.

"I recon' I did. This 'un ain't nothin next to them in yonder." The buxom figure in the polka-dot print disappeared and reappeared like a bear on stage. "You like double wedding band or lone star best?" The dip of snuff in her lower lip was now too noticeable to be ignored.

"They're all very nice. I..."

"Hand stitched and quilted," she boasted.

"How long does it take to do one?" Helen asked, now more curious.

"You or me?" she said.

"I don't think you could time me without a calendar," Helen laughed, still standing in the grass below the rough mill lumber porch.

"Now, that first 'un'll neerly make you lose your religion."

"That will give it back to you," she nodded at the mountain she was now at the base of. "Can you drive up there?"

"All but the last little piece. Just take that dirt road yonder where you see the new looking drain tile," she said, finally spitting off the end of the porch.

"Thank you." Helen got into the car and drove across the highway and onto the designated road. The road was narrow and steep. It had several wash-outs that caused her concern for Andrew's car. At the end of the road, which was obviously not the top of the mountain, she steered to an area below a large four-wheel drive pickup truck. She got out, glad that she had worn tennis shoes and followed the indications of a path on the ground. It led to a large mound of dirt that had been intentionally dumped there to prevent any further vehicular intrusion. She continued on the trail through laurel thickets and jackoaks to a point of decision. The left fork went sharply up while the straighter route appeared to break out of the woods just ahead. She chose the straighter route and followed it in twenty yards until she was standing roughly halfway up on the edge of the rock face. The valley and craft store below her were dwarfed by the panorama of farms and ponds and villages and more mountains in the distance. She took a couple of steps onto the solid granite and leaned back on her hands and shoulders, feeling the rock's cool, rough surface.

After a glance up the climb that remained, she ventured a few more steps out, this time using hands and toes while facing the rock. Since the slope was not perpendicular at this point and the surface had no loose material to slip on, she easily made her way to an area that was almost the size of a surfboard. Again she turned and pushed her back against the mountain and absorbed the experience.

"This is great," she thought as she could now see the top in clear sight. She had become comfortable using alternating hand and foot holds to continue nonstop up what would soon be half the climbing area. She reached the top of the climb and could stand on the now gently sloping ground and see almost 180 degrees.

"Wow," she whispered. As she turned and walked to the firetower in the very center of the top. She could see across the remainder of the whole plateau and out in the other direction.

After a few minutes of strolling around the top, she returned to a ledge near the place where her assent had ended. Taking a seat with her knees up and her arms wrapped around her legs, she gently rocked back and forth and fell deep into thought.

"What did I tell you?" he whispered through clenched teeth.

"Are you sure she's alone?" came the response.

"Yeah, come on, Fool."

The two shabby characters slinked out of the laurel thicket toward their objective.

Helen was oblivious to their presence until she suddenly felt a rough yank of her hair, causing her to gasp sharply.

"Jes you sit tight, sweet thang," he said as his enormous face came into view with its scrappy beard and breath that smelled of stale beer.

Fear gripped her like a cold vice and she felt her ears and neck respond to the almost audible rush of blood from her heart as she realized a second man to her left holding her arm.

"You know," said the first one, reaffirming his hold on her hair while pressing his leg hard against hers, "This could work out to be right nice for everybody if you behave yourself."

She could not speak. She no longer knew the mechanics of what it would take to speak.

The second man slid his left hand between her knees and she instinctively slammed them together.

"Now, that ain't what my cousin meant a'tall," he said, squeezing her arm to the point of pain now and showing a gold tooth and grimy grin.

71

"She don't like you, Leon," said the first captor. "Watch here."

He thrust his fist between her thighs halfway above the knees and forced her legs apart.

"Hang on to her, Leon, it's time to go to work."

She gasped and found her tongue. "Lord, save me," she cried.

Boom! Boom! The unmistakable sound of gunshots split the crisp mountain air, and sent both would-be assailants to their feet searching for the source of their turmoil. They both froze at the sight of the ominous form less than twelve feet away with something on its back, a huge beast by its side and what appeared to be a cannon leveled at their faces.

"GET OFF MY MOUNTAIN!" "Boom!" The gun discharged again and both offenders went tearing headlong back through the laurel thicket, ripping clothes and flesh in their flight.

"It's okay now. They're gone," he spoke softly to the tightly tucked form on the ledge.

She lifted her face from her knees and forearms and turned to face the familiar voice of her rescuer.

"You?" she exclaimed.

"Helen! Are you okay?"

She jumped to her feet and lunged into Stuart's arms. He held her close to his chest with his cheek firmly pressed on top of her head.

She cried softly for a moment before she loosened her embrace and stood back. "Oh, Stuart, I've always thought if something like that happened, I would kick or bite or scream," she said wiping her eyes with her fingers. "I couldn't move."

"That would have been the case for anyone. They were two, big men! There was nothing you could have done."

"When I think of what could have happened," she shook her head and continued, "Thank you! Did I thank you?"

"You're welcome. Sit down." He moved her a little back from her previous spot to a fallen tree which they could sit on.

"So, how have you been?" she laughed.

"What on earth are you doing here?" he asked.

"It's a long story and I'm not really sure where to start."

"Don't worry about all that now."

"I've been doing a lot of thinking....". She stopped. She wanted to tell him of her struggle but didn't want to be presumptuous or appear patronizing.

"You don't owe me any explanation. If you wanted a place to think, you couldn't beat this one."

"Well, today didn't provide the most peaceful experience...."

"It had some rough moments, but I think things are looking up now," he smiled.

"Who's your pal?"

"That's right, you haven't been introduced to Maggie." He turned and whistled with the fingers of one hand in his mouth. In less than a minute, the sleek pack lab trotted up to them.

"She's beautiful."

"So, how about lunch?"

"Okay," she inhaled. "What do I do?"

"Build a fire," he said and kicked out an area about eighteen inches across.

She got to her feet and began helping him stack twigs and sticks, then watched as he lit the wood with a match. With the larger sticks safely burning, they slowed the work and she sat back.

"Here," he said and pulled a ground cloth from Maggie's pack and spread it out so she could sit on the ground with the fallen tree trunk supporting her back.

She glanced at the fire and then turned her gaze to the view she had been enjoying before the interruption. "This is nice," she said.

"I'm glad you think so. I agree."

"What did you mean when you told those jerks to get off *your* mountain?"

"It's just a male thing. You know, like territoriality. Kind of a chivalry thing defending the virtue of a beautiful woman." His eyes sparkled with sarcasm.

He looked into her eyes and thought she was beautiful. The sun was high and highlighted the occasional auburn in her hair. Her brown eyes were soothing and genuine. The cream ragwool sweater softly accentuated her figure.

She smiled when she looked at his pack where the gun was half visible and sticking in the open sidepocket.

"Smith & Wesson, 9 millimeter," she said, remembering. "Everybody else in high school exchanged rings or broken medallion necklaces. I had to fall for a guy who bought us a matching pair of pistols."

"Do you still have yours?"

"Yes, and I actually carry it a good bit."

He was sitting on the ground cloth now and reached to drop another medium-size stick on the fire. He pulled the pack between them and took out a bowl and began to pour the contents of packets in. Finally he produced and emptied a small box of milk and stirred it for about a minute before covering it and setting it aside.

"So, what brings you to Yonah?" he asked innocently.

"I came down with a friend to attend a pastors' retreat in Atlanta."

"Andrew."

"That's right. How do you know him?"

"I met him the afternoon I stopped in to see you. You know, the day you were in Gainesville," he said very matter-of-factly.

She felt her ears turn red. How could he have possibly known? "Who said I was in Gainesville?"

"Really, it was an informed guess," he smiled.

He didn't ask the point blank questions and she didn't volunteer any more.

"How do you like this part of the world?" he asked, looking at the view.

"Beautiful. It's so full of energy," she marveled.

"That's a strange description," he noted.

"There's nothing more powerful to me than peace. That's what I feel, is peaceful."

He smiled and watched her look for a moment, then reached into the pack and brought out the small grill and a container with something inside. He set the grill across a couple of rocks and took a pair of tongs and began to arrange shrimp on the grill.

"Mmmm," she approved, with raised eyebrows. "That sure beats...."

"Don't speak too soon," he cautioned. He reached into the pack again and presented a wrapped article that was fist size.

She smiled knowingly and took it. "Hoop cheese," she said without unwrapping it. "Where did you get it?"

"Caragan's in Sawdust," he said dryly.

Her mind was already entertaining memories of Sunday afternoons when they were in high school. Those long walks and picnics on sand bars had confirmed to her then she wanted a man who was her best friend, too.

"This shrimp will be done in a second." He pulled yet another, sealed container out of his pack and opened it to reveal a beautiful cut of beef swimming in a marinade.

"What on earth?"

"Chateaubriand," he laughed, putting it on the grill and sliding the shrimp to a cooler spot. "Just add imagination."

"What next? Wine and a serenade?" she asked.

"You'll see," he said, reaching for the pack.

"Red or white, since we are having seafood and beef?"

"Green," he said producing the squeeze bottle of Gatorade he had mixed at home.

She squeezed the cold liquid into her mouth and realized she had not had anything to drink in several hours. "Nice. A good year, no doubt."

"Do you come up here often?" she asked leaning back again on the tree trunk.

"Some. I haven't been going to church every Sunday lately and I've found myself either here or Blood Mountain. You know, God promises to meet us where we are, so I figure I'll pick someplace we both like." His tone was more reverent than humorous.

He reached with the tongs to turn the meat and then set the blue-speckled bowl of sauce next to it on the grill.

"I'm sorry about the single serving of dinnerware, but I had thought I would be forced to eat alone when I packed."

"I hope I'm not intruding," she said smiling.

He seated her Indian style and put his bandana in her lap and brought from the fire the beef and sauce. Taking his hunting knife from its sheath, he carved the medium rare entree' and slid the medallions at a shingled angle on the grill that was now on the 'table'. The sauce was added and the only plate was positioned so that both could use it while sitting on the same side of the 'table'.

"Shall we?" he asked, reaching for her hand, palm up.

She placed her hand in his and bowed her head.

He prayed a short, direct prayer about mountains, safety, and at the end, the food. He then cut a piece of meat and put it in her mouth.

"Delicious," she said still chewing. "You don't rough it like some people."

"I don't have much to prove," he smiled, taking his own bite. "I guess if I wanted to test my resistance to discomfort, I would have gone to the city today," he continued.

She smiled at the old Stuart she had known. Simple, unpretentious and not overly concerned about his image. "I wish I cared less about what other people think."

"And sometimes I wish I cared more," he admitted.

"If you wish that, you probably care more than you think."

"I know I care what you think," he said, looking at her and not smiling.

She looked at him for a moment and did not speak.

He continued. "I have always admired you. I've even tried to emulate you. You're secure in your convictions and it's encouraging to be around you."

"I'm not as neat and packaged as you might think."

"Life is not as neat and packaged as you sometimes think. But I have never appreciated you like I do right now." Stuart said thoughtfully.

She could feel her mouth getting dry. The compliment felt good and almost embarrassing.

"You are blessed to have come to where you are in your character and maturity," he continued.

"Thank you." She looked into his eyes and added, "I could stand a lot of this."

"There's something I need to say that you don't need to feel responsible for." He took her hand and turned her to squarely face him.

"I love you Helen. Right now it's probably hard for you to understand or trust my feelings, or yours."

She interrupted his declaration with a gentle finger over his mouth. "I love you Stuart. And I feel I have permission to love you now."

"Would you permit yourself to marry me Helen?"

"Yes" she said softly and without question.

They embraced and for the first time in this second chapter of their lives, they kissed. And though their eyes were moist, peace and security were realized.

CHAPTER 16

"You did WHAT?!? How?"

"That's right," Helen said calmly. "It's a long story," she said, putting the phone back to her ear.

"Well, where are you now?" Ruth asked a little more settled.

"I'm still in Atlanta. Stuart followed me back to the hotel so I could return Andrew's car."

"This is wonderful, Helen. I'm so excited I can't think. So now what? I've heard of being tacky enough to leave a dance with someone other than the guy who brought you, but this takes the cake."

"Stuart wants to drive me home tonight. We should be there about eight your time. He wants to talk to Daddy."

"What do you mean 'my time'? Have you already moved? This is too much. When is the date?"

"We haven't talked about that yet. We've been in separate cars since...since we got engaged." She felt good about the title.

"Be careful. I love you."

"Thanks, I love you....bye."

She hung up the phone and walked with Stuart to the doors where his car and the black Lab waited.

"I hope it wasn't unpleasant talking to Andrew," he half-asked.

"Not at all. He seemed quite happy for us."

"If we wait until March, that will give me a week off for Spring Break," she said, flipping through the calendar in her checkbook.

"That's kind of long, don't you think?"

"You're probably right. I don't guess I need to plan around work in Columbia anyway."

"Not unless you want to get married and finish out the year in Columbia, then move to Gainesville and join me in the summer."

She thought back a few years to how he had left for college and things ended soon after.

"I'm not interested," she stated. "We're together for good and the details will just have to fit."

"I was not even remotely serious," he smiled, pulling her over to him.

They drove straight through, both still full from lunch, until they got to her house. They walked up the walk and she invited him to come in before going to his parents' house.

"Surprise! Congratulations!" screamed what sounded like two dozen female voices in unison. Helen found Ruth in the chaos and they embraced. She leaned around and hugged Stuart with one arm.

"Do you know how lucky you are?" she pointed her finger at him.

"I learn slowly, but I don't forget," he assured her.

"She's earned every bit of this, one skull session at a time."

"I'm out of here," he laughed. "See you sometime tomorrow," teasing Helen as he left.

"You two are unbelievable!" Helen was crying, as were a couple of her co-celebrators.

****

"Congratulations, son," his father said, extending his hand across the kitchen table.

"Oh, Darling, this is wonderful," his mother said, giving Stuart a hug from behind his chair. "We just love Helen so much."

"When is this going to take place?" his father asked.

"We want the wedding to be before Christmas," he responded.

"Is she going to quit her job at that time?"

"Yes, sir. We hope she can find something in Gainesville. She has a speciality that is in pretty high demand."

"How are things going with your work?"

"Pretty good, actually," Stuart answered, thinking as he spoke.

"Well," burst in his mother, "we have a wedding to plan," she pronounced. "And just enough time to do it."

"Shouldn't the bride concern herself with those arrangements?"

"Yes, of course. But we get to do the rehearsal dinner," she said, clapping her hands together.

"What a joy," his father said disgustedly. "Duck manure on crackers, 'shampain' and all balanced on my knobby knee."

"Fiddle, faddle. You'll have more fun than everybody else combined." Stuart's mother mused.

"Probably not an overly burdensome standard," he muttered, winking at Stuart.

The drive back to Gainesville seemed shorter than ever the next day. The air was clear and he could see the mountains plainly when he turned onto Dawsonville Highway. He stopped by Joe's house on the way in.

"I can't stay long, but I want to tell you what's up," he began as he walked up on the deck. "I've gone and done it. I'm engaged."

"That's great," Joe said, shaking his hand. "I can't wait to meet her."

"Well, you're pretty quick. I thought you would ask 'Who'?"

"No need to, there are only two possible choices, and one of them is in there talking to Linda now," he calmly mentioned.

"What?"

"Yeah, Elise is in the den with Linda."

"I might ease on...."

"Joe! Is someone on the deck with you?" called Linda.

"Yes, Hag. It's Stuart. Come on out."

"Well, well, I thought I heard a familiar voice."

"Hi, Elise. How have you been?" Stuart asked.

"Fine. Were you out of town this weekend?"

"Yes, as a matter of fact I stopped here before even going home. I'm just back from Columbia."

"I'm sorry I didn't know. I had to contact some high schools in Nashville and you could have saved me a trip. I could probably postpone it for a while, though. Do you plan to be going back any time soon? I'd like to ride with you." Elise said.

"Yes, more than likely," he nodded.

"Well, I've got some things to finish up before work tomorrow. Linda, if this book is all you had to bring me by here for, I'll ask you to run me home."

"I'm ready, now," she said, taking her keys off the table on the deck. "I'll be back in 10 minutes, Joe."

"See you later," Elise said to Stuart.

"Bye," he waved.

"So," Joe began as they got into the car. "the single life failed your test."

"Maybe I failed its test. At any rate, this was not so much a negative driven decision and not liking where I was, as it was a positive decision and knowing what I want."

"When do you walk the plank?"

"Some Saturday in December."

"I'll be there. Then what?"

"It's off to a week of honeymoon and then housekeeping in the valleys of Hall County."

"Good for you. What about her job?"

"She'll quit mid-year. I hope she can find something here."

"Funny you should say that. I heard Linda talking this past week about someone being needed at a new program for handicapped children that is using one of the churches during the week for its facility."

"I don't think I've heard of it."

"I don't know a lot about it, myself, but it's fairly new. It was started by a doctor whose child is confined to a wheelchair. My understanding is that it is funded by several different sources and has a need for teachers because the student/teacher ratios have to be so low."

"Helen mentioned to me once that she had an interest in working with stroke patients and older people who need communication skills rehab. I guess if she's interested in this at all, it would be in that light."

"Why don't you tell her to call Linda in a day or so?"

"I'll do that, thanks."

"Besides, we need to meet this new addition."

"I'm looking forward to getting her down here."

CHAPTER 17

"I hope you don't mind going someplace cold," Stuart apologized.

"I don't mind at all," Helen comforted. "I just can't wait to see you. Do you realize we haven't seen each in three weeks?"

"You don't have to tell me. I've been less than functional at work for a month."

"Why, are you nervous?"

"I'm fine."

"If you want to back out, I'll understand. I guess you probably think you rushed into this. I mean I know it was romantic and all, but you don't have to push yourself through this if you are having second thoughts," she enabled.

"I was thinking of eloping tonight," he assured.

"I'm sorry I seem nerved. It's just that a girl starts thinking about her wedding day when she is five years old, and here I am on the phone with my fiance just four days away. I can't believe this is happening."

"So, how about the honeymoon? Do you understand that the effort of someplace warm this time of year is a little much in terms of expense?"

"I really am fine with anything. I am looking so forward to getting out of this circus of cakes and photographers and decorators...."

"And even spending a couple of days with me?" he checked.

"Of course. I'm looking forward to every day of the rest of my life with you as my husband. Everybody has been so good at work. They are giving me a party tomorrow. I'm going to miss these people."

"And you will be missed, there's no doubt about that."

"But I'm looking forward to what's next, too."

"You're going to love it here, and this place will love you," he guaranteed.

"I may need a second and less biased opinion."

"Linda was telling me that the director of the special needs learning center got your resume and is looking forward to setting up an interview with you."

"That sounds good. I hope I can adapt to that type of situation. I've been around handicapped people before but I'm not really sure I'm the one for that job."

"She can probably help determine that for you."

"I'd better run. I love you."

"I love you. Bye."

He hung up the phone and called an old friend of the family who had a travel agency in Athens.

"Jean! It's Stuart."

"How and where are you?"

"Gainesville. What's new with you?"

"I'm just leading this old boring life of spanning the globe, but I hear from Middle Tennessee that the same is not true of you."

"That's what brings me to call."

"Honeymoon cruise time?"

"Not cruise, but something special."

"Hot or cold?"

"What have you got that's hot?"

"How much time do we have?"

"We'll probably spend Saturday night in Nashville and want to fly out Sunday."

"This weekend?"

"Is that a problem?" he asked.

"Not if you have a magic carpet."

"I kind of changed my mind. Helen would like some warm weather."

"Well, it is your honeymoon and Helen probably wants something special."

"No, that's just why I want to do this. She would really be content camping out somewhere if we didn't freeze to death."

"It's nice to see that some things never change. Is she still like she was in high school?"

"Better."

"I'm very happy for you, Stuart. Now, let's see what kind of rabbit I can pull out of my hat. I'll get back to you. I need to dig around a minute."

They hung up and he immediately picked up the phone and started punching the buttons again.

"Maury?"

"Hi. How's the groom-to-be?"

"I'm fine. I need your help to pull off a surprise."

"Sounds great. What do I need to do?"

"When are you going to Columbia?"

"Tomorrow. I'm going to help Mama with the rehearsal dinner. Why?"

"I need you for about two hours Friday morning."

"You've got it," she promised.

★★★★★★

"Okay, where's the photographer?

Stuart looked back at the scene he had just left. The small, rural Methodist Church had been Helen's family church during her childhood. He had visited several occasions when they had wanted to get an early start on a Sunday afternoon date. Today the church was bustling with the activity of two families renewing old friendships while creating new ones. Time seemed to hang suspended for a moment as he watched his mother laugh with her brothers, and his father learn that a niece was pregnant. "family"....he thought, "What a great concept."

"Come on inside," Helen called, standing in the center of the concrete front porch and looking like a queen bee in a hive of attending workers. "We are going to get some shots at the front of the church." The gaggle of relatives parted slightly to allow him to pass. The members of the wedding party followed close behind before the crowd sealed in again.

"That does it for the church," announced the photographer. "Let's get some at the reception, uh, the cake cutting and that should do it."

They all filed into their respective cars and drove the 15 miles to the reception where applause greeted the newlyweds and champagne was passed to everyone over four and a half feet tall.

"Where are you going on your honeymoon, dear?" Aunt Judy asked.

"Stuart isn't telling. He has been able to keep it from me."

"Well, that sounds great, but how did you pack?"

"Emphasis on lingerie," she smiled slyly.

The pictures, cake cutting and conversation with friends, cross-friends, in-laws and obligatories continued until late afternoon.

"We better think about a move, Sweetie," Stuart whispered to Helen in the midst of a trio that had ridden together from a central meeting point in North Mississippi.

As the reception neared its end, Stuart's parents pulled up to the hall in their car. Helen threw the bouquet to the anxious unweds and the newly joined couple waved goodbye and slipped into the provided get-away car.

They pulled off slowly, waving through the open passenger side window. Helen began to cry and Stuart wondered what to do about it.

"What's the matter?" he asked compassionately.

"Nothing," she sobbed softly. "I love all those people so much."

"And you want them to go with us?"

"Of course not."

"You want us to stay here with them?"

"Not at all," she objected, sliding over next to him and tucking her head under his jaw. "That's the trouble with men; they won't talk enough when they're supposed to and they talk too much they shouldn't." Stuart communicated with a firm squeeze to her shoulder with his right arm and drove in silence.

"Where on earth are you taking me?" she blurted less than ten minutes later.

"Surprise," he smiled, knowingly.

They continued on to the airport and parked in the long-term parking. She did not concern herself with details at the point of checking the luggage. They proceeded to the gate.

"Huntsville?" she asked when she saw the confirming flight number and time.

"I hear it's beautiful this time of year." was his only qualifier.

"Suits me fine," she replied sincerely.

They boarded and in no time were being told the plane was landing in Huntsville. The flight attendant began her delivery of connecting flight information. Helen listened half heartedly and they stood when given the signal, holding their rather large carry-on bags.

"Atlanta?" Helen asked, again observing the sign behind the desk at the gate. "You said it was Huntsville."

"I said Huntsville was pretty, I never said we were staying there."

"Are we staying in Atlanta?" she enunciated clearly.

"We'll see," he teased.

Again they boarded shuffled, buckled and scarcely finished a glass of wine before the plane touched down. Helen had listened more carefully this time to the flight attendant's advice on connecting flights, although she didn't quite know why.

"I don't guess we're through even when we get to Miami?" she asked as they boarded the flight so marked.

"Is this a basic insecurity of yours?" he smiled.

"Knowing where I'm going has become habit forming for me. I guess I picked it up in the Girl Scouts," she said putting her carry-on bag under the seat in front of her.

"You'll have to get used to a few changes."

"That sounds like a great idea," she said taking his hand.

The next flight change was a long walk through the Miami airport. They took their place in a long, but quickly moving line.

"Citizenship?" asked the uniformed middle aged, somewhat harsh woman at a checkpoint located as an obstacle to a group of three boarding gates.

Stuart pulled a folded paper from the extension pocket on his overnight bag. "I was told that a passport was not required," he explained as he handed her a copy of his birth certificate.

"This will do nicely," she said not smiling. "Ma'am?"

"I, uh, uh" Helen said looking at Stuart.

"It's here, too," Stuart said presenting it with a little too much delay.

"What is all of this?" she asked as they were herded through the area. He took a seat and gestured for her to do the same at the middle boarding gate. She looked at the logo on the lady at the desk and on the sign behind the desk.

"Caymen Airways?"

"That's right," Stuart said in a canned disc jockey monotone. "You, Mrs. Kerr, will be wisked to the tropical emerald paradise of Grand Caymen on board Caymen Airways, the official airline of the newlyweds. You'll be staying on that British West Indies colony for six days and nights amid palm trees and sea turtles while dining on conch fritters and French-fried parott fish."

"Are you serious? I wonder what was behind door number two?"

"You'll learn that on our tenth anniversary."

"I'm snowed," she said softly.

They boarded the plane and she glanced at her carry-on bag.

"I guess I've carried this across four states for exercise," she said, laughing. "It's full of wool."

"Maybe you can cut the sleeves and legs off and look like a lamb in a tank top," he offered as he thought of how she would react when she opened it to find the new clothes he and his sister had spent three hours buying the day before. Maury had given him that confirming nod at the reception, indicating her accomplished mission of making the switch.

"I'm sure not going to let clothes be a concern on a trip like this," she assured, squeezing his hand.

CHAPTER 18

"How do you like it?" Helen asked.

"It looks great. You changed almost all of it around since this morning when I left for work," Stuart replied.

"My interview went so well that I thought I'd better spend the time, while I had it, getting things straight."

"How in the world did you get the big chair across the room?"

"We have the nicest man living next door. He's single and semi-retired, and he was outside when I was trying to get my bike up the back steps. He came over and then came in and moved several things."

"How did the interview go?"

"I start Monday. I actually worked with Sharon, that's the director, for two hours today."

"That's something, Sweetie. We've only been back from the honeymoon a week and you've already settled us in this house and yourself in a new job. You're my hero. Let's celebrate."

She took him by the hand and led him around to the view of the small dining nook with the English pub "dining" table fully extended and set with the wedding china and a gardenia in a crystal bowl, floating.

"Wow, what's for dinner?"

"Chateaubriand," she said matter-of-factly. She led him into the galley kitchen, reached behind the door on a hook and brought out the chef's apron he had been given for a wedding present. She slipped it over his head and tied it behind his back.

"I feel as though I've been enlisted."

"I've been wanting it since we got engaged. You should have never let me see you cook it that day."

She opened the refrigerator and took out several packages and containers.

"This is going to be great," he marveled.

"So, tell me about your day," she inquired.

"I talked to Savannah today and they are mailing us the notice to proceed on the project we bid a few weeks ago."

"What is that? Notice to proceed, I mean," she asked.

"You bid the job first, having to provide a bid bond even then. Next, you are declared the apparent successful bidder."

"The lowest price?"

"Usually," he acknowledged.

"Then you get all the paperwork in order, like insurance and performance and payment bonds and everything, from financials to dental records. If they like all of that, they will award the job to you."

"So, then you go to work?"

"Not until you are given a 'notice to proceed' which shows that they have gotten all of their drawings approved and permits purchased and monies allocated. Then the clock starts running."

"You're not paid by the hour, are you?" she wondered aloud.

"Very rarely. In most jobs now, you are paid monthly on a basis of periodic completion, less a retainage that is held in escrow until the end of the job."

"Why did you say the clock starts running?" Helen asked.

"There's usually a clause in the contract called 'liquidated damages'. It's really a form of penalty, even though they won't call it that. It's for dragging a job out too long. It is rarely a factor, because if you ever took as long as they allow, you would lose your shirt on the job anyway. But, they put in some daily dollar amount and I do know of rare cases where it was imposed on a contractor. It happened to a guy up in Rabun County once on a Georgia DOT job. He was from Waycross.

"He hit rock and tried to get by with spot drilling by hand and using a backhoe to chip it out of the way. He crawled around Tallola Gorge like the fog coming off the lake. The company I used to work for owned a couple of rock quarries beside the road building crews. We took a couple of track drills up there and started one on each end and three days later, they met in the middle. The fourth day, we loaded drill holes all day with dynamite and at 3:00 that afternoon, we pulled a shot that, I believe, blew a hole in the ceiling of Hell."

"That must have still cost that contractor a ton."

"No, we had the stuff to do it and the owners of the company were not the kind to take advantage of a man down on his luck. He actually probably didn't lose anything on the job."

"That's neat," she marveled.

"Yeah, it seems things are changing now. Things seem less personal.....but that's not a matter for this committee. Tell me more about your job."

"It's mostly support-related. We obviously have an objective to teach, but a lot of what we teach is more of how to get along in a world that only partially accepts the handicapped."

"We?" Stuart asked.

"Excuse me?" she asked.

"You said 'we teach'. You adapt quickly."

She blushed slightly. "I feel like the director really accepted me. The pay isn't that great, but I'll be through most days at two o'clock, so I think it will work out when we start planning our family."

"Sounds like you found your calling."

They continued talking through dinner and into the bedroom.

★★★★★★★

"Make sure you crossbuck those tracks," Ken called to the transport truck driver.

"She ain't going nowhere," he assured, popping the chain with the cheater-pipe he had used to cam the chain binder to its tension. "Tighter'n a banjo string," he confirmed.

"Stuart, the two scrapers are on the site and the pusher dozier is probably halfway to Savannah by now. Is there anything else you need this week?"

"No, that ought to get me started. I'll need the sheepfoot when we go back next week."

"Be careful: This old dragline can be tricky to haul," Ken cautioned the driver.

"I'll be back in a day or two, Ken. I'm going to let a couple of the men take my truck and I'll ride down in the lowboy with Larry. I will bring my truck back probably day after tomorrow."

"I know, I know, newlywed."

"You're just jealous," Stuart laughed.

They climbed into the cab and Larry throttled up the big Peterbilt 600 Horse Diesel, popped the airbrake with a high pressure hiss and eased slowly out on the clutch. The gears found each other and the monster crawled without the slightest lurch.

"You got to baby her from a dead stop or that cat engine will ring the driveshaft like a dishrag." he boasted. Soon all fifty tons and six axles were cruising at fifty miles an hour.

"Mind if I take a snooze?" Stuart asked, positioning himself as if he had already gotten permission.

"Help yourself. I ain't much for talking according to my old lady noway. Now there's one more mouther for you. She could talk the horns off a billygoat. One time I had to pull a load of watermelons from Cordeal to somewhere in Maryland and she decided she wanted to go. We bobtailed out of Gainesville and by the time we got to Macon, I knew I was in for...."

The hum of the wind in the cab, coupled with the sun shining through the non-tinted glass quickly took Stuart away from this monologue into a deep sleep.

****

Helen took advantage of Stuart's absence to get a head start on her new job. She drove to the school and walked down the quiet, deserted hallway to the room that was to be her classroom. As she entered the empty room, she stood in awe hoping that her efforts would result in some positive change to the life of someone, anyone. The click of the light switch drew her attention to the door of the classroom.

"Well, hello again. Back so soon?"

"Sharon, I hope you don't mind my barging in. My husband, Stuart, is going to be out of town for a couple of days and I didn't have a lot to do, so I hoped I could hang around here."

"Sure. I hope you understand that this is one of those board-run and hardline-budgeted operations. In other words, I'd love to have you, but you don't officially start until Monday, so I can't pay you."

"I understand and that's fine. I just don't really want to sit home in a new town and all."

"Okay, let me show you some things that you didn't have time to see yesterday." And with that, Sharon took her down the hall to what would soon become their new physical therapy room.

"You're here, Rip Van Winkle."

"What?" asked Stuart, in the middle of a dream that had nothing to do with trucks or draglines.

"Savannah," Larry proclaimed.

"You've got to be kidding," Stuart said, looking at his watch.

"You ever been here before?"

"Yes, I came down last month to get a look at this job we're going to start tomorrow."

He looked through the streets from the bridge they were crossing and remembered them with the chaos of a parade and green beer.

"A college pal of mine and I came here for St. Patrick's Day. We stayed about three days and went to every party and danced every dance." He thought more specifically for a minute and added, "He had a cousin that stole my heart. We stayed in her parents house and she was, of course, staying there for the week. You know, home from school."

"How convenient," Larry said with a roll of his eyes.

"In my dreams. She didn't even notice I was a male," Stuart laughed.

"Good thing. If you fell for her like you say, you might have wound up down here for keeps."

They turned off the main road and followed a track, now becoming road for a hundred yards and slowed to a stop. The big tractor seemed to sigh as the engine was idled, then shut down. Larry walked around to the trailer and reached behind the frame just under the fifth wheel where he found the rubber covered starter button. The pony engine cranked on the first try and its eight horses strained to supply the hydraulic pressure needed to extend the single cylinder to the ground and support the load previously on the fifth wheel.

Larry pulled the keeper shafts from each side and threw the 18" lever that would allow the lowboy to separate from the portion of itself still coupled to the tractor. When the cylinder was again retracted, the deck of the trailer sat on the sandy soil and Stuart assisted by cranking the tractor and pulling out of the way while Larry now assigned himself to firing off the big 30B dragline and walking it off down the incline like an elephant down a gang plank. Stuart watched in the sideview mirror until Larry had descended, pivoted and lumbered out of the way, then knuckled the shifter into reverse and rolled straight back into the small, curved forks and redocked the assembly.

"The boom's coming on another load," Stuart announced. "Put it as far over there as you can get it. We're going to start running the pans in the morning."

They both got back into the tractor with the empty trailer in tow and started for the motel that would be home for four nights a week to a crew out of nearby Thompson for the duration of the job.

CHAPTER 19

"My name's Diane," she said, extending a hand.

"Hello. I'm Helen," Helen said, smiling and taking the surprisingly firm, full handshake.

"When did you start working here?"

"Actually, I'm scheduled to begin Monday. I've just recently gotten married and my husband is out of town on a new project he's working on in Savannah, so I wanted to kind of familiarize myself with things."

"Good, you can sure be a help to me today if you want."

"Doing what?"

"PT."

"Excuse me?" helen asked.

"Physical therapy. At least, that's what we call it. I'm not exactly finished with all of my training as a therapist yet, but I'm volunteering my time, and Sharon lets me do some of the less technical things."

"Sounds fine. How can I help?" Helen volunteered.

"Come in here where we are setting up some of the equipment." They walked the short distance down the hall and into the room Helen had seen yesterday. There had been considerable progress made since Helen had last seen it. About the time she was going to ask Diane for some explanation, Sharon followed a wheelchair into the room.

"Helen, this is Darren," she introduced.

Helen turned and saw the nine or ten-year-old boy sitting in an elaborate motorized wheelchair. His atrophical legs were nonfunctional and his arms were diminished muscularly. He looked up and smiled but did not speak.

"Hi, Darren," Helen welcomed.

Sharon said in a low voice, "Darren was hit by a car while walking across the road in front of his house. It has been almost two years now and he is showing some sign of promise in his arms. There is not really a lot of hope for his legs, but we feel like we may be able to help him develop some very valuable use of his arms."

"Okay, so how do we start?"

"I'll let you and Diane work on that," she smiled in Diane's direction.

"Darren, can you come over here by the mat?"

Without answering, he thumbed the toggle switch and the chair clicked, then hummed to the point Diane had indicated.

"Now, Helen, give me a hand. We're going to set him out of his chair and onto the mat."

"Okay."

They positioned themselves on either side of the wheelchair and Helen watched to be sure to mirror Diane's actions as much as possible in lifting the obstinate passenger first up then over to the slightly elevated but level approach deck covered with a mat similar to a tumbling surface.

"Okay, Darren, first I want you to put your hands down beside your hips and just sit straight up. We're going to be right here but I want you to try to keep yourself from falling to either side by using your hands."

Diane placed her hands on his shoulders as he sat like he would in a wheelchair. She watched the surface of the mat close to his hands for any depression that would indicate pressure. There was none.

Helen sat now facing him with her feet straight out almost touching his and put her palms squarely down on the mat on either side of herself.

"If she can do it, you can do it too, Darren," challenged Diane. She felt his muscles respond in her hands and carefully began to remove her own support. "That's it, you're doing it," she said softly.

In only a moment, the indention on the mat under his left hand disappeared and his body began to topple left and backward. Diane quickly compensated with her hand and knee in her squatting position and sat him upright.

"Great start, Darren," congratulated Helen.

"Darren, why don't we rethink this thing a little while and we can try again later?"

"Okay," was the first word Helen had heard from Darren.

"Darren," she said, wanting to keep the exchange going, "Could you show me how to drive your chair?"

"Sure," he agreed.

Helen sat down in the chair and positioned her feet on the step plates and looked at him for instructions.

"Forward makes it go forward," he said simply.

She clicked the joystick and was startled at the speed. A few feet and she came to a full stop before leaning the stick slightly to the right and feeling the drive engage to start a sharp pivot.

"This is okay," she said as she spun past the mark that would have lined her up to return to her original position.

"Girls!" Darren remarked shaking his head in mock disgust.

"Give me time," said Helen. "You teach me this and I'll teach you the mat. How's that?"

"Okay," he smiled as she lurched to a stop close to her starting place.

Helen got out of the chair and walked over to him. She and Diane now assumed their lift positions and raised, then began taking steps to the chair. The new position required Helen to have her back to the chair. Her foot struck the step plate and she stumbled.

She shrieked in pain as Darren's full weight landed on top of her despite all she could do to maintain control.

"Are you alright?" she asked him.

CHOICES

"Sure, but I'm already paralyzed," he smiled.

"Helen, are you okay?" asked Diane, getting the increasing impression things were not good.

"I can't get up. And my back is hurting pretty bad." she grimaced. Diane worked herself directly behind Darren and lifted with her hands locked in front of his chest and her arms under his arms until she had him in the chair.

Helen was now flat on her back with tears streaming across her temples. Sharon had come in when she heard the noise of the fall. "What is it?" she asked anxiously as she responded to Helen's painful expression.

"Her back," answered Diane.

Helen tried to hold back the sobs.

"I'm sorry," said Darren sincerely.

Helen looked up and smiled. "It's okay," she assured him. "I should have been paying closer attention to what I was doing."

Sharon leaned down and slid a panel corner of the mat under Helen's head. "Can you tell if the pain is more to the side or in the center?"

"It seems like it's everywhere," Helen winced.

"Let's call a doctor," said Diane.

"No. I'll be better in a little while, I think."

"Have you had this happen before?" asked Sharon.

"Yes, in college when I was moving from one apartment to another. It stayed sore for a week or so, but got okay."

"Do you remember the pain being this intense?" Diane pursued.

"No, but that was a few years ago and I think I did wind up staying down for several hours."

"Let's see if we can slide a mat under you and leave you alone for a while."

They worked slowly and carefully to maneuver a mat under her and a pillow for her head. Diane brought in a tape player and recited the selections, asking for Helen to make a choice.

"Anything slow that doesn't make you want to move your hips," she smiled with a contorted upper lip.

****

Back in Savannah, the track was showing the wear of the earthmovers and Stuart motioned for the motorgrader to blade over it and remove the shallow ruts and pockets. The fill was even now taking on the characteristics it would maintain for 75% of the project. The slight incline to a higher dumping area, then a more abrupt one to the yet unfilled subgrade or in this case, natural ground. The motorgrader made short work of the haul road. It made its way over to the borrow cut to smooth some of the gorges the scrapers made by lowering and raising the moleboard while trying to find just the right depth for the particular material that would load at the ideal speed. Stuart watched over the rim of the cone shaped paper cup as the next load became the first one to cross the freshly dressed ten-foot-wide path. The operator snatched the highest gear, now that the bouncing had stopped.

Suddenly without warning, the great yellow beast dropped and stopped with such abruptness, the operator flew headlong out of the open cab.

Stuart lowered his hand and allowed the empty cup to fall from his grasp. The operator climbed into the lowered cab and selected first gear. He began to throttle up, but the pulling axle on the front of the two-piece tractor threw the enormous tires into a spin in the muck that had devoured the lower portion of the scraper. The front end lashed now from side to side, straining for footing. The endeavor proved hopeless. It looked like some pathetic prehistoric myth in a tarpit.

The motorgrader was on its way to extend its blade to offer a push when it too toppled, first one side then the other, into the expanding mire. When Stuart saw it, he waved the other scrapers to a halt and signalled to the operator on the dozier.

"What do you think, Ernest?"

"Beats anything I ever saw," he concluded.

"I mean about the dozier. Will it walk on that stuff close enough to winch those two out?"

"We can try."

Stuart got in his truck and followed behind the dozier in the direction of the expanding problem. The dozier's wide tracks offered lower ground pressure and it was hoped they would snowshoe it close enough to reel a cable off the winch drum to one of the helpless pieces. No such luck. Even fifteen feet away, the dozier dropped to the belly pain as though it had wandered onto thin ice.

Stuart stepped out and declared "It's lunch time. Let's take a break before we lose the whole fleet."

They clamored out of their respective seats and got into the back of the truck. He pulled up to the crew truck they rode in and said, "Let's go down to the cafe across the bridge and drown our sorrows in a moon pie."

The workmen declined, opting rather for luncheon meat which they had brought to the job. They invited Stuart to join them. In light of the impending doom, he felt it would be the diplomatic thing to do so he joined them. Spam never tasted so bad.

"Trouble?" a driver asked, his moon face now looking sincerely at Stuart from behind a thousand freckles. He had pulled his rig beside Stuart's truck.

"An hour ago. We were trying to build a dike on the river bottom across the bridge, and now my equipment is halfway to China."

"Pans?"

"Yeah," Stuart answered, surprised by the familiar question. "And a dozier and motorgrader. We were hauling fine for several hours and then....."

"The surface crust broke through into blue gumbo." the stranger diagnosed.

"I don't know what it is. It looks like black bean soup with an attitude. But you seem to know."

"That's gumbo. If it's sun dried, you can't drive a nail in it, but if its wet and in one of its moods, you can't fly a plane over it without getting stuck."

"Well, this education is going to cost me more than my daddy paid for my college."

"Not necessarily," he said, finishing his sandwich. I've got a little something on my lowboy that might help."

Stuart lit up. "You sound like you may know better than I do what I need."

"Come on out and let's see," he offered, jumping from his seat in the cab. The piece of equipment on the trailer was unlike any Stuart had ever seen. The tracks were in concept like a dozier, but much wider and lighter material. The cab was higher and the engine much higher off the ground than conventional.

"What is it?"

"I call her Swamp Guinnea. She can climb a cypress and pull it up by the roots while she's sitting on the first limb. Lemme show you what she'll do."

Within minutes, the big, redheaded operator was whistling his machine toward the quagmire like Brer Rabbit loping toward the brierpatch.

Stuart motioned for two of the operators to join him in the truck. They soon had cabled the entangled equipment to safe ground. As they were getting out of the truck, the project engineer drove up.

"Problem?" he asked Stuart as he stepped from his state embossed truck.

Stuart's mind raced past several choice responses given the obvious scene. "Yes, some unexpected subsoil failure," he censored. "This fellow here saved my equipment, at least."

"Kirk's the name," the savior offered.

"Well, how do you plan to haul the rest of that material?" the engineer asked calmly reminding Stuart of the unmet contractual obligation.

"This is none of my business, but it don't really matter how you get it there, it ain't gonna stay," Kirk put in.

"What do you mean?" questioned the engineer obviously less sure of himself in this new conversation.

"If it won't hold a dozier, it won't hold the dike. It may take months, but if you put in a 10-foot-high dike on no more width than you've got staked, it'll disappear. The only way to fix your problem is to dredge pump the river channel and silt this area, or at least a couple of hundred feet of it, with what comes out of that river."

The young engineer had no rebuttal. "I'll have to talk to my boss and he's out until Monday."

"Sounds like 'Miller time'," came a voice from behind the discussion.

The engineer drove off and Stuart turned to his benefactor. "Kirk, I don't know how to thank you. Let me get you a check for the time."

"No need. It was my pleasure."

"Let me do something," Stuart persisted, not surprised at the response.

Kirk stopped and turned from what was his intention to board the Swamp Guinnea for loading.

"Several years back," he began "my brother and I decided we would expand our business. We had been doing work in this part of the country for years and thought it was time to go North. He agreed to run the job if we got it, so we headed to Rabun County to put in a widening lane. About a week into the job, we hit rock bad. He found a crowd out of Gainesville that sent equipment and dynamite to pull our fat out of the fire. We would have busted if they hadn't done what they did. You wanted to do something in return? Next time you see somebody stuck, if you've got the way to pull them out, take the time to do it. It might just be the real reason you got up that morning."

Stuart smiled and thought quickly of whether he should claim credit for the rock-blasting relief, small world story. "Thanks," he decided, "I'll remember that for a long time." He shook Kirk's leathery hand and said goodbye.

CHAPTER 20

Stuart pulled his car into the driveway/parking place which seemed to welcome the weary traveler. He opened the door to his new home and scanned the room for signs of life.

"Get all the strange men out. I'm home early and unexpected," he joked.

"In here," a reply sounded softly.

Stuart walked into the extra bedroom that was not furnished and found his wife lying on the floor amidst several pillows with one knee pulled up to her chest.

"What's going on?" he asked, kneeling down.

"I hurt my back this morning at work."

"How?" Stuart kneeled.

"I slipped while I was lifting someone into a wheelchair."

"Is it bad?"

"No, just slipped out or something. I couldn't move for a couple of hours. They insisted that I get it x-rayed, so I did because I was pretty scared at that point, myself."

"And?"

"They must have taken 100 different angles. One thing's for sure, if it could show up on x-ray they would have found it. I haven't had that many pictures taken since our wedding day."

She slowly lowered the left leg and raised the right, bending the knee and bringing it almost to her nose.

"Much better," she observed. "I'll be back to normal in no time."

"Can you walk?" Stuart asked.

"Yes. I just have to be careful getting up and down," she said.

"And not pick up anything that weighs more than a straw hat," he prescribed.

"Right. What are you doing home?"

"It's a long story. I'm going to get a shower. Grab my suitcase and bring it back to our room," he laughed.

"Don't even joke about that yet. The thought makes me ill."

"Do you feel like getting up?" he asked.

"Yes, give me a hand."

They walked down the small hallway to the larger master bedroom at the back of the apartment. With Stuart's help she was soon propped on the four poster queensize bed that looked beautifully out of place in the small apartment bedroom.

"How about a beer?" he offered.

"I'd love one, thanks."

He was back in a matter of minutes with two full frosty mugs. He glanced at the size of the heads and extended to her the one with less foam.

"Scoal."

She gestured a toast return and turned it up. "Mmm, that's the best thing all day."

He leaned over and kissed her softly on the lips. When he raised, her eyes were still closed.

"The service here is great," she said slowly.

"We aim to please," he said, touching her cheek with the back of his fingers.

"Tell me about how all this took place," Stuart requested, making his way over to his side of the bed.

"Well, everybody was great. The precious boy I mishandled was a really good sport. I could have hurt him badly, you know," she pondered. "I spent a couple of hours on the floor before I could even move-it hurt so bad. Later, when Diane drove me to the hospital, it took three people, one I didn't know at all, to get me into the car. I think three more got me onto a stretcher at the hospital. They gave me a pain killer that helped and a prescription for a muscle relaxer that is still helping. It was just unusual for me to have to be assisted in everything. There was even a trip to the bathroom before the hospital adventure. It gave me a taste of what it's like to be on the receiving end of the kind of work I'm going to be doing."

"How did that feel?"

"To be honest, I didn't like it much. Not so much from the standpoint of not being able to run and jump and play, but the fact that I didn't like having my needs affect someone else every inch of the way." she noticed. "And Heaven forbid that I should need to change my clothes or go somewhere while in that condition."

"Are you having second thoughts about working there?"

"No. I just am a little more focused on what the objectives of our work really ought to be."

"And what would that be?"

"To help these kids know that their handicap is not handicapping anyone else, regardless of their level of dependence."

"Sounds like a good plan."

****

"Morning, Stuart, I didn't think you'd be back yet."

"Hi, Ken," Stuart said, sitting at his desk and going over some blueprints. "I ran into a problem in Savannah," he said, putting down his pencil and inviting Ken to a sincere discussion.

"Tell me the story," Ken attended.

"The haul road the pans were taking fell through to what looked like black bean soup and smelled worse than an alligator farm at low tide."

"Gumbo."

The word that so used to stimulate his salivary glands was quickly becoming an irritant.

"You know the stuff?" Stuart asked.

"Mississippi Delta region, 1967," Ken said conclusively.

"You make it sound like a plague," Stuart said desperately.

"It can be, depending on the contract. Where do you stand now?" Ken wanted to know.

"The engineer is going to check with the regional guy, his boss, and get back to me."

"What's that?" Ken asked pointing to the drawings on Stuart's desk.

"Job down around Pendergrass. I wasn't going to bid it, but even if they force my hand in Savannah, I don't think I can use those scrapers, so I thought I'd try to find them some work."

"Good thinking. When does it bid?"

"Ten o'clock this morning at the D.O.T. office on 129."

"I better let you get to it, then."

"I'm finished. I came in early so the phone wouldn't interrupt me and the takeoff went a little faster than I thought. It's a unit price bid with a preset rock clause, so I feel safe."

"Mind if I take a look?" Ken asked, reaching for the drawings.

"Not at all," Stuart answered, handing the drawings and bid workup sheets to Ken.

"Who's on it?"

"I don't know. Like I say, I wasn't even going to shoot at it myself."

"How much you got in the dirt?" Ken checked.

"A dollar and a dime."

"Any pipe?"

"None other than this one line that runs into a retention basin."

"Where does the retention pond empty?"

"Close to the easement of I-85."

"Drainage structure?" Ken wondered.

"It's on sheet number seven." Stuart turned pages and pointed. "It's a standard box; poured in place with a wire outlet. I put $325.00 a yard on the estimated concrete quantity to cover forming, steel, pumptruck, concrete and labor."

"Okay," Ken approved. "You scramble pretty good for a college boy." Ken picked up the phone and dialed from memory. "Alice, is Wayne in?" he asked.

Stuart could only hear one end of the conversation.

"Wayne?" Ken began. "You bidding the Pendergrass job?"

Stuart watched as Ken thumbed to the worksheet showing the line item bid summary.

"Well," Ken continued, "Stuart's in a tight spot. I'll explain the details later, but he's needing work," he said, now poising his pen. "I've got it in front of me,......item number one, I'm at a dollar and twenty cents," he lined through Stuart's figure and noted $1.20 as he talked.

Stuart walked to a better vantage point and watched as Ken raised the price of most of his items and hung up. Ken kept the worksheet and calculated the extensions before initialing all the changes and dropping the revised bid in an envelope. The new bottom line was $176,540.00.

"We better move it," Ken announced.

"Sure, let's go," responded Stuart as he looked at his watch. They drove the short distance to the D.O.T. office and parked out front in one of the visitors slots.

"We're here for the bid opening," Ken informed the receptionist.

"They are just going into the conference room," she said and directed with her hand.

They walked into the large plainly furnished room where three D.O.T. representatives sat in a semi–circle around the end of the conference table.

"Hello," nodded the older man in the center of the three. "What company are you with?"

"Blue Ridge Contractors," Ken answered, sliding the large envelope down the table and pulling out a chair.

Stuart sat next to him and nodded hellos in the general direction of the end of the table and looked at his watch. It agreed to the minute with the one on the wall, five minutes till ten.

"I hope there will be another bidder, gentlemen," said the man at the end of the table. "Takes two to open," he said, reminding them of the law that no Georgia D.O.T. job would be considered on a single bid.

Suddenly a large bearded man rushed in and slid his envelope the length of the table.

Ken nodded cooly, "Hi, Wayne."

The director cleared his throat. "I'm going to declare the deadline for receiving bids is...closed. Now, let's open these in the order they were received." He proceeded in his monotone to call contractor's names and prices. "Apparently, the low bidder is Peachtree Grading. Blueridge Contractors is second, and the bid we received last seems to be the highest. We will let you gentlemen know officially in a few days. Thank you."

Stuart was numb as they filed out. He didn't know what to do with the overwhelmingly obvious situation. Ken had illegally breeched confidentiality decorum by disclosing his bid to a competitor prior to the bid opening. This process is known as "complimentary bidding." Many states require that at least two bids be proposed for each project. Often times two contractors will collude to ensure that there are in fact at least two bids and they know who will be awarded the job. They went to the office and Ken excused himself to a jobsite.

Stuart picked up the phone and called his father. "No sir, we didn't get the job...no, sir, my original price would have been beaten by Peachtree as well."

"You know that confronting Ken will be a moral accusation," his father described. "It is likely you will jeopardize your relationship."

"Yes sir," Stuart agreed.

"You will jeopardize your self-respect if you don't confront him."

"I know," Stuart admitted.

"Son, I can give you some ideas on how to live broke, but this thing of living with a compromised self-respect is something I have no council for."

CHAPTER 21

"Ken, I need to talk to you. I'm not comfortable with what happened Friday, and I need to know before we go another inch that it will never happen again. Do I have your word on that?"

"Who on earth are you talking to?" the unexpected female voice required.

"Nobody. I was just shaving," admitted Stuart.

Helen walked into the bathroom and put her arm around his toweled waist. "I'm glad you're going to Ken. I don't care what happens, it'll be alright and we will be together."

They drove to the church where the center was housed and she walked up the long concrete sidewalk. Stuart lingered a minute to watch her.

"Hi, Helen." Darren met her at the door grinning as wide as his mouth would spread.

"What's all this?" she asked of his appearance.

"My brother's football helmet and elbow pads. I thought if you and I were going to be working together today, I'd come prepared."

"Good idea," she laughed.

She grabbed his wheel chair and spun it around. "Hey, where's the motor?"

"Miss Sharon wanted me to start trying to get around in this by using my hands," he said.

"Well, I'd like a chair, too, if we're going to be working together."

"That's an excellent idea, Helen. There's one in the classroom past my office. The furniture has been taken out to wax the floor."

She took Darren's chair and pushed it in front of her.

"Now, let's see," she began. "How do you get into this thing?"

"Put the brake on and flip up the little steps. Be careful sitting back into it."

"Oh!"

"Your back?"

"No, a little lower. I was pinched by something." Helen blushed.

"Okay?"

"Yes, but I can't push hard enough to go."

"Let me see you try."

He grabbed one wheel in each hand and strained. The chair did not budge. "See?"

he complained.

"It's been a long time since you asked anything of your arms. They need to re-learn coordination and redevelop strength. I've got an idea."

Helen went to the closet and started moving things around.

"Just the thing," she exclaimed.

She came out with a jumprope. She took one end and tied it to the back of her chair, and the other end to the front of his.

"Now," she explained, "I'll begin by pulling you so you can get used to the movements of grabbing and working your hands and arms forward. The chair will move, so you won't have to actually produce much energy. Ready?"

"Sure."

"Okay, stroke," she instructed. "STROKE" with the rhythm and cadence of a Harvard crew. "STROKE", I can't see you so you are on your honor. How's it going?"

"Fine as long as I remember to let go," he laughed.

They circled the room three times before Helen ran out of steam.

"That's going to have to do for a minute," she panted.

"Helen? Are you able to come...."

Sharon walked into the room in midsentence.

"I told someone I was looking forward to your innovations, but I didn't know just how forward."

"Miss Sharon, we went around three times and I was getting the hang of it when Miss Helen tuckered out."

"I can imagine," she smiled.

"I'll be back in a minute, Darren." She turned to Sharon. "Who could be here to see me?"

"It's your husband."

Helen looked at her watch. "Ten-fifteen. He was not going to be here until noon. I wonder what's going on?"

"Hi, Sweetie. What's up?" she asked when she reached the small office.

"Can you excuse us just a minute?" Stuart asked Sharon.

"Of course. Actually, I was on my way to town for ten minutes. Helen, would you be able to hang around and kind of keep an eye on things until I get back?"

She looked at Stuart for the answer to which he silently responded in the affirmative. "Yes, I'll be right here."

"I talked to Ken this morning," Stuart began sadly.

"How did it go?"

"Worse than I ever thought," he prepared.

"Oh, no. I'm sorry. What does it mean?"

"Simple enough to understand. I'm through, my desk is clean."

"Okay, that's his loss in a lot of ways. If he is unwilling to change his practice, he can learn to live with it himself."

"Five thousand dollars severance pay."

"Well, that's certainly a start," she comforted. "You'll bounce back in no time. Just chill out here for awhile."

"No...thanks. One thing I'm sure of. I don't want to sit and do nothing until 5:00 on any day."

"Okay, I'll see you at noon." She leaned over and kissed him, "You know something? You're my hero," she added.

He left and drove to the library. After parking the car, he went up the walk and into the large entrance. The lady at the desk invited him with her expression to ask for information.

"Hello," he greeted in a quiet voice. "I need to get a book on....he hesitated. It suddenly dawned on him that he would raise a suspicion that he was unemployed. Out of work for two hours and already a laughing stock. How would he finesse this?

"A book on what?" she beckoned.

"Human resource management," he pivoted.

She directed him to the general area. When he got to the aisle, he noticed several books with categorically similar titles. After several minutes, his eye was caught and he retraced its scan for the key word. There it was. "How to Draft a Job Winning Resume." Now all he had to do was get out of the building with it. I wouldn't be stealing he thought. This is a public library and they loan books all day. All he wanted to do was borrow it anyway. He looked at the publishing information. Maybe he could order the book himself and have it shipped to him. This was all ridiculous, he thought. It was not like he was a teenager buying pornography. He took the book and marched to the counter, completed the paperwork necessary to be granted a library card.

He looked at his watch as he backed out of the parking place and drove down Green Street toward the church.

"You're punctual," said Helen as she got in the passenger side.

"It's not as though I have much else to complicate my schedule," he mumbled.

"I'd like to say something about that, if I may."

"Feel free. You certainly have a vested interest."

"You did what you had to do. I supported it before you did it and we both agreed that confronting it was imminent. We also agreed to accept the consequences."

"You're right. I'm just not used to dealing with being unemployed."

"You dealt with college while cutting classes," she reminded him.

"Not as much as I let on."

"Anyway, you've got an assignment. You and I have to put your resume together and go door to door with it. It will be fine. Something better is waiting."

They walked through the door of the Cakebox and found a booth halfway down the window.

"Hey lady, how much is he paying you to sit with him?"

Stuart turned to see a casual friend. "What's up, Jerry? Do you know my wife, Helen?"

"Wife? Now I know there was a bribe. I'm Jerry and you have my sympathy," he smiled.

"How's the poultry business?"

"It's hard, but fair, I guess. What county are you raping the land and promoting erosion in?"

There it was again. Two for two in meeting people and dealing with the awkwardness of the job situation.

"Now, you like to drive on nice highways and fly into nice airports as well as the next guy," he avoided.

"I suppose. Nice to meet you, Helen. By the way, I'm having some folks over Saturday night. We're going to get a keg and barbecue some chicken. You want to come?"

"Thanks. Sounds good."

He walked to a table on the other side of the restaurant.

"Was that someone you spent a lot of time with in your first marriage?"

"Yes, for a while. But you know how things are. I don't think I'd be seeing much of him regardless of that. Do you want to go this weekend?"

"I think you should decide. You would have a better idea of whether it's something we would enjoy."

"I'm not that excited by the thought, to be honest."

CHAPTER 22

The next morning, Stuart was up at 5:30 and showered and dressed by 6:00. He went into the den and got out the materials necessary to write cover letters and address envelopes. He decided to handwrite on nice stationary rather than go to the time-consuming trouble and expense of getting everything typed. He was well into his fourth letter toward a goal of 25 when he heard something from the bedroom.

"Are you okay?" he asked Helen as he came into the bedroom. She was coming out of the bathroom with a pale and distant face.

"I don't feel so hot. I just threw up. I guess it was the pizza from last night."

"You didn't eat that much. Has pizza ever made you puke before?"

"I hate that word," she said in a whisper.

"Pizza?"

"No," she said flatly. "But I do feel better. I think I'll lie down for a while. If I'm not up in twenty minutes, come check on me."

"Okay."

He went back and resumed his work and twenty minutes later, went back to check on her.

"Well, you must be the substitute they sent me while my wife recovers," he said, seeing Helen up and dressed and looking better. "I'm glad to see you feeling better."

"I don't know what it was, I'm just glad it seems to be over."

"What time will you be in?" he asked as he kissed her goodbye.

"About 2:00, I guess."

"Have fun."

"What are you going to do?" she asked.

"I have a meeting at the bank that's kind of an interview and kind of a hope on my part that will be a 'please forward if necessary' stamp."

"Knock 'em dead," she encouraged and kissed him again.

He looked at his watch and walked back to his closet and thumbed through the limited selection of ties. His years in the construction industry had not given him reason to accumulate much in the way of dress wardrobe. He did the best he could and slipped on a sport coat, picked up the sealed envelopes and dropped them in the apartment mailbox on the way to his car. He was out of the elevator and into the hallway when he realized he had not totally formulated a purpose for this meeting.

He introduced himself to the receptionist and watched as she pressed a single button and waited. "A Stuart Kerr to see Mr. Taylor," she announced to someone on the other end that was obviously not Mr. Taylor. She continued waiting.

"Mr. Taylor will see you now," a new face announced.

Stuart nodded his appreciation and followed her to the door of the large office where she motioned that he was on his own.

"Come in, Stuart. How are you?"

"Fine, thank you, Mr. Taylor," Stuart answered, shaking hands over the desk.

"Have a seat," he gestured with his hand then sat back down behind his desk. "So, Stuart, what puts your capable services to the point of market available?"

He had not anticipated the need of this type of explanation. The full facts were not something to be discussed in his opinion. "Personal reasons," he smiled.

"That's fine." His expression redirected the conversation. He leaned slightly forward and asked, "Do you think you could handle my job?"

The question was the second of two that had caught Stuart completely off guard. "It would probably take a couple of weeks," he answered, appearing to be giving the idea consideration.

The executive smiled and continued, "Seriously, I would not be interested in hiring someone that did not aspire to someday have this office."

"And I would not apply for a frozen position," Stuart confirmed.

"There is a test we have all of our applicants take that helps to profile certain characteristics and preferences. When do you think you could take it?"

"How much time does it take?"

"About five hours, if I remember correctly."

"Tomorrow is fine with me," Stuart answered.

They parted company with a handshake and Stuart was given the name of the person he would see the next day at ten o'clock. He got in his car and as he was going to put the car in gear, it occurred to him that he had nowhere to go. This was a new feeling and more than a little unpleasant. Should he go to get Helen for an early lunch? No, that didn't seem right. She would be off midafternoon anyway so they probably wanted her to work while she was there. He decided to increase his volume of resumes.

He drove to the bookstore and bought a city directory. Remembering the checklist that he and Helen had put together, he began to prioritize a list of who he would contact. The day picked up speed as he imagined himself working in one capacity after another. He only noticed the time when Helen came in.

"Hi," he greeted, looking at his watch.

"I made a couple of stops on the way home," she answered the implied question. "Looks like you've been hard at it," she said, observing the cluttered materials all around him on the couch and coffee table.

"It doesn't feel much like work," he admitted, putting his pen and legal pad aside.

"I thought we'd take a quick run up to Yonah if you want to drink some wine and try some of the new cheese I picked up," she stated.

"You're something, you know that?"

"The important thing is that you think it. So, what do you say?"

He watched as she walked down the small hallway and into their bedroom in the back of the apartment. He couldn't help feeling how she should have someone better than him, someone more stable, someone with....someone with a job. He shook his head in disgust at himself and then picked himself up and tried to muster what it would take to avoid adding self-pity to his dilemma.

They were in the car in a matter of minutes and driving towards Cleveland. She was in the passenger seat and arranging the items she had brought in the daypack to be carried to their picnic spot.

"You know," she began, "I was thinking today about how you would fit in the ministry."

"I have an economics degree, three DUI's, one of which was actually accomplished on horseback in the Magnolia Parade and I've been divorced. What self-respecting session would be able to keep a straight face at the news, let along recommend me?"

"Aside from all of that, does the idea appeal to you?"

"I have never entertained the idea for a moment. And now that I am, it is not entertaining me at all."

"Why?" she asked innocently as she zipped the pack.

"I've never thought of being an astronaut either."

"You've never been in a rocket, but you've been in a church," she disqualified his analogy. "You've taught Sunday School for three years and I've heard you speak at a Fellowship of Christian Athletes gathering. You really are more qualified than you think."

"But what about seminary? The tuition is a consideration and I don't think I could expect to knock down a six figure salary as a student."

"We'd make it, if it's what you want."

"I didn't even bring it up. But, no! It's not what I want, thanks."

They rode in silence around the square in Cleveland and took a right on the road toward Helen, Georgia.

"I don't know....it just feels wrong, not working. We have a few dollars left, but I'm scared that we're not far from hitting bottom. It takes about $2,000 a month to run our train and your job brings in about $1,000 clear. I'm not sure that choice is going to be a luxury we can afford."

She slid over next to him and put her head on his shoulder. "I'm not scared," she assured him. "I'm not sure why, but I'm not scared."

He took his right arm and embraced her. "Thanks," he said. "I know that was not necessarily meant for just me, but I'm glad that you don't seem to be holding me in contempt for any of this."

"Well I'm not hungry yet," she qualified. "The fury of a female with a growling stomach is a frightening adversary."

CHAPTER 23

"Do you have to get up so very early?"

"It's the same time I've been getting up for years. Just because I'm unemployed, doesn't mean I'm free to become a sluggard," Stuart qualified.

"Do you expect to have an interview at six o'clock?"

"No, but I have to keep the tubes packed by sending out resumes every day. I've got to take some kind of psych test at 10:00 at the bank and I want to get a few things done before that."

Helen stopped the interrogation. She was thankful he was approaching the challenge with commitment, but mindful of the potential letdowns this kind of energy could bring. "What kind of test?"

"The interview I had yesterday resulted in this next step," he began. "It supposedly helps to show what you should be doing and how you're expected to respond in certain circumstances."

"I've heard of tests like that. I've never taken one, but I think more and more of them will be cropping up."

He nodded and looked into an accordion file to see which resumes he had sent out three days ago. The stack had five in it. He set them out on the coffee table. He picked up the phone and began dialing with the first one in hand, then the next, then the next. He was met with consistent indifference.

The indifference bred frustration which began to dominate his emotions.

★★★★★★★

"Helen?"

"Yes, Sharon. I'm in here."

Sharon walked around the corner and motioned for Helen to follow her. "I'm going to the courthouse to get some paperwork straight. I need for you to take Darren to the bathroom."

"Darren?" she asked, thinking of the potential embarrassment for them both.

"That's right. He knows how to position the chair and can talk you through the process. It's really one of the easiest things we do with him, especially now, since he's beginning to strengthen his arms."

She walked to Darren and said goodbye to Sharon.

"Are you ready to go to the restroom?"

"Yes," he answered with less concern than he would have if she had offered him a doughnut.

She wheeled him down the hallway and stopped the chair just outside the large door. When she pushed the door open, she awkwardly tried to pull the chair in from the hall and got herself between the chair coming in and the door whose hydraulic arm was putting pressure in the other direction.

"I'm sorry," she offered.

"If you'll get behind me and push, the door should open fine," he suggested.

"Thanks for your patience," she apologized.

They got into the bathroom and the door closed behind them. She began to position the chair and Darren said, "If you don't mind, I would rather be on the other side of the commode. It's easier for me to help when I'm moving to my left."

"No problem," Helen said, turning the chair around and aligning it with the provided bars.

"That's fine," he said. "The first step is to get my pants down."

She was not comfortable with this unskippable step and tried hard not to show her discomfort.

"It's okay, modesty is the easiest thing to lose," he smiled.

"Now what?" she asked after she had pulled his pants down to his knees. He instructed and helped as much as he could and the transfer to the toilet seat went quite well.

"I'll just be outside. You call me when you're ready."

"Okay."

In a few minutes, she heard his call. "Helen?"

"Coming."

She walked around the toilet and asked "What first?" Then he looked at the toilet paper very obviously.

"Up until a couple of weeks ago, that would have been the next step. Thanks to you and Miss Sharon, I can handle that myself now."

****

Stuart sat in a vacant office at a secretary's desk. He had been there a little over an hour and felt he was halfway through the test. He looked disgusted at the new page he had just turned. It showed a drawing on the left of an elaborately dressed man posed in the profile. The instructions simply said, "Duplicate the drawing on the opposite page." The opposite page was blank. He looked at the figure and then at the drawing page; back at the subject, back to the space provided. The opposite page didn't just look blank now, it looked sterile.

"I can't draw flies," he muttered to himself.

He wondered why he had to be subjected to this humiliation and remembered that he had been told there was no right or wrong on this test. It's purpose was to evaluate the individual and determine strengths and weaknesses. He reasoned his weakness in drawing was not something he wanted to invest a lot of time in, or try to overcome. Without much more thought, he sketched the figure at the interest level and detail of a third grade behavior-disordered child and moved on to the next test section.

The remainder of the test took two hours, and he decided to have a late lunch or midday meal of some sort and drove to the Cake Box where he reflected on the test and got no satisfaction trying to understand why questions like "Would you rather be fishing or reading a book?" had to be answered without any information about the type of book or the weather being provided. The multiple choice format left no room for answers like, "It depends."

He drove out to one of the older small parks with a boat ramp and slowly circled through the concrete picnic tables. He considered parking, but knew he had to go back to his apartment and do something so he kept the wheels barely rolling. "Whatever you have to do in a given day, if you are able to select the order, do the most unpleasant first." The words his father had used when he was ten years old on their small farm had become second nature to him. But now he faced days that had no redeeming events scheduled.

He climbed the brown-carpeted stairs of the four-unit building and walked through the unlocked door. The stack of index cards was still waiting for its follow-up phone calls. He sat down and picked up the next one and remembered how his call had gone earlier that day. He was just about to dial the number when he heard someone on the steps. In a matter of seconds, Helen was standing just inside with a frightened look through eyes that had been obviously crying.

"What's wrong?" Stuart stood and reached for her.

She dropped to her knees and buried her head in a throw pillow on the couch. She sobbed softly, and in a moment, looked up like someone slipping over the edge of a cliff and clutched his hands.

"I'm pregnant," she blurted and continued sobbing.

He pushed the coffee table out, slid to the floor and put her face into his neck. "I know the timing is bad, but something will work out. Don't worry. This is great news!"

"You don't understand," she cleared her throat. "I was pregnant while I was getting those back x-rays and while I was taking the pill and everything."

He knew very little about prenatal care, but he knew what she said could not be disregarded.

"What are we going to do?" she asked desperately.

"I don't know. Nothing has to be done today. We'll just have to get some advice as to what our options are."

CHAPTER 24

Stuart picked up the phone and looked again at the directory for confirmation. He called a doctor who had been referred to him by his friend Jerry. He was told the office was closing early today and that the doctor would be out of town the following day.

"I don't want to push, but this will only take a few minutes of conversation. It's about some details regarding my wife's activities before we learned she was pregnant."

"I see," she answered, suspecting drug usage. "Let me take your name and number and I'll call you after I've spoken with him."

"Thank you very much."

"What did they say?" asked Helen silently through the tear-stuck eyelashes.

"They want to call us back for an appointment," he explained.

The phone rang immediately.

"This is Dr. Hansel. I had a message to call you at once."

"Yes, it's about my wife. She has just been found to be pregnant and she has had an exposure to x-rays as well as being on the pill."

"When?"

"Listen, Doctor, this is something that we would really like to meet with you about because she obviously can tell you better than I can the when and how much. Could we see you?"

"Yes. Can you drive to my office now? I'm finished for the day and I'll be out of town tomorrow."

They hardly reached for anything but the car keys and quickly drove the three or four-mile distance to his office. The parking lot was empty when they turned in and they could see two cars at the back. Stuart didn't bother to lock the car before they walked arm in arm up the aggregate concrete walkway. The door was waiting slightly cracked, and the muted lighting suggested a specific purpose. Stuart wrapped his knuckles on the opening door as they walked in.

"Dr. Hansel?" called Helen.

"Come in," came the reply in a cheerful voice.

A man looking approximately fifty years of age rounded the counter. His white coat complimented his deep tan and white hair and he smiled slightly.

Dr. Hansel shook Stuart's hand and ushered them toward the only bright light in the building. They followed his invitation and were surprised to find a woman standing just inside the door.

"This is Ms. Kelly," Dr. Hansel introduced.

"Hello, Helen. Nice to see you again," greeted the redheaded attendant.

"Well, this office a bit tight, but I think we can all have a seat for a few minutes at least," offered Dr. Hansel. "Now," he continued, "Tell me as nearly as you can, exactly when and what has taken place to concern you."

"Last week I was working at the developmentally delayed preschool and trying to help a child in a wheel chair. I hurt my back rather badly and couldn't move for some time. The director suggested that I have it examined. I went to the emergency room where they x-rayed my back."

"Did they ask you if you were pregnant?" Dr. Hansel interjected.

"Yes, but I said no, because I had been on the pill and had no idea of being pregnant."

"Okay, I'll talk with the x-ray technician and the radiologist in a day or so to get some details," he offered.

"The best thing is for me to check into this from my end, but while you're here, Ms. Kelly and I wanted to discuss a concept with you and I think now is as good a time as any to begin. Have either of you ever given any thought as to when you were planning to start your family?"

The question came as a surprise, but somehow it was cushioned by the complexities of the day.

"No," responded Helen, and then she added, "I haven't even given any thought to pregnancy or parenting."

"I see," soothed Ms. Kelly. "Often when a young couple starts planning for marriage and a life together, things like a car and place to sleep seem to take precedence over more long-range goals like parenthood. Had you discussed how large of a family you wanted?" she asked compassionately.

"We had mentioned waiting a couple of years," remembered Stuart.

"Do you remember the reasons you wanted to wait?"

"I'm sure it included financial considerations," he stated confidently.

"Do these considerations still exist?"

"More than ever," he admitted and dropped his head.

"And now is the added concern of potential difficulties," she consoled. "You know," Ms. Kelly leaned toward Stuart. "You still have the ability to maintain a good proactive plan. Abortion is a simple procedure and would allow you to get control of this mishap before it gets control of you and burdens your marriage to a level neither of you wants."

"I guess I just thought this was something we couldn't do much to change. We were just wondering how serious the threat of birth defect was, that's why we wanted to meet," Helen explained.

"We will have that information when we check with radiology in a day or so, but the main thing is for you to know that this option can be made available to you safely right here. Dr. Hansel does the procedure regularly and it is no problem for most patients."

"I don't know," questioned Helen. "I mean, I know it's not the best timing, but shouldn't we give some thought to the baby?"

Now Dr. Hansel leaned toward Helen. "The fetus is not a living being until a much later point. You and your husband need to think about this from your own perspective. This decision will in no way hinder your plans to begin your family on your own terms, when you can apply yourselves to the responsibilities of parenting."

"We need to talk about this and get back to you," Helen concluded.

"Okay," settled Ms. Kelly. "There's someone I want you to meet in a couple of days. She has done a lot of work with people in similar circumstances over the past couple of years and I think you would benefit from spending time with her while you decide."

Stuart stood and reached for his wife's hand. "At least we don't have to pull this trigger tonight," he sighed. "Let's go. Doctor, Ms. Kelly, thank you. We will be in touch in a day or so."

"Incidentally," warned Dr. Hansel, "I wouldn't delay this decision needlessly. The sooner the better as far as the procedure is concerned."

"Good night, Dear," Ms. Kelly graciously squeezed Helen's hand.

"Bye." Helen smiled with her mouth only.

Stuart and Helen walked to the car silently and opened their own doors simultaneously. They drove out the way they came in and were waiting to turn onto the main road when Helen said, "Do you mind making a stop on the way?"

"No, what do you need?"

"I was going to say I'd like a snack, but I think I'll die if I don't get a chili dog."

"Boy, for something that isn't alive yet, the....fetus....is sure letting himself be known. First you were hurling beets in the morning, now you're pigging out in the evening."

"Himself?" Helen asked.

"Whatever."

"I don't feel like he's an 'it' either."

They drove through the Dairy Queen drive thru and Helen added onions and mustard to her order, and then for good measure, she ordered two; not so much that she wanted both, but she was insuring against tempting Stuart to share in the craving.

He took a bit and looked at her for a reaction. "Help yourself," she smiled. "I figured for you."

"I had a friend in college," Helen reflected as she chomped on her chili dog, "that was not married and got pregnant her senior year. She didn't talk much about it, but she had some kind of skin cancer develop on her lower back. Anyway, she had radiation treatment before she realized she was pregnant. As soon as she learned that she was definitely pregnant, she aborted the baby."

"Because of the radiation?"

"There were a lot of reasons in her mind, but I do remember her telling me that the doctor was particularly concerned about the chances of a birth defect."

"How do you feel about an abortion?" Stuart asked.

"I've never really thought about it. I've heard some people I respect a lot talk about, and clearly make stands, that it is wrong."

"What do you think they are basing it on?"

"One lady in particular comes to mind. She has gotten on the subject more than once when she took her turn of leading our Bible study. She bases everything else on scripture so I feel sure that's what she's doing."

"Why don't you talk to her?" Stuart suggested.

"I guess I should."

"Ms. Kelly wanted you to meet with someone else, too."

"Yes, I guess I should do that too. Did you get any kind of funny feeling about her?"

"No, why?"

"I don't know. Something about that meeting gave me an uncomfortable feeling and I'm not sure whether it was what she said or how she said it," Helen recalled.

"Let's go in and get to bed. I think we should try to talk to some of these people we've mentioned, and I think we should begin that process tomorrow."

CHAPTER 25

Stuart shook his head in self pity as he thumbed through the index cards on the coffee table. The stack of those to follow up on was growing daily at a rate of two to one since he was not enjoying the call back process.

The phone rang and Stuart almost jumped.

"Who could that be?" he asked out loud as if Helen were still standing there. "Hello."

"Hey, I wasn't sure what the deal was when I called the other day at your office."

"Hi, Joe. I can't believe I haven't even talked to you about it. How are you doing?"

"Talk to me about what, exactly? I gathered you had made a change."

"It's a long story. Bottom line....I'm not working there anymore."

They agreed to meet for lunch and talk about it.

Later, the knock at the door reminded him of his lunch date.

Joe followed his knock into the den before Stuart could answer. "What's up?" he greeted.

Stuart was in the process of standing. "Not as much as I'd like."

"Where do you want to eat?" he asked as he walked back through the open door.

"Crab Trap."

"St. Simons would be nice, but I better not take ten hours round trip for lunch. How about the Box?"

Stuart thought for a minute of Hazel's knowledge of his unemployment and the small chance she might say something in front of the familiar crowd.

"No. Let's change our luck," he suggested.

They drove to the back of the Brenau campus and parked closed to an old brick building. The hallways inside branched and turned until they were standing at a small counter writing their own short order on a preprinted pad. They sat at a table in the back corner.

"My wife wants an explanation when I come to the Tea Hole," Joe pondered.

"I thought that was only in spring when the girls come through here on a sunbathing break," Stuart recalled.

"Things have tightened up at our house during family planning talks."

Stuart felt his stomach react to the subject.

"So, tell me the deal," Joe cut to the bottom line.

"I really don't know how much of it ought to be public knowledge. The long and short of it is, I'm not there anymore and am needing work among other things."

"Among what other things?"

Stuart thought of how nothing was going to come of this time together if he wasn't willing to open up. "Joe," his game face was on, "I need to talk about something in real confidence."

Joe sat silently, giving him one last chance to change his mind about opening up.

"Please don't discuss this with anyone."

"Not a soul," he assured.

"Several days ago, while I was out of town, Helen hurt her back. She seems to be fine now, but that day the people helping her encouraged her to get it xrayed. She went to the emergency room and they took a lot of them from all angles. Well, now comes the kicker. We found out yesterday that she's pregnant." He stopped and took a deep breath as though he would continue, but didn't.

"Well, what are you thinking?"

"I don't know."

"When did you and Helen plan to have another child?"

Stuart sincerely appreciated Joe's acknowledgement of Brooke and felt, himself, that the question was worded accurately. "We, of course, would not consider this addition under the circumstances of finances alone, but what do you do at this point?"

"Have you talked about aborting?"

"Not really. We kind of found ourselves in a discussion about it but have not really hammered it out."

"Well, for what it's worth, I think it applies here; and the good news is that the government agrees. Look at it this way. You've got a lot of years to get a handle on things and all this is going to do if you go through with it, is further set you back. This baby could bring you and Helen and Brooke a lot of pleasure when the timing is right. If you let it happen now, it could ruin you financially."

"Besides," Joe continued, "think of the odds of a birth defect. They've got the technology to predict and sometimes even diagnose these things to where it's not such a crap shoot anymore. I say it's no big deal and something you should take advantage of. After all, it's not like what you're going through with work right now, you know, like depending on others to hire you. This thing is in your total control."

"Would you like anything like ketchup?" the waitress asked.

"Yes, please," nodded Stuart.

"Here's your ketchup." The small packets were laid beside Stuart's plate.

"Thanks."

★★★★★

"Yes, I've now spoken with Ms. Kelley and she said that she will pick up the other lady and meet you here at Dr. Hansen's office at 2:00."

Helen jotted down the time and said, "Thank you. I'll be there then."

Helen hung up with her index finger and dialed another number.

"Hello."

"Hi, sweetie. What cha' doing?"

"I just got back from lunch with Joe and I was thinking about calling you."

"I just wanted to tell you that I'm meeting with Ms. Kelley at 2:00 and I'll be a little later getting home than I had thought."

"Well, that's what I was going to call you about. I have been thinking about going to see someone in Nashville."

"Who?"

"Do you remember Bill Argon?"

"Sure. What makes you think of him?"

"I don't know. I have no desire to move to Nashville, but I do want to talk with someone that at least knows me and maybe even cares about the outcome of this job hunt."

"Why don't you call him then?"

"If I get him and he can see me, "I'll leave you a note about when's and where's."

"Okay. I love you."

"I love you."

Stuart was lucky that his friend was available to meet with him at 5:00 that afternoon. He jumped from the couch and ran through the shower. Then he dressed quickly and stuffed a couple of extras in an overnight bag. The note to Helen was scratched on the back of one of his index cards, stuck to the TV with a piece of tape and he was on his way.

The traffic was light and he continued to confirm his schedule to be safe with the target time. In his hurry, he had not paid much attention to the gas gauge and he was now able to tell it would not make it all the way. He decided he would try to coordinate with a strategic bladder relief stop. The top of Monteagle Mountain seemed logical and he pulled into a station with all the convenience store extras. He pumped an even thirteen dollars on the mechanical dial.

The counter inside had no line, but several people milling around caused him to decide he would rather have a speedy exit than something to drink. He went up to the cash register and handed the cashier his Visa. In a few seconds, a beep alerted everyone in line of its decline. The cashier smiled awkwardly and tried again. The machine seemed to increase the volume.

Stuart confirmed his suspicion that his wallet contained only a ten dollar bill. Two places back in line stood a well-dressed yuppie in Ray Bans.

"Is there a problem?" the well-starched customer snipped.

Just as Stuart was about to step aside and try to figure out how to handle the situation, a young, barefoot, tattooed man with stringy hair walked up to him. "Here you go, Bubba. It's my turn to pay for the gas." He then handed Stuart a twenty.

The exchange was made with the cashier and Stuart stepped out of line and to a less crowded spot in the store. He reached out the seven dollars change and opened his wallet to add his own ten.

"Keep the ten," refused the benefactor. "You aren't home yet, are you?"

"No, in fact I'm headed the wrong way. How did you know?"

"Hall County, Georgia, unless you stole that car. I saw the flag."

"Listen, I want to pay you back. How can I get the money to you?"

"Don't worry about it. I'm home."

"Will you give me your address?" Stuart requested.

"Naw, not likely."

"I guess I should have planned better, I left in such a hurry...."

"Planning ain't everything. And it ain't nothing if something unplanned comes up."

CHAPTER 26

Helen took a seat in the waiting room of Dr. Hansel's office after telling the receptionist she had arrived. She thumbed through a dated magazine and glanced toward the clock on the grasscloth wall. Her eye was caught by the movement of the door as it opened and she instinctively focused but saw no one enter. Presently, a middle aged woman appeared, but her stride seemed hesitant. A four foot high planter obstructed Helen's view of the entryway and the woman was in with the door closed behind her. She bent over oddly and now Helen was consciously trying not to stare. The next full view of the woman as she emerged fully solved the dilemma. In an unusual wheeled walker was a girl Helen's age that was barely three feet high from the top of her head to the floor. Her position in the contraption was seated and she now propelled herself to the transition of carpeted floor.

Helen's eyes met with hers and the new proximity required verbal exchange.

"Do you mind if I park right here?"

"Not at all," Helen said as she slid the end table to open the traffic pattern a little more.

"Thank you." The smile radiated more meaning than the simple phrase. "I'm Judy."

"Nice to meet you. My name is Helen Kerr." She also nodded to the lady that had escorted her into the room.

"Are you here to see Dr. Richland?" Judy asked Helen as she watched her mother through the door.

"No, I'm here to see...." She hesitated. "Actually, I'm here to see someone who works with Dr. Hansel. Her name is Ms. Kelly. Why?"

"No reason. It's just that when you're sitting in the center of the waiting room, it's hard to tell. These two doctors share a building, but not much else, I'm afraid."

"Oh?" Helen asked.

"You can't pay any attention to me. Dr. Richland has been my gynecologist forever and I just think he's a prince. So," her face changed the subject, "are you going to have a baby?"

The question was not exactly something Helen was prepared for. If Judy had simply asked if she were pregnant, it would have been easier. "I'm not really sure, yet," she said without much emphasis on the final word.

Judy glanced at Helen's left hand. "How long have you been married?"

"Not quite two months," Helen answered.

"Are you working?"

"Yes, at a new center for developmentally delayed children. It's meeting at a church facility right now."

"I've heard of it. I wish it had started when I was young."

Helen thought of how things were in her own grammar school in the sixties. "Did you attend....I mean were you in some kind of..."

"Not at all," she laughed, "I was right there with all the other kids. And they were a big help. I never knew anything else, so it was no big deal."

Helen was beginning to see that this was no small person. "Was it tough watching other kids do things you couldn't?" She couldn't believe she had asked something so personal of someone she didn't know.

Judy, on the other hand, was not phased. "Not really. Oh, I'm sure there were times I pouted, but I had some great friends and I was always included." She shifted and chuckled as she remembered a story.

Helen felt herself giggle.

Judy got what was now a contagious laugh under control. "I was in high school and several kids picked me up. We were in Jack's dad's Cadillac and I had to be put on the armrest in the back. We were going down the bypass when a policeman pulled us over."

"Too many people in the car?" Helen guessed.

"No," Judy burst out again. "There was some kind of a break-in reported at a furniture store. The policeman thought I was a stolen T.V." Now the laugh came all the way from her toes and Helen joined in.

"Helen Kerr?" asked a nurse.

"Yes?"

"Ms. Kelley has just phoned. She has had a number of difficulties and will not be able to make your appointment."

"Nothing serious, I hope."

"No, she was picking up someone that was to meet with the both of you and a garbage truck dropped a dumpster at the end of this person's driveway. When that was finally cleaned up, they were on the bypass and had a blowout. Ms. Kelley was so upset on the phone that I didn't fully understand the rest of it, but it involved a chicken truck."

"My goodness," exclaimed Judy, "it seems that your meeting was not supposed to take place."

"Anyway," concluded the nurse, "she asked that you call again in a day or so."

"Sure, thank you," Helen said.

"Judy?" The call came from the receptionist. "Dr. Richland is ready for you."

★★★★★

"You must be Stuart."

"That's right."

"Go right in. Bill's expecting you."

"Thank you." He thought as he walked back how nice it was to be welcome.

It didn't take long for the two to end up somewhere besides Bill's office. They were soon having a beer downtown.

"Now," Bill took a swallow, "tell me what brings you to Nashville."

"I'm looking for your council. I had a situation develop in my previous job that turned sour. Without dragging you through the details, it left me out of work."

"How long?"

"Several weeks."

"Any interviews?" Bill asked.

"Quite a few."

"Offers?"

"None." It was nice to state it frankly and Stuart was glad that he had not avoided the question.

"What about employment agencies? Have you tried any of those?"

"No, do you recommend it?"

"That depends. Think of it in terms of sales. Insurance companies think it wise to market their product through a store front like mine. The analogy is not great, but the point is that the manufacturers usually want a focused effort on sales. In this case, you would be the manufacturer."

"Okay, I'll contact some people when I get back," Stuart committed.

"Meanwhile, have you ever considered the insurance industry?"

"No, I've never been in sales."

"Your dad told me the last time we talked that you were bidding work all over the state."

"That's right. Why?"

"That's all I do. Tell people what I do and ask them if I can have a chance to do it for them," Bill explained.

"I guess I never thought of it exactly like that."

"Let me do this, Stuart. I have a friend in Atlanta that I've gotten to know casually over the years on insurance company trips. He's a guy I think you would like. He's several years younger than I am and in the city. He does a lot more business than I do, and chances are, he might just make you an offer."

Bill proceeded to explain to him how the sales industry operated and what he could expect from it.

"It's more like what you've been doing than you think. For example, if you bid on a project in Alabama, if you don't get it, they don't pay you for the work you did, do they?"

"Not a dime," Stuart rolled his eyes in obvious realization of the times it had happened to him.

"And," continued Bill, "if you do get it, there's no guarantee you'll make a profit."

"True again," consented Stuart.

CHAPTER 27

Helen stopped at the grocery on the way home. She was not really motivated to cook for just herself, but didn't even have anything to snack on.

"Helen?" The unexpected voice startled her.

She turned to see a friend from church. "Becky, how are you?"

"Fine. How about you and Stuart?"

"Doing well. Stuart is out of town tonight, so I'm going to junk out."

"Sounds like you ought to go to something with me tonight. Peter is out of town, too, and I'd love to have some company."

"What are you talking about?"

"Younglife. Were you ever involved in it?"

"No. Not as a teenager, I mean. While I lived in Jackson, I did a little volunteer work as a leader."

"There is a bit of a special meeting tonight. It takes place at the regular club meeting, but they are bringing another high school and having a speaker and all. Why don't you go with me and we can do the junk-out later, together?"

Helen was a little surprised at Becky's push, since she didn't know her that well, but finally agreed to go.

*****

Stuart stopped in indecision at the parking garage exit. He had learned from an earlier conversation that his parents were out of town, so he really hadn't planned on going to Columbia this trip. However, he didn't feel like driving all the way back to Gainesville. He thought of getting a motel room and physically touched his hip pocket as he recalled the ten dollar bill and the hamstrung Visa card. He decided to drive the fifty miles to Columbia and use the hidden key to spend the night in his parents' house.

*****

"Sorry I'm running a few minutes late," Becky apologized. "It shouldn't matter since the old folks like us will be at the back of the room. We can slip in even if the meeting has started."

"No problem. I'm just holding you to the junk food frenzy afterward." They parked behind the huge civic building and wormed their way to the low ceiling meeting room on the lower level.

The music was guitar and clapping with what looked to be a hundred teenage bodies seated Indian style on the tile floor. The music subsided after its proclamation of "He's Alive" and the Area Director took the small stage and began a twisted rendition of what he called "Render Cellar." It took the crowd only a minute to recognize the plight of this peasant girl who would dance with a "princom hance" and "slop her dripper" to their epidemic laughter.

"Next," announced the director, "we have someone who I think has a great deal to say on the subject of selfworth."

To Helen's astonishment, the familiar walker of her recently-met friend wheeled out. "Hi, I'm Judy," she began, "and it's great to be alive. My particular challenge is called ostiogenisis imperfecto and it has from time to time given me fits."

The words that she continued with were not necessarily new and on their own. They could have been written in a book, but what this person brought to the message was an undeniable evidence that concerns of life need not be controls of life. She talked about the concerns of unclear skin and a girl in front of Helen laughed as tears ran down her blemished face. Judy's words were well planned to encourage and not patronize and she held the entire audience in her tiny hand.

"My status of selfworth," she pointed out, "comes from my eternal significance. God created all things. And all things He created for His glory. I'm just glad to be one of those things that will last forever."

Becky turned to Helen as the applause was giving way to a new skit being assembled on stage. "She can speak volumes without ever opening her mouth."

"Do you know her?" asked Helen.

"Everybody knows Judy. I've been able to say she's a friend for several years. She's remarkable and contagious. The kind of feeling you get from her is not one of those 'thank goodness I'm not handicapped' feelings. It's the ability to see beyond appearances. Becky turned her attention toward the stage and almost unconsciously said, "And in today's planned parenthood culture, we are aborting for a whole lot less."

The impact of the statement sent Helen to the door. She excused herself but the noise of the skit drowned her alibi of a need for fresh air. She stood for a moment on the small walkway alone and looked at the sky over the high school football stadium. She couldn't understand her feelings. She knew she could not handle the possibility of a birth defect. As she walked, she tried to get comfortable with the memory of the meeting she and Stuart had had at Dr. Hansel's office with Ms. Kelley.

She was now sitting on the grass that bordered the driveway. "Hey." The voice from behind startled her and now she turned to realize she didn't know exactly why she was where she was.

Becky stepped into the security light she was under. "I guess I didn't hear you say where you were going."

Helen's expression was such that Becky asked, "Are you okay?"

"I was going to walk if I had to," Helen smiled, "I'm starved."

The smile did not fool Becky, but she didn't persist. "What did you think?"

"I was encouraged to see so many kids. We never had that many at the club in Jackson while I was there."

"Do you think you would be interested in being on the committee?"

"I don't know. I would need to talk to Stuart."

They got into the car and started toward the road. "The committee is a lot of fun, but it is work and now they are asking for a three-year term. I'm sure you and Stuart have to see how that fits into your family planning."

That did it! Helen sobbed into her hands and was unable to speak for almost a minute. Becky stopped the car and waited. When Helen was able to look, she saw that Becky's eyes had welled up. Helen spoke first. "I'm terribly sorry. I've had a lot on me lately."

"Do you want to talk about it?" Becky invited.

Helen didn't know. Her relationship with Becky certainly did not merit anything like this.

"Yes," she consented.

"Okay, we'll drive through Dairy Queen and go back to your apartment."

"Thanks."

They got back and walked up the steps to the second level.

"Excuse the mess," apologized Helen.

"Call this a mess and risk being barred from my house forever," laughed Becky.

Helen sat in the large chair and motioned for Becky to have a seat in the wingback cornering it. She took a small bite of the fudge sundae and set it on the steamer trunk used as a table. After a deep breath, she began, "I don't really expect you to understand all of this, but I appreciate your willingness to listen. Stuart and I have been married less than two months and he has a precious little girl from his first marriage. We had not talked about adding any children to our family in terms of a timetable. To make matters more complicated, Stuart is currently unemployed."

Becky sat silently and piddled with her dessert.

"Now the kicker. I'm pregnant."

Still no reaction from Becky.

"And I've been exposed to a lot of x-rays. I understand that carries some risk."

"Do you have your mind made up as to what you are going to do?"

"Stuart and I went to meet with the doctor when we learned I was pregnant. There was a woman there and we talked for an hour or so. I think they are steering us toward an abortion, but we just don't know what to do."

"What do you think you should base your decision on?" Becky probed.

"What do you mean exactly?"

"Well, should you get more technical information about the degree of risk given the x-ray or what?"

"I don't know what I think."

Becky sat back in her chair. "Can you tell me what you feel?"

"It changes from hour to hour and I can't trust my feelings." Helen conferred.

"Can you remember what you were feeling when you were meeting with the doctor? You said that they were steering you in the direction of an abortion."

"I'm not sure," Helen recalled. "I didn't like the way it was sounding though."

"I wonder why?"

"It felt selfish. I felt like everyone there, including us, was concerned with what was best for Stuart and me; for our financial situation and our calendar."

"Well," calmed Becky, "you are the two involved in this, aren't you?"

"Not the only ones," Helen qualified.

"What do you mean?"

"My baby. I mean, what about my baby?" Helen pointed to her stomach.

Becky leaned forward. "But parents make decisions all the time for the good of their children," she answered.

"When in Hell would that include killing the child!!?" Helen's eyes burned at Becky.

Becky now smoothly moved to the ottoman in front of Helen and lightly touched her knee. "Never," she smiled.

"What?" Helen regained her composure in response to the understanding face looking at her.

"So long as your life is not in jeopardy....never."

Helen was still trying to get a picture of the whole conversation. "So you are against the whole idea?"

Becky's eyes dropped for a moment. "Peter and I killed a child three years ago." Her eyes filled and slightly overflowed. "We were engaged and the wedding was only weeks away. We even said that no one would do the incriminatory math, and the idea of starting off a marriage with a child didn't appeal to either of us. We both wanted to work and my job would not have been easy to get a leave for maternity reasons. We didn't even have health insurance."

"We are in bad shape financially, and will be worse off if we go on with this full term. You were obviously in favor of abortion as an option at one point. When did you change?"

"Right after the operation. I was depressed and I knew I had done the wrong thing. My doctor never told me anything about that tough side of the whole thing. He always referred to my baby as the product of conception. The funny thing was that I had a friend who was pregnant at the time and she miscarried. He was talking to me about her and learned that I knew. In her case, he said that she had lost her baby." Becky's eyes welled up again and spilled down her cheeks.

"I'm sorry I'm requiring so much," apologized Helen.

"It's a mistake that will last the rest of my life." Becky sat upright. "But you can avoid it. You have realized what's going on before it's too late. You are carrying a child that has a right to live."

Helen nodded with her lips pressed together in a thin line. "I'm scared, Becky. Things are not good for us right now."

Becky looked at the tennis racket on the couch. "Have you ever lost the first set and gone on to win the match?"

"Plenty of times."

"I think this can be your biggest win. Don't give up. It's so early."

"I'll need Stuart's okay."

"I know and that's none of my business. As for now, I'm concerned about your ice cream intake." She pointed to the gray puddle in the clear container on the steamer trunk. "Let's make another run."

Helen cut her eyes. "What I could really go for is an all-the-way chili dog."

"Let's do and say we didn't," challenged Becky.

CHAPTER 28

Stuart stepped into his jeans and tucked in his shirt. The bed was easy to make; it looked like he hadn't slept in but a three foot line of it. He walked out through the front door of the old homeplace and locked it behind him. He walked the dry laid brick walk between the boxwoods to the splitrail opening that held no gate. The lower pasture to the northwest was now developed with the bulge of Sunnyside and he reminisced to a time when he had a crewcut and that pasture had only one house. He would bounce down the limestone terrace to the fence and do a synchronized crawl with his springer spaniel underneath before breaking into a dead run for the small frame house of his second parents.

Lilly and Rabbit had come to live on his father's farm when Stuart was three years old. Rabbit, a magician with iron, was a blacksmith by art and their basic arrangement was for him to tend the needs of several Tennessee Walking Horses. His skills soon proved essential in every area to the small farm and his influence in the life of a wide-eyed boy would be indelible.

Stuart laughed to himself now as he recalled the conversation between Rabbit and his father the week he was to begin school. "Ain't no need, Doc. He knows where every nail on the place is. He can bareback and he ain't scared of a twelve-hour day." The funny thing was, Stuart remembered his father's temptation to consider the argument as having grounds for an alternative to school.

Lilly was truly a friend to Stuart's mother. The old house needed more than one woman and they made the perfect team. Lilly's humor was of a marketable quality and the childless couple had been an all-around fit that lasted twenty-three years.

That was it. He would go to visit Lilly and Rabbit. They had since moved to Theta, which was about fifteen miles away. The idea made him almost trot to his car.

The drive out Santa Fe Pike was not so familiar. He had not been up to their house in some time and they had spent most of his life on the same property with him.

The frame house had smoke climbing from the chimney on one end and he knew the inside would be warm. The storm door had to be pulled in order to knock on the wooden front door.

The jolly face that met him was timeless. "Come in, come in. My nose was itching this morning and I told Eddie we would have company."

"How are you doing, Lilly?" He hugged his old friend.

"A lot better than I deserve and not near as good as I would be if I had my say."

"How's Rabbit?"

"Come on in here and see for yourself. Ain't nothing wrong with your eyes."

He had seen Rabbit in the hospital some few months ago when a vascular problem claimed one lower leg.

"How's it going, Rabbit?"

"The leg don't bother me near as much as this ornery woman."

The pair sat in the front room in opposite chairs and left the couch for Stuart.

"Tell me about married life. Nothing changes for us, we want to hear what's going on with you. It sure seems to be agreeing with you."

"Thanks. I love it. You know Helen. She's just like she always was and better than you can imagine with the kids. I'll have to take you down to see her sometime."

"I'm not much on long road trips," Lilly alibied.

"I can fly you down. I've been flying long enough for you to trust me," Stuart countered.

Lilly shifted in her seat. "No, thank you."

Stuart could not pass up the opportunity. He had spent most of his life debating simple issues with Lilly's priceless vernacular attached to her razor sharp mind. "Now, Lilly, you know that you are not in any danger. Nothing is going to happen to you until your time comes." He sat back confident he had trumped any possible argument.

"I've studied about that thing. If it's just us up yonder in that plane, what would me and Eddie do if your time was to come?"

He shook his head. "Undefeated and still champion," he muttered.

"What?"

"Nothing," he said, smiling in mock disgust.

"Well, how's Helen?" Lilly asked.

"She's fine."

"I remember going fishing with you and her when ya'll were teenagers," put in Rabbit. "She's a good'un," he declared with more scrutiny than Dunn and Bradstreet.

"When we going to get more young'uns?" Lilly asked.

"We can't afford much planning along those lines just now."

"That's the Lord's planning. You just do what comes natural."

Stuart hesitated. "Who's going to raise your tobacco crop this year? You still have your allotment, don't you?"

"What makes you think something would change that ain't changed since Eddie got sick?"

"I was just wondering..."

"Wondering how to dodge my question."

His missing smile would have escaped most trained observers, but not her.

"What's bothering you?" she asked.

Stuart looked at Rabbit and back at her. He had two options. He could tell them the truth or he could tell them it was none of their business.

"Nobody knows this...Helen is pregnant." His face fell slightly and he sat silently.

She used the silence as skillfully as she did her glib tongue. The next statement must be his too.

"We don't know if we're going to keep it," Stuart blurted.

"It ain't no bluegill to be thrown back," she admonished without laughing.

"There's more. Helen was exposed to x-rays and there's a chance of birth defect. We want our baby to have a normal quality of life."

"If your six-month-old son was in a car wreck and the doctor said he would never walk again, would you have him put to sleep?" Lilly asked.

The question did not expect to learn.

"I'm scared," he confessed.

"Now you've told the truth," said Rabbit. "Don't hide behind some tale about the quality of life when you know the Lord don't need no help deciding who ought to be born. If it ain't to be, Helen will have a miscarriage. If it is to be, you'll be fine. Don't never doubt yourself."

The subject was finally changed successfully but Stuart was numb the rest of the visit and soon was saying his goodbyes.

The drive was as automatic as if he had been on rails, and his mind raced from left to right on this critical issue. The timing could not be worse, he thought. The sandwich Lilly fixed had been eaten somewhere between Ringgold and Tate. He couldn't remember where. The gas gauge was showing a little less than a quarter of a tank and the mileage remaining was a little more than a half tank. His watch and stomach agreed it was getting close to evening but the ten dollars would have to feed the Cutlass.

He drove into Gainesville just at dusk and crossed the glass-smooth lake via Thompson Bridge and turned up into the apartment complex. A car was at the bottom of the drive and slowly climbed the hill in front of him. The bumper sticker read: TO BE OR NOT TO BE—Creator's Choice. Helen's car was in her parking space and he climbed the steps still vacillating.

"I'm home," Stuart called through the door as he pushed it open.

"Hi," came the response followed by a full embrace.

"Sweetie, we need to talk," he began.

"I know."

They sat down on the couch and shifted to almost face each other.

"I mean we need to talk to God," he qualified.

"I know."

CHAPTER 29

"Mike, I was calling to find out if we could get together and see if we have anything to discuss."

"I'm going to be out of town from tomorrow through the middle of next week. And you know how it is just getting back in the office, so I'm afraid it will be a couple of weeks out."

"How about right after lunch today for fifteen minutes?" Stuart allowed his hope to show in his voice.

"Well, I don't see why not," he empathized.

"Thank you. I'll be in at 1:15. You're just outside the perimeter at the Georgia 400 exit, aren't you?"

"That's right. The agency name is on the sign at the entrance to the office complex. See you in a couple of hours."

Stuart went quickly through a shower and put on a suit. It had been a week since he had gone to Nashville and he really appreciated Bill calling Mike for him.

Later, in Atlanta, Stuart walked into the large atrium and looked at the directory. Southeastern Insurance Center was the occupant of the entire third floor. After a few minutes of waiting, Mike Norman was available to meet with him in the main conference room.

"Thanks for seeing me so quickly. I was hoping I wouldn't have to wait a couple of weeks."

"Bill had a chance to say some nice things about you, but not much in terms of experience and so forth..." Mike put his coffee cup to his mouth and waited.

"I have no direct sales experience and only a buyer's awareness of insurance in any form. My degree is from Georgia, in Economics, and my experience since 1979 graduation is all construction. I'm married with one little girl and another child on the way."

"Why insurance?"

"I don't know. It's almost a 'why not' question, I guess."

"So, it's not something you have always hoped for the chance to do?"

"It's not something that I've given much thought to one way or the other," Stuart answered.

"Do you think you can do it successfully?"

"Yes, I do."

Mike smiled. "There's going to be a problem. In insurance, it takes a while to get started so that the money flows. When you first get going, you could starve waiting to get paid for the first sale. Depending on how the customer pays for his policy, it could take you a year to get all of the money due you from the deal. Obviously, as you have more deals under your name, the gaps fill in and there is more predictability in the income stream."

"Bill said that sometimes a draw is used."

"Not here. I am personally opposed to it."

"I see. I asked for fifteen minutes and I can leave you with five in change...or...I could be so bold as to ask you what you have to lose by giving me an 'eat what I kill' contract to see if I can produce."

"What I have to lose is my peaceful conscious. You don't have a cash reserve and you have an obligation to a young family. I don't want to lead you down a rocky path. I need some time to consider this. Leave me with a number."

"Thank you, Mike." Stuart stood and shook his hand. "I'll wait for your call."

*****

"You better give the doctor a call, Helen."

"Maybe you're right. Can you watch this group while I go to your office and use the phone?"

"Sure thing."

"Hello, is Dr. Hansel in?"

"He's with a patient. May I help you?"

"My name is Helen Kerr and I'm pregnant. I've been having a lot of pain today and a little light spotting. Do you think there's anyway he could see me?"

"Not today, if it's not an emergency, I'm afraid."

"When is the soonest?"

"Day after tomorrow, but I would be glad to let you speak...."

"Thank you anyway." She hung up and started out of Sharon's office. The pain surged again and Helen went back to the phone. She flipped to the yellow pages to see if she could recognize the name. There it was in OB-GYN category. She punched the number.

The next ten minutes were a blur and Helen was amazed to be in an examining room answering the questions of a lady with a clipboard.

"Everything seems to be fine," he assured. "I just want to confirm what my stethoscope is telling me."

The ultrasound was arranged and he soon was viewing the monitor with a smile. He shifted his eyes and tapped his stethoscope with his finger as the ear pieces were not in his ears. "I think I have some news for you," he began.

Helen could not read his expression. "What is it?" she asked suspiciously.

"You have a bit of a housing problem you are adapting to. You see, you are carrying twins."

"Are you....I'm not ready for this. Stuart is really not ready for this. What am I going to do?" Her face was not as fearful as she felt with these people she didn't know.

"I want to set you up on some regular visits, but for now, I need to know that you can take it easy."

"What do you mean? No work? Because things, I mean circumstances, will not allow me to stay home."

"I don't mean go to bed. I just mean you are going to have to avoid lifting and over exertion and, in general, be smart about what's going on with your body."

"Thank you. This is all new to me and I didn't mean to sound so....scared. I'm sorry."

"No problem. I'm glad it worked out for you to come in. We have some literature that you'll need to take advantage of, but that does it for now."

After getting back to work, she decided to call to see if by some chance Stuart was there.

The answering machine clicked, then sputtered and she heard a garbled message, then a crisp beep. She held the phone for a second. "Stuart, it's me, Sweetie. I can't believe I'm telling this to your stupid machine, but I had a problem today and went to the doctor. I'm okay, but....he told me that we are going to have twins." She sighed. "I love you."

*****

Becky had just gotten in the back door with the groceries when her husband appeared to greet her and ask about her day. Once they both knew how the other's day had been, her husband said, "I want you to hear something on the answering machine." He moved toward the phone.

"I thought that thing was broken."

"Just the part that plays the answering message. It records the call fine." He pressed the play button.

"Stuart, it's me, Sweetie. I can't believe......" The full message continued in perfect clarity.

"What do you think of that?" he asked, pressing the save button.

"Peter, I don't know how, but that's Helen Kerr. I know it is. Redo it."

The message played again.

Becky looked up the Kerr's number in the phonebook. "Their phone number is only one digit different from ours. This is unbelievable. Bless her heart."

"It's only been a week since you were over at her house. Has Stuart found work yet?"

"No, not two days ago, at least. She sounded scared."

"I guess so. They don't have but half an income and she'll probably have to quit soon because of this, and no insurance....man, oh, man."

*****

It was almost dark when Stuart finally pulled into the apartment parking lot with another car behind him. It was Helen and he walked around to meet her. She got out with some papers in her arms.

"Mind if I carry your books?" he said, bowing.

"Are you just getting home?" she asked, handing him the small stack.

"Yes, and you?"

"Yes. I worked on a couple of letters to parents and lost track of the time."

"You look a little beat."

"It's been quite a day. I want to take a bath and then tell you about it when I can deal with it. How did your interview go?"

"He was nice enough to give me the fifteen minutes like I told you he agreed to, but I'm afraid it would take a miracle to be a fit."

When they opened the door they stood in shock at the scene in front of them. The den was covered in boxes of infant cereal and diapers. There were clothes still in the packages and garbage bags of used baby clothes. A crib was fully assembled next to the pub table. Cans of formula were stacked up pyramid style on the coffee table.

"Wow!"

"Yeah."

Stuart pushed the door closed behind him and tiptoed his way to a small spot left open on the carpet and sat down. Helen joined him.

"This is unbelievable," she marveled.

"Who....I mean, how would...."

"I don't have a clue. I didn't talk to anybody after I left the doctor's office today."

"You went to the doctor's office?"

Oh, that's right. I haven't even talked to you yet. I was having some trouble and had to call about it. Anyway, I called and left you a message on the answering machine. I'll sit here while you play it."

Stuart slid over to the end table and pressed the play button. "Stuart, this is Mike Norman. I wanted to tell you before I left town that something happened after you left my office. A representative for one of the insurance companies contracted in our agency came by. They want to test a new sales idea that would involve a captive contract between that one company and a producer. They would provide training, a benefit package with full hospitalization coverage and a salary of two thousand dollars a month. So contact Nelda in my office if you are interested. See you, Stuart."

Stuart stared at the room full of new supplies and silently cocked his head at Helen. "I feel as though I've been given a financial reprieve. Could it be so much better so quickly?"

"This is unbelievable," Helen said as she slowly shook her head.

"I almost forgot. You said you wanted me to hear your message on the answering machine. There isn't another one." He looked at the answering machine and back to Helen.

She took a breath and began, "Today while I was at the doctor's office...."

A knock at the door interrupted her.

"Come in," yelled Stuart from his seated position.

The door opened and a blue canvas-covered chrome baby stroller began to roll in with their next door neighbor behind id. "The people I let in this afternoon asked me to hold on to this until both of you got home for some reason."

Stuart looked at the unmistakable design of two seats and turned to his bewildered wife.

"That's what I have been trying to tell you, but I don't know how anybody could know already," Helen said as she pulled it into the room. "Thanks Rene."

"No problem. Congratulations! You folks have got some pretty special friends." She closed the door behind herself.

"Play that message again, Sweetie," Helen smiled. "Somehow I think this is going to work out."

Stuart pulled the two rattles out of the sack he had brought in from the car. "Is this really happening?! Twins?!"

Helen nodded "yes" with a teary smile.
"We're having twins! What a day!"

CHAPTER 30

"Do you want any more shrimp salad?" teased Helen.

"No," popped the little cherub voice. "It's not good, it's yucky."

"Brooke, you know the rule, try one bite of everything," reminded Stuart.

Helen held up one finger in passive protest. "Even on a picnic?"

Stuart turned and looked at the view. "Things are just a little different on Yonah," he consented. "Come on, Poco. Let's climb the fire tower."

"Stuart!" This protest was not so calm. "Don't you think she's a little young for that? You've already brought her all the way up to the top of the rock face."

"I had to so I could show her where we decided to get married. Besides, the fire tower is a cakewalk compared to the repelling we did last year."

"I refuse to look. I just want to go on record as contesting this decision."

"She loves heights." He put her on his shoulders and strutted toward the center of the small plateau. "What do you want Helen to have, darling? Girls or boys?"

"Yep, sister, brother," Brooke voted.

"I suppose that's a possibility. I know one thing, whatever they are, they are going to have a first-class big sister, that much is a given."

She giggled as though she understood every element of the conversation.

"That's high enough," called Helen after they had climbed a little higher.

"What difference does it make. If we fell, they would have to bury us in the same coffin now."

"This sign says not to do what you are doing," she noticed as she walked to the bottom step.

"This is career day for Brooke. She might want to become a ranger. Besides, she can't read."

"No higher, Stuart," Helen returned to business.

"Yes, ma'am."

"You've seen it, come on down."

"It's not just something you see. You don't get up from the table after one bite and say 'Now I've eaten'." He was coming down and Helen didn't care about being right so long as she had her orders followed.

"Don't you think we ought to be going?"

He checked his watch. "You're probably right. My flight is at 4:15, but you need to have Brooke back by 5:00, so we'll have to run ahead of schedule a little bit. When he was almost to the bottom step he acted as though he had tripped and stumbled with Brooke shrieking her delight.

"Very funny. I'm not laughing."

"I wish I could take both of you with me."

"I know. I don't like the idea of you being up there three weeks without coming home. Who all is going to be there?"

"There will be about twenty agents from almost as many states according to Mike. The training will cover several aspects of insurance. I don't know much else."

"Who is going to teach it?"

"I don't have a clue. Somebody with the company, I guess."

They were picking up the picnic supplies and putting everything into Stuart's daypack.

"Anyway," he raised his eyebrows, "I'm looking forward to getting home already. I don't know much about insurance, but I know it saved our necks to become part of this company and get maternity coverage when we did."

They drove down the rutted rocky road and found their way on toward Atlanta. The goodbyes at the airport were done at the no parking zone of the relatively new midfield terminal.

"It's hard to believe, this is the first road job I ever worked on," he remarked, looking down the curved approach to the deck of the terminal. "We did all the work on the aprons and a couple of taxiways in the summer of '79."

"Well, it seems to be holding together well," teased Helen with a well-communicated 'Who cares?' look in her eye.

"Don't grow until I get home, Poco," he changed the subject. Her flaxen ringlets bounced as he picked her up to kiss each dimple.

"Are you going to write me some of your letters?" Stuart asked of Helen. "That's the only thing about being married that was a letdown. Now that we share the same address, I don't get anything in the mail from you."

"Call me with your address. I love you."

Helen buckled Brooke into the childseat and slid under the wheel just as she was being approached for a reprimand. She sang softly and by the time she was on the expressway, her voice and the warm sun had sent Brooke into a well earned nap. The nonstop drive took a little over an hour and she delivered Brooke at home still asleep. By the time she climbed the stairs to her own apartment, it was dark. The red blink on the answering machine indicated one message and she walked over to play it.

"Well, I have to find out from other sources that you are going to have twins! Maybe you should call your old buddies once in a while. You know I can still take partial credit for you two getting together."

Helen smiled at the voice as she picked up the phone and dialed Ruth's number.

★★★★★

The contact at the Philadelphia baggage claim was holding a small cardboard sign which read, "STUART KERR," just as arranged.

"That's me." Stuart pointed to the sign.

"Hi, I'm Diane and I'll be taking you to the facility."

"I have a couple of bags to get and I'll be ready."

"They said you were from Georgia, but the accent is something you have to hear to be prepared for."

"So, you haven't been around many of God's preferred people?" he asked.

"No, I'm a northerner, born and raised."

"You seem to be overcoming it, at least," Stuart teased.

"How so?"

"I've always been warned about how people will treat you 'up here'."

He took the last of his bags off the carousel and she motioned the direction and assisted by taking one of the bags.

"It's about twenty minutes to where you'll be for the next three weeks."

"I'm homesick already," he said, buckling his seat belt.

"Married?" she asked.

"Yes, with a little girl and twins on the way," he smiled.

"You and your wife are going to be busy."

"I hope we can just stay out of debtor's prison."

"It's expensive, at least that's what I've heard."

"You married?"

"No, not a chance."

They rode on another ten minutes with Stuart mainly asking questions about various buildings until they arrived at the facility where Stuart took his bags to a check in area.

"Let's see, Mr. Kerr...you'll be staying with Kevin Bosman. Do you know him?"

"No, I don't."

"It says here that he is from Texas. He's already checked in so you'll probably meet him right away." She handed Stuart a key and pointed to the elevator. "Let us know if there is anything you need."

"Thank you."

He walked to the elevator and managed to get all of his luggage in without dislocating anything, then followed the desk clerk's directions to his room. He inserted the key, but the door swung open before he could turn it.

The man at the television turned and smiled all the way to his receding hairline.

"You must be Stuart."

"Kevin?"

"That's right. Glad to know you."

"It's nice to meet you. I understand you're from Texas."

"Right again. You're not going to tell me you know somebody from Texas, are you?"

"Not at all. I was one of the few people in college from my state and got tired of the 'do you know' game before the end of my freshman year."

"Funny how people think you should know everyone in your state."

"It would probably be true if you went to Amsterdam.....'I knew someone in the states, once'."

"So," Stuart said, changing the subject as he hung up some of his clothes, "when did you get in?"

"Couple of hours ago, I guess. I've had a chance to take a tour. There is a pretty good health club complete with hot tub and sauna. The food is supposed to be outstanding. There was a guy in our agency that came to this thing several years ago. He came back talking more about the food than the training."

"How long have you been with the agency you are in?" Stuart asked.

139

"About five years, I guess," Kevin said after a moment. "How about you?"

"I'm brand new. In fact, you mentioned a guy coming to this several years ago; it was my understanding that this was a new concept."

"Oh, you mean the captive contract within the independent agency. That is a new concept, but this agent training school has been going on for years. They used it in the past to build relationships with agents. With the program you're on, it will be even more helpful."

Stuart finished putting away his clothes and shoved his bag into the end of the closet. Then he began to question Kevin about more important things like dinner.

CHAPTER 31

"Hi, Sweetie."

"How is everything?"

"It keeps me pretty occupied, to be honest. The material is new to me and it takes me most of the night to catch up for the next day. They are following the schedule of the agenda pretty closely so you can tell from day to day what will be next."

"What are you going to do on your first weekend?"

"I couldn't get a date," Stuart laughed.

"What a pity."

"I probably will study this stuff some more. How about you?"

"I don't know," she said distantly.

"I know I've only been gone a week, but you sound like you're talking to someone else with your hands while you're talking to me with your mouth. Is everything okay?"

"Actually, there is something I need to tell you. I had hoped to wait until you got home," she admitted.

"I won't be home for two weeks. Tell me now."

"When I dropped Brooke off last Sunday after taking you to the airport, she was still asleep when I drove into her driveway. I tried to be as quiet and quick as possible, but Wednesday, I noticed her sweater on the floor of the back of the car. There's not much cold weather left, so I called and was offering to take if by when her mother told me."

After a couple of seconds, Stuart anxiously asked, "Told you what?"

"They have been talking about it for some time, but they have decided to move to Valdosta."

The news impaled Stuart with helpless confinement, "DAMN!"

Helen sat for a moment in the silence that followed. "This is a simple job change and at least is not born of any hidden agenda."

"I've got to go," Stuart concluded.

"You don't plan to call, do you?" she asked quietly.

"I don't 'plan' anything. Everything is 'planned' for me," he snapped bitterly.

"Sweetie, I wish I had waited."

"When is the move?" he asked more calmly.

"Next month some time."

"Okay, I do want to hang up, still. I love you and I don't intend to make any call."

"It will be okay. You'll see. Please don't feel you have to carry this alone. We can do this thing as long as you don't shut me out. Remember, I love Brooke, too."

"Thanks."

Helen lightened her voice. "For loving Brooke?"

"No, for loving me. Brooke can thank you for herself."

"We'll see to it that she has plenty of opportunity."

"'Night."

"I love you."

"I love you."

★★★★★

Helen got up from lying half under the cover and went to the door.

"Come in. And which one of Santa's elves are you?"

"What do you mean?"

"Come on, Becky. I don't know how you knew I was expecting twins, but nobody could have done this other than you."

"Done what?"

"The clothes, the bed, the....everything."

"I was not alone and we all would just as soon remain anonymous."

"Stuart and I will never forget it. Thank you."

CHAPTER 32

Helen walked through the security check and on toward the gate Stuart's plane was to come to.

"Daddy!" Brooke shouted as he came into the sitting area.

"Welcome home." Helen kissed and hugged him.

"Well, the whole gang is here." He patted Helen's stomach that was making the news public. "I missed you pretty bad."

"Three weeks is just too long," Helen said shaking her head.

"How are you?" he asked as he picked up Brooke and carried her on his hip.

"I'm fine," Helen said.

"Have you been feeling any better since Thursday?"

"Kind of. Dr. Richland says that it's just going to be a day to day thing and I should be prepared to spend the last few weeks in bed."

They waited for and gathered up Stuart's luggage, then walked to the shuttle step and rode to the zone where Helen had parked the car.

"I meant to tell you, your second check came and I deposited it in the checking account."

"That was fast....or I guess it was. It felt like I've been gone two months. And by the way, Brooke, you grew a foot without my permission." He turned his attention toward Helen. "How is the checking account holding out?"

"We're in pretty good shape, actually. But I haven't faced the hospital bills for my x-rays and all."

"I'm going to contact them tomorrow and see what kind of payments they will accept."

"You'd better get in good with them before the big day," she said and patted her stomach.

"I knew I had something to tell you," he began, "I talked to the office yesterday and it has been confirmed. The pregnancy is technically viewed as any other illness, and this particular hospitalization plan that we're on will not exclude it as a pre-existing condition."

"That simple means we're covered?" Helen asked.

"That's right."

"What a blessing and relief."

"It's tough enough to face whatever is coming without being certain you're going to be bankrupt."

"You don't have any regrets, do you?" she asked.

"Not even for a minute. I just get scared from time to time thinking about the tough stuff that could happen."

"I know. But the results are not up to us. We just have to play the cards we're dealt. And I don't have any regrets, that's for sure."

Stuart took a deep breath and checked the traffic before merging onto the interstate. "Not many more days until they move." He tilted his head toward the back seat where Brooke was buckled into her carseat.

"I know." Helen slid a little closer and took his hand. "I want you to know how important it is to me that we keep up the contact necessary to maintain our relationship."

"Do you know how far it is to Valdosta?" he reminded without asking for a specific answer.

"I've looked at the map. It is under 300 miles, I think."

He smiled at her optimistic expression and choice of words. "I thought I married you for your gentleness. You don't quit easy, do you?"

"Not when the prize at the end is worth so much."

"How in the world are we going to effectively get the kind of time with her we need?"

"No one has set a minimum on what it takes to build a relationship. We will just set a priority of driving and when she gets a little older, phoning. The bottom line is, we'll have to do the best we can and hope the results pan out."

In other words, there's no point in pouting about it?" Stuart asked.

"I hope you don't think that's an insensitive statement. I know this hurts you very much. I just want you to know I'm in it with you for the long run and I think we'll make it work."

Stuart squeezed her neck and turned on the radio. "Let's stop at the 'V' for a gourmet dinner," he suggested.

"Where?"

"The Varsity. Haven't you ever eaten there?"

"No," she confessed.

"There were two in Athens when I was in school and we used to hit there for a late night grease relief after we had been...." he hesitated, "studying at the library." His face showed the disbelief it would have if he had been told the same story.

"You must have been exhausted," Helen rolled her eyes.

"You'll like the ambiance the indoor experience offers," he said in explanation of the unasked question of why they weren't at a speaker of the world's largest drive-in.

Brooke was groggy and draped over his shoulder as he escorted Helen to the entrance. He opened the dingy glass door and ushered his wife into the wide hallway that dead-ended into a counter with an anthill of activity behind it.

"Two naked stakes walking through the garden and a PC," an employee behind the counter shouted to his right as he filled a cardboard container with hot french fries.

Helen recoiled and stepped on Stuart's foot. "What did he say?" she said without turning around.

"Two hamburgers with lettuce, tomatoes and onions and a chocolate milk."

144

She played the order back in her mind. "I don't get the chocolate milk," she stated, rather than asked.

"PC....it means painted cow." Stuart deciphered.

She stayed back a few feet and decided to gather more data. The counter with a surface of stainless steel ran the length of it's portion of the building. The conveyor behind it was running like a ticker tape. Other rooms included onions in huge sacks and roller racks of buns for hot dogs and hamburgers. Several large rooms were furnished only with a couple of dozen school desks and a large television mounted in a corner about head high. A ledge ran around every room with oversized plastic squeeze bottles of ketchup and mustard and three shakers; salt, pepper and red pepper. The smell was chili, onions and fried.

"How do I get mine?" Helen asked shyly.

"You walked into the middle of their assembly line," he said turning her gently by the shoulders and nodded to the right of their present position. "We need to go down there to order."

"What'll it be?" the man in the paper hat demanded.

"I haven't had a chance to...."

Stuart stepped up. "May I?"

"Sure, thanks."

"Four all the way, two fries, one ring and three PCs."

Helen raised her eyebrows. "What's that going to be?"

"You'll love it," was his only answer. "Take her and let's get a table in the upper deck." He pointed to a glassed-in area as he handed Brooke to her. "I'll bring up our order."

Helen walked up the wide steps and found a clean table. She put Brooke in a chair and retrieved a highchair from a table that had not been bussed.

Stuart soon joined them. His eye was caught by someone walking down the connector part of the building.

"Just a minute, Sweetie. I think I see somebody I know...yeah, that has got to be him. Swamp Guinea," he spoke out.

The big redhead stopped two feet away with a confused look on his face. He cocked his head like a St. Bernard determining sound direction and then lit up with recognition. "Hey, aren't you my Savannah mud turtle?"

"That's right," smiled Stuart. "Meet my family. This is my wife, Helen, and my daughter Brooke. You'll have to help me with your name. I'm terrible at remembering names."

"Kirk, and I can't call yours either."

"Stuart Kerr. Pull up a chair and tell me what you're doing in Atlanta."

"Letting. I thought you'd be there."

She nodded. "Nice to meet you Kirk. It's a small world. Imagine you two running into each other twice as strangers on opposite ends of the state and then finally again in a restaurant."

Kirk's face twisted slightly. "We only met in Savannah that one time."

Helen took a swallow of her chocolate milk and turned to Stuart. "I thought he was the one in Rabun County that you said you went up and blasted rock for," she remembered.

Stuart thought for a second, then corrected, "It turns out it was Kirk's brother in Rabun County."

Kirk looked blankly at Stuart. "You never told me that was you."

145

"I just worked for that company," he explained.

"Still...I, well, anyway, I thought you would be at the letting yourself."

"No, I've changed jobs and I'm not in contracting anymore."

"What are you doing?"

"I'm in the insurance business," Stuart answered.

"Man, I wish you could do something about my work comp. That stuff is about to eat me alive."

"I've had my head stuck in the sand for several weeks, but I will look into it. Where can I get in touch with you?"

Kirk reached into his pocket and produced his business card. "Call me, really. I'd like to have some help."

Stuart smiled. "I'll look you up sometime when I'm down that way."

CHAPTER 33

"Kevin, it's Stuart Kerr," he spoke into the telephone.

"Hi, Stuart, what's going on with you?"

"I want to run something by you and get your opinion."

"Shoot."

"What do you know about contractors?" Stuart asked.

"They promise to be done in two weeks for one thousand dollars and it takes two months and four thousand dollars."

"No, I mean a different kind of contractor. Anyway, I told you I had spent several years in the construction business and I still know several people in it. What I want to know is what you know about worker's compensation coverage."

"It's regulated. The premiums are set and the claims are set for unambiguous damages like the loss of an eye or hand or something, but where are you going with all this?"

"I have written a letter that has a clip and return request at the bottom. It asks a couple of questions like premium presently being paid and number of employees and so on. The gist of it is that I wanted the people not satisfied with their work comp to mail me back the inquiry. I got a forty percent response to my mailing when I sent them out to the Georgia's bidders list."

"I need more help, but I'm warming up."

"I have spoken to three insurance companies and none is interested in writing it monoline."

"I'm not surprised. It's a mess here in Texas and our companies are telling us that they are losing their shirts in it. Most of them have stopped writing it except what is assigned to them through the state pool."

"That's about the size of it here."

"So, without calling you a dufus, why did you go to all the trouble to learn what you could have been told by anybody in the insurance business?"

"I guess it goes back to simple economics. The demand is high so capitalism should be able to respond with supply."

"How do I fit? You said you wanted to run something by me," Kevin continued.

"The companies I've talked to rejected my first idea. I wanted to bundle up a group of contractors and combine their businesses in a single policy to make a larger premium base so the company would be able to reduce the surcharges. They didn't like it for a lot of reasons, but the main one was profitability."

"I'm still listening."

"My next approach was to share in the risk by putting up a front line entity that would retain ten thousand dollars on any one claim. That entity would then purchase reinsurance. The company I'm contracted with is interested in that."

"Any idea of what it takes?" Kevin asked.

"Some idea. Mechanically, the front line has to be an insurance company. It can be an offshore company, but since it will be collecting premiums and will be involved in claims, it must be an insurance company. Then what happens is it must be capitalized to the extent that what the actuaries determine is expected. Depending on how many we put in the group and their payrolls and classifications, it could go to a quarter of a million dollars just to be in business. Whatever the amount, the insurance company would have to see escrowed or irrevocable money available. What is purchased then is reinsurance on each account so there is no stacking of limits, so the $10,000 per claim stays available."

"How much premium are you talking about?"

"I feel the response I got was a start. If I take that response and just calculate according to the people I know who would at least know who I am, I can see $25 million of premium."

"So what do I do?" Kevin asked slowly.

"I need capital. The amount of reinsurance that has to be purchased will determine how much of a reduction this idea can offer. The amount of capital raised will translate into the size of the facultative share or the retention. If we can retain ten thousand dollars, for example, we can probably purchase the reinsurance with what would represent the normal rate less a surcharge. It could mean a fifteen percent savings to the contractors."

"You want me to raise the money?"

"That's right. Without the capital, all we have is a good idea. What do you think?"

"If I had the money, I'd be doing something else, like fishing and not worrying about it," Kevin laughed.

"I don't think 250 cabbages is much of a retirement fund for someone of your age and obligations, but what we need is a venture taker or several. The risk would be limited to a certain amount of money. The return could be projected from actuarial work, so the idea could be sold to a few," continued Stuart.

"Do you think the fact that I'm in Texas and you're in Georgia would have anything to do with the outcome of this mission to raise cash?"

"We have to start somewhere. You've been in the business a lot longer than I have..."

"In percentage years, yes, but...."

"You can work with me on making sure the coverages don't get left out and all the detail stuff stays in order. You also know of some people, I'd guess, that are financially capable of hearing such a proposal and participating if they should want to."

"What does that leave for you, exactly?" Kevin let his voice ooze with sarcasm.

"Selling the contractors, administering the claims through a contracted service and purchasing reinsurance. Besides, I would guess that there may be some contractors who would like to throw in with us as investors as well as being policyholders."

"Claims through a contracted service?" Kevin singled out.

"Yes, I don't think that area is one we need to trust to ourselves. One bad claim experience and our reputation is shot."

"I agree to an extent. Doing business means having problems to some degree. The problem becomes real only if it goes unfixed."

"Are you saying we don't need to farm out the claims work?" Stuart asked.

"No, what I'm saying is, that even when you do, it will not guarantee a worry-free operation."

"I understand," said Stuart, "and agree."

"So, what do you plan to do first?"

Stuart looked up at the secretary in the doorway of his office who was telling him Helen was holding on another line.

"Kevin, I need to get with you again on all this when you've had time to give it some thought. I need to go, my wife is on the other line."

"You need to handle that the way I did."

"What do you mean?" questioned Stuart.

"We are separated," Kevin said flatly.

"I'm sorry to hear that. How long?"

"No problem. Less than a week."

"What was the objective when you decided to do it?"

"What?"

"The objective." repeated Stuart, "Were you trying to take a step toward divorce a little at a time, or were you trying to step back ten yards and punt so you could later improve your marriage?"

"I'm not sure we have any plan," Kevin said slowly.

"I've got to go. Give me a call if you feel like it."

Stuart pushed the blinking light on the multiline set. "Hi, Sweetie, I'm sorry to keep you holding."

"That's okay. I just called to tell you I had to go to Dr. Richland's office. I was feeling weird so I called. They told me to come on by. After he saw me, he told me I was going to have to quit work right away."

"You've still got a couple of months to go. I didn't think he was going to shut you down this fast."

"We hope there will be another couple of months. He doesn't seem to think we're going to make it that long. Anyway, as of this moment, he has not really shut me down completely. He has just told me to discontinue work."

"Have you talked to Sharon?" he asked.

"Not this afternoon, since I've been back. Why?"

"Well, it's just going to be tough for her to hold a spot for you for an indefinite amount of time."

Helen changed ears and shifted in the chair by the window. "I know we really haven't talked this through, but I don't see how I'm going to be a likely candidate for that job anyway. Even if everything goes the way we hope it will, I could never generate enough income from that job to offset the expense of not being at home, with daycare and everything."

"I can't talk about it just now. I know you're right, I just can't see how we can make it without you working. But the doctor's orders are simple for today's agenda....no work for the rest of the pregnancy."

"I'm sorry," she offered.

"I hope you don't feel like I needed you to apologize."

"No, I just know how tight things are and I want to help."

"I know. But now we have to take it one step at a time and I know the first step is for you to tell Sharon you're out of the game, for a while at least."

"She's gone by now. I'll give her a call tomorrow. I'll see you when you get home, somebody's at the door."

The door opened and Helen smiled, "Hi, Becky. How are you?"

"Fine. I just dropped by to see how your were doing."

"Well, I went to see Dr. Richland today and he has asked me to stay home from work. He hasn't put me to bed at this point, but he just wants the pregnancy to run as long as it can before these guys make their appearance."

"So, how are you feeling?" Becky asked as she sat in the other chair.

"I don't feel bad. I think this is a precaution. I just hate the consequences of all this."

"What consequences?"

"Look at me," Helen interrupted herself. "I haven't so much as offered you a Coke, let alone got up and act like I'm glad you came by."

"No problem. And yes, a Coke would be nice, thank you." Becky was already halfway to the kitchen.

"I guess I'll just sit here and watch you get it." Helen shook her head at herself.

"No, worse than that, I'm going to get you one while I'm at it and wait on you hand and foot. Where are the glasses?" She set the Coke out of the refrigerator.

"Over the sink. Thanks, that would be good."

Becky returned in a minute with both glasses. "What consequences?"

"Work. Stuart is trying to get started in this new job and things are really tight for us. I don't know where we would be if all of this stuff hadn't arrived. I doubt if I'll ever be able to thank you enough."

"So, what are your plans after the twins get here?"

"I don't know. It would be hard to find something that would justify the cost of me being away. Daycare alone would probably eat up most of what I could make. And then you add the things that some jobs require, like clothes, transportation and everything. I wish there were something I could do that would provide income and let me stay home at the same time. But I guess that's asking to have cake and eat it too."

"Not necessarily," Becky said thoughtfully. "Do you have time to take a ride with me?"

"I need to be back in an hour if that's okay."

"It won't take that long. I just want to show you something that might interest you."

"Sounds mysterious."

"We'll be back in thirty minutes."

They drove north to an area near North Hall High School. The rolling hills were steeper and closer together and in the shadow of the mountains. The road they turned down was paved but older and wound its way for a couple of miles into a valley that was wooded on the left and healthy green pastures on the right. They rounded a bend in the road and Becky stopped at the bottom of a small hill that had recent ruts and scattered gravel leading over the top. A log chain from an oak tree to a treated four-by-four post formed the night barricade. Becky pulled the front of the car onto the gravel and stopped.

150

"Do you feel like walking up the hill?" she asked Helen as she got out and closed the driver side door.

"We may have to stop a couple of times, but I'm the one with the time commitment."

The hill was not steep and the short distance was covered in one attempt.

Becky asked just as they were reaching the top, "Do you know the Bartlets?"

"I've met them at church. It's Robin and Chip, isn't it?"

"That's right."

"What makes you ask about...." Helen stopped as the view took her by surprise. The renovation of an old farmhouse was well underway and there, without warning to Helen, was the lake.

"This is beautiful," she marveled, looking at the irregular shoreline that ran out of sight in two directions. "I had no idea we had gone all the way back to the lake."

Becky smiled. "That thing is everywhere. It goes to Atlanta on the other end."

"Why are we here, by the lake?"

"I want to talk to you about it on the way home. But what I have to say only makes sense after you've seen this place."

CHAPTER 34

When Stuart got home he was greeted by the sight of Helen and Becky waiting for his return.

"Becky and I want to talk to you about something," Helen said.

"Should I have a lawyer present?" he asked.

"Sit."

"Yes, ma'am," he said as he sat on the couch.

Helen began from her chair, "Do you know the Bartlets?"

"Just by name, why?"

"Robin and Chip are several years older than us and they have a situation that Becky suggested we talk to them about. Becky, you tell Stuart what you told me."

"They moved here several years ago from South Carolina. About a year or so ago, Chip's father died, and since Chip is an only child, they talked to his mother about moving in with them. She did not want to then, but just recently, she's had a stroke and she wants to now. Anyway, she has sold her home on Lake Hartwell and is now moving here. The next part of the story is where I thought you might fit in. For some tax reason that I don't understand, Mrs. Bartlet is advised to spend the money from the sale of her house on a house here."

"Yes," nodded Stuart. "Otherwise, she would have to pay tax on the difference in what she and her husband paid for their house on Lake Hartwell and its sale price."

"Whatever. Apparently they had a nice place because I understand they are putting a lot of work in the house they are renovating. So, as the story marches on, I took Helen out to see the place just a few minutes ago. When it's finished next month, they will all move into the house and they are looking for someone to move into the old guest house and look after Mrs. Bartlet."

"Are you sure they're not just looking for a nurse?"

"My understanding is, they just want someone to be around. Chip has to travel two nights a week regularly and even more at certain times of the year."

Helen put her hand up and said, "For what it's worth, I want us to talk to them. The guest house is a two bedroom cottage and the den is bigger than this one."

"I'm fine with that. Give them a call tomorrow," he permitted.

"I thought we might give them a call tonight, if you don't mind," Helen persisted.

"As if I could prevent it," Stuart said smiling.

"Good. I have the number on the table if you would be so kind as to make the call."

"Helen, I don't even know what we're doing or the people involved."

Becky cleared her throat and spoke up. "Listen, why don't you two talk about the prospects and if you're interested, I'll mention it to the Bartlets. If they are still thinking about getting someone to come and stay with Mrs. Bartlet, then you can all discuss the details."

Stuart sat back and nodded. "That sounds reasonable to me. Is that okay with you, Sweetie?"

"Sure, thanks Becky," Helen said, turning her attention toward the door where Becky was now preparing to leave.

"My pleasure. I'll wait till I hear from you." She closed the door behind her.

Stuart shifted to face his wife. "Now, tell me what this is all about, if you please."

"I was telling Becky about my having to quit work and how it will be difficult for me to find something to do after the twins are born. She told me about the Bartlets and took me out to see the most beautiful place I have ever seen. The guest house looks like the gingerbread man lives there, or it will when it's finished. It has two bedrooms and a balcony sleeping nook. There's a fireplace in the den and a scaled down kitchen. I think it would suit us fine for a few years. I understand it's part of an old farm that was half-flooded when they built the lake in the fifties." She squeezed his hand. "I think it would be great and would allow me to help without being away from the kids."

The phone ring interrupted her. "I'll get it," Stuart offered. "Hello."

"Stuart?"

"Yes, it is."

"This is Kirk. Kirk Mayes in Waycross."

"Hi, Kirk. How are you?"

"I'm fine, but I got this letter today from my insurance company saying they are going to cancel me."

"Does it say why?"

"Something about them not writing this kind of insurance anymore."

"What kind is it?" Stuart asked.

"Something called Employers Liability," he repeated from the letter in his hand.

"That's workers compensation. Does the same company cover your other exposures....do they cover your equipment and truck and everything?" Stuart asked.

"Yes, why?"

"Well, Kirk, I'm not your agent, but I would imagine they are not exactly cancelling your policy in the middle of the term. I suspect they are non-renewing your policy, which means they won't write the work comp when the expiration date comes up. Have you called your agent?"

"No. It is with an agency that belonged to a friend of mine for a lot of years. He sold out six months ago and retired to Florida. The guy that bought it is some mega owner of several outfits. He's in Savannah. I was hoping you could take care of it for me."

"Well, I would be glad to so long as I don't get you in a mess. We ought to have plenty of time if you just got the notice."

"It's a couple of months away."

"Tell you what, you mail me a copy of the letter and I'll call you when I see if what I think is true. Meanwhile, you be sure you have coverage if you have to call the company."

"Okay, it will go in the mail tomorrow."

Stuart gave the address and phone number of his office, they said their goodbyes, then he called over his shoulder, "I'm going to get a shower."

"I'll be out in a minute." Stuart disappeared down the hall and into their bedroom.

The phone rang and Helen hesitated to see if he would get it. The second ring prompted her to get up.

"Hello?"

"Uh....is this Helen?"

"Yes. Who is this?"

"I'm Kevin Bosman. Stuart and I were roommates in Philadelphia."

"Yes, I've heard him talk about you a lot. How are you?"

"Fine, thanks. Is Stuart there?"

"He's in the shower, do you want me to have him call you?"

"Please. Let me give you my number."

Later, when Stuart walked in, Helen gave him the message and Kevin's number.

He dialed the number from Helen's note. "Kevin?" he said when the phone was answered.

"Nobody else lives here. That you, Stuart?"

"Yes, and I thought your living situation was by choice."

"I didn't call to talk about that."

"What is on your mind?" Stuart asked.

"I talked with a money man today and he is interested in meeting with you."

"Is he going to be in this part of the country anytime soon?"

"I don't know, but I suggested that the two of you talk on the phone before you go to the expense and effort to meet," Kevin suggested.

"Why don't we set up a conference call tomorrow. I'll be in the office most of the day."

CHAPTER 35

The next day Stuart got his friend, Kevin Maxwell, to hook up a conference call for them with Ricky, a potential third party in their insurance plan and an acquaintance of Kevin's.

Stuart began the conversation with, "Do you currently involve yourself with the purchase of workers compensation insurance in your company?"

"Not much. We are heavily into agriculture and mostly exempt from regulations that mandate the coverages."

"Then are you familiar with the growing difficulty business owners are having finding and paying for the coverage?" Stuart boundaried.

"To a degree."

"Kevin and I want to propose a plan that would put more supply back into a system that has unbalanced demand. We think we can form an offshore company to take the frontline risk and subcontract the claims work and reinsurance to a domestic carrier. The result would be identical coverage to the insured and escalating retention limits to us. Ultimately, we would be purchasing lower and lower reinsurance limits."

The three-way connection was momentarily silent. Then Ricky asked, "What is the incentive for the company owners to buy this plan since the price is regulated?"

Since Stuart was fielding the questions he answered. "The rates are regulated according to class codes. But recently, the companies that would normally offer work comp along with a package and auto account are no longer writing it. They are required by state law to participate in the assigned risk pool, but the pool has gotten so fouled up with surcharges and upfront downpayment plans, that the net result to the insured is high price and low service."

"I see," began Ricky, "but I would certainly think no one originally intended for this to happen. What makes you think you won't end up in the same predicament in the near future? I mean, if the rates are set and the claims adjustments are set, apparently there is not enough premium to provide the coverage....in other words, it looks like a proven loser."

"One of the major problems is fraud. The incentive to misrepresent the facts is too high. Claimants are typically disgruntled employees who get medical bills paid and receive reimbursement for lost wages. The incentive for the doctor is a regular office visit with whatever tests he wants to order. The insurance company compiles records of no profits to merit its pleas for surcharge increases. The insurance company probably finds it cheaper to carry a deadbeat than to spend money contesting his ambiguous back injury. I would hope we could put together a group that has some incentive to do the right thing."

"What kind of group?" Ricky asked.

"The problem is, the victim in this situation is the insured. In the specific program we hope to develop, the contractor is the one who suffers. He has the downtime of the employee with no incentive to return to work; he faces increased bottom line to his insurance premium through overall market conditions as well as individual experience modifications to his base rate, and he has nothing to say about any of it because the law demands he buy the coverage. The law sets his price and requires him to get the claim reported and then get out of the way."

"Stuart, you sound like you're personally involved in this thing. I see every point you are making, but how do you propose to get started?"

"I want to make this thing large enough to spread the risk, but small enough to control. Incentives should be offered to remain claim free. These incentives should be offered to employees in enough substance to offset the temptation to defraud what they are now living under. The healthcare provider should be controlled somehow too, but that's an area I don't know how to get my hands around. Penalties would be nice but almost impossible to police."

"Will the risk to your investors be limited?"

"Yes, I don't think I could go in otherwise. Remember, this does not function without insurance, this is taking a portion of the risk, and hopefully, a portion of the profit."

"Have you formed the upfront company yet?"

"No, this is mechanically still in a fledgling stage."

"I have had some experience in offshore charter work. Maybe I could provide a couple of shortcuts for you."

"That would be most helpful," Kevin put it.

"What do you see my role being?" Ricky asked.

"Ricky, I don't know how to really answer that without saying primarily money."

"As long as I know that, I don't have a problem with it. Of course, I would like to get as much information as possible on the feasibility of your idea, but for the moment, I'm interested."

And with that, he said his goodbyes while Kevin and Stuart remained on the line.

Stuart looked down and realized he was actually on his feet. He was not sure when he had stood up, but he was standing at his desk. "Well, Kevin, what do you think?"

"I think he is just what he said....interested. What do you plan to do next?"

"I plan to talk to some contractors and see what kind of interest I can get from them. I don't think we need more than three investors other than ourselves, so we can keep a handle on the communication. Meanwhile, I need for you to work on the details of the offshore company, the limited partnership offering, so we can't go to jail for trying to sell stock in some securities exchange violation. And we both need to be trying to find out about reinsurance treaties, whatever they are."

"I've got a couple of people in mind to talk to. Why don't we plan to talk again day after tomorrow."

"I'll expect to hear from you then."

Stuart hung up the phone and immediately called his potential client, Kirk.

"Kirk, this is Stuart. I'm glad I caught you in. There is something I wanted to talk to you about regarding your work comp."

"Tell it."

"How would you feel about being part of a group that had a risk retention pool that provided the insurance coverage and also paid you a dividend if the pool was profitable?"

"What is my risk?"

"If you were a principal in the pool's ownership, you would have to ante your part to make the pot right."

"I'm not interested in being in the insurance business. I would also think that my ante would be paying claims for other contractors. That is, if you're talking about putting together a crowd of contractors."

"That's right. But what about buying your insurance through the group?" Stuart asked.

"I'm fine with it, so long as they pay claims and there's no way my premium will be more than it was quoted to me."

"I need to make sure you understand a couple of things. First of all, just like your workers comp premium is treated now, the payroll is the rating basis. In other words, you might estimate your payroll to be $100,000 for the year. Then you might get more work than you figured on and wind up hiring a bunch of people. If your actual payroll went to $200,000 instead of the $100,000 estimate, your premium would be double what you had originally thought it would be. But, that is because your exposure increased and that is exactly the way it is for you now anyway."

"I'm fine with all that. I just don't want to be put into one of those things where you can owe more just because they lost money even if your payroll didn't go up."

"No, Kirk, you're talking about a program that is assessable. In fact, those things can demand more money from over a year in reverse. They are not all bad, though, and if I were trying to pick one, I would think of it as picking a fund. Some of them turn out okay, but I would want to see several years of performance. The thing that I am talking about is not assessable, but if it is profitable, a dividend would be paid back to each one of the policyholders."

"Sure, who wouldn't want to be a part of that? Does the coverage cost more?"

"No, the per payroll rates will be the same, but since we can get rid of the surcharge, the net to you would actually be cheaper. Then on top of that, there would be the chance to get a dividend back."

A beep from Stuart's secretary interrupted them, "It's your wife. She asked me to interrupt you."

"Kirk, I've got to grab the other line. Give it some thought and I'll call you in a day or two.

"Hey, Sweetie. What's up?"

"Stuart, I'm not sure. I called Dr. Richland and he told me to meet him at the hospital."

CHAPTER 36

Stuart arrived at the hospital to find his wife already admitted for an over-night stay.

Stuart walked in and Helen was sitting up in bed. "You got checked in pretty fast," he observed. "How're you doing?"

"Fine, but that is a question better handled by Dr. Richland. Have you two met?"

"We've spoken on the phone," Stuart said, extending his hand.

"Andrew Richland, nice to meet you." He took the handshake and offered Stuart a seat in the chair toward the head of the bed. He stood facing both of them and his face was reassuring in its expression. "What we are doing now is everything we can to prolong the pregnancy to as close to full-term as we can get it."

"I'm all for that," smiled Stuart.

"I'm not overly concerned; the worst that can happen at this point is that Helen will actually go into labor. I would obviously rather that not happen just now, but that is what the Brethine is for. I think we've got it under control for the time being."

Once Dr. Richland had left Stuart asked, "So, what's for dinner?"

"I don't know. They will probably feed me at 4:00."

"Do you have any appetite?"

"Not much, although I really don't feel that bad."

"That's good. From what he said, it doesn't sound like we've got a lot to be really scared about." Stuart walked to the head of the bed and caressed Helen's cheek with the back of his fingers.

"Dr. Richland wanted to buy a couple of weeks if we could. He thinks that this thing will probably happen three to four weeks earlier than a non-twin pregnancy."

"That's funny, I would think twins would take eighteen months to hatch."

He laughed and paced to the other side of the foot of the bed. "Can I get you anything?"

"I'm fine, thanks," she declined.

"I think I'm going to go home and get a shower and maybe a drive-through burger. I'll be back up here about 5:30 or so."

"Did you have any lunch?" she asked.

"No, I came when you called and then spent some time in the holding tank here."

"You must be starved. Go on and I'll see you when you get back."

He kissed her on the cheek and went out the door. The exit door reminded him that his car had been parked some distance from the building. He thought as he drove home of the concerns they had discussed early in the pregnancy. He whispered a prayer for healthy babies and stopped next to the lighted menu sign in the drive-through.

He picked at the fries in the sack until they were half gone by the time he got home. He scanned the paper for headline news as he ate. The phone interrupted the over-anticipation of both events.

"Stuart, this is Robin Bartlet. How are you?"

"I'm fine, thanks."

"Do you know why I'm calling?"

"Does it involve a conversation with Becky?" he qualified.

"Yes, as a matter of fact, it does. Actually, I had called a couple of times and missed you and Helen. I really didn't want to leave a message, but I would have if it had kept dragging out. Anyway, I understand Helen has ridden out to see the place."

"That's right. She was quite taken by it," he confirmed.

"Thank you. We are really looking forward to finishing everything up and moving in. Do you think from what you've heard, that you and Helen would be interested in meeting with Chip and me to talk about some of the possibilities?"

"Yes, I think that would be fine. The timing is a little off right now. Helen is at the hospital trying to postpone labor. I hope you are not in a big rush to finalize things."

"No, in fact, the place will not be ready for several weeks, in my opinion. But the guest house, which is what we will be talking about needs some cosmetic work, and it would be nice if whoever was going to be living there had some input."

"What kind of timeframe are you looking at on that?" he asked.

"I would hope to get a commitment from somebody within the next couple of weeks."

"I see. Well, why don't we plan to meet after church on Wednesday?"

"Sounds great. I'll see you at church," she agreed.

He hung up and was enthusiastic to tell Helen what he knew would make her look forward to Wednesday. He put the uneaten half of the cheeseburger into a plastic bag and into the refrigerator before driving back to the hospital. When he got in her room, she was finishing her meal.

"Hi. You know I didn't think to tell you when you left, but there was no real need for you to come back tonight."

"Well, I couldn't get another date on such short notice," he explained.

"How hard did you try?"

"I had one she-male call while I was home and she actually asked for a meeting."

"Do I know her?" Helen inquired playfully.

"Robin Bartlet."

"Really?" Helen asked excitedly, "What did she say?"

"She had talked to Becky and briefly to her husband. They want to meet us."

"When?"

"Well, I knew it was important, so I told them to come up here. They should be here any minute," he said without a smile.

"Be serious. When?"

"I told her we would get together after church Wednesday."

"I think this might really be the ticket for us, Stuart."

"It would be great for you to stay with the kids and still be able to work, or at least do something that would be a net gain to our household."

"How long do you plan to stay up here tonight?"

"I don't know. Why?"

"I was just thinking of how good a chili dog would taste."

★★★★★

"Ricky, I'm not sure, but I would say it's fine. I tried to call Stuart at home and got no answer," Kevin said while he double-checked Stuart's number.

"Normally, I would have more notice, but something has come up and I have to fly to Atlanta anyway. I would like to book my return flight with enough cushion to meet with Stuart at the Atlanta airport," Ricky outlined.

"I understand. Let me do this. You book your flight just that way and let me know what time you will be on hold. I'll tell Stuart to be at the airport at that time. I feel sure he can push things around enough to do that tomorrow. The main thing is for me to get in touch with him tonight and tell him when and where."

"Tell him the Admiral's Club at 2:30 Eastern Time."

"I'll tell him."

Kevin assured and pushed the hook button and dialed the 404 area code and number.

"Hello?" Stuart answered after the first ring.

"Stuart, where have you been? I have tried you three times and got no answer. Something sounds crazy on your answering machine and I didn't trust it. Did you even get my message? You have got to be in Atlanta tomorrow."

"You seem a bit excited," Stuart teased.

"I just talked to Ricky. He wants to meet you tomorrow at the Airport at 2:30. Can you do it?"

"Sure, where? Meeting at Hartsfield is like arranging a meeting of Woodstock."

"The Admiral's Club."

"What did he say?" Stuart wondered.

"Nothing else. Apparently something came up and he had to go Atlanta. Anyway, he wants to meet you."

"I'll be there."

CHAPTER 37

Stuart found Ricky waiting for him in the Admiral's Club. After introductions they got straight to business.

"Tell me all about this idea of yours," said Ricky.

"Since we talked last, I have found out a couple of things. The reinsurance we will need can come from a segment of a company I am contracted to represent. The blends of percentages would have to be worked out later. The first step is to set up a company in an offshore charter and fund it. Then we would have to start haggling for reinsurance in the same way large corporations negotiate different premiums for different deductibles."

"What about investor interest? Have you raised any money? Ricky pinpointed.

"I haven't really tried, but the answer is no."

"How much money will it take?"

"I think we should meet with a reinsurance company and start sparing with some actual numbers. The amount of capital will help determine the deal we can cut."

"What about buyers?"

"I have confidence in that area. I have polled a lot of contractors in the state and the need is there."

"If you don't have some of your insured's investment money, what is their incentive to control claims?"

"We'll show them a profit share. The group could be assembled in such a way as to pay dividends above a certain reasonable profit margin. That dividend would be paid to all policyholders whose loss ratios were under sixty-five percent."

"Make sure I understand a loss ration," Ricky said.

"The simple comparison of premium to claims incurred and defense cost. In other words an account with a $100 premium and a $30 loss year would have a thirty percent loss ration in pure numbers."

"What if a lawsuit is filed and the settlement or judgment is still pending?"

"You would set up a reserve and then calculate someone's entitlement to a dividend based on that reserve."

"Why do you think it has been so unprofitable in the past?" Ricky tried again.

Stuart sat back in his chair. "Basic human nature. The insured is pushed out of the way at claim time and his policy gets exploited. I think companies should contest more claims, but it is a touchy area. Since the days when labor unions were the life-saving voice of sweatshop slaves, there has been an over-swing of the pendulum to the side of more pay for less work. The employer is held responsible for anything remotely related to the job as though he were malicious. The corporation is viewed as a non-personified target whose bull's eye is a bottomless pot of gold called insurance and the archers are a dime a dozen. All they have to do is pass the state bar to get a third of the take.

Then there is the ambiguity of the rules of the game between the insured and the company. Particularly in the construction industry, it is unclear as to what an exposure is. On the one hand, you have subcontractors who are sole proprietors working on the same job as the insured. They don't want to be covered, willingly sign a hold harmless agreement and show themselves to be independent entities operating at more than arms' length from our insured. Yet, because of chinks in the law, some companies view this as auditable exposure. On the other hand, the system is not uniform in its criteria for inclusion or exclusion."

"Okay, okay. What if I told you I had the company chartered?" Ricky cut to the bottom.

"What do you mean?" Stuart said leaning up to concentrate.

"I have a company that is more or less a shell now. I formed it several years ago for the purpose of export and am not using much of that now. I would have to shift some assets around, but I think there are instruments in place to do this thing. Now, what is the next step?"

"The company would have to declare itself an insurance company and we would then try to get the reinsurance contract. That, in my opinion, would require a trip to Philadelphia."

"I'm ready for that trip. I need to know what those numbers are going to be before I completely make up my mind," Ricky stipulated.

"I understand. I will arrange it for us as soon as they say it's convenient."

"Next week is good for me. Let's shoot for Thursday."

"I'll let you know what happens," Stuart committed.

They shook hands and Stuart almost bounced down the steps from the Admiral's Club. His feet were just hitting the high spots as he made his way to the short term parking lot. The drive home took almost a full tape on his handheld recorder to be sure he got every note and concern to be later investigated. He walked into the door of his apartment and without hesitating, stumbled into what looked like a meeting.

"Going to a fire, Sweetie?" Helen laughed.

"I'm sorry...I was...." His tongue was hesitating even if his feet wouldn't.

"Do you know Robin?"

"Yes. Hi. I was kind of preoccupied. Sorry we missed you Wednesday."

"Good to see you, Stuart. Today is better anyway."

"Thanks for coming, or..." He looked at Becky. "Did you have a choice?" he smiled.

"Actually, it was my idea and when we called, Helen seemed like it was fine."

"Well, don't let me interrupt," he said starting to leave the room.

"I think you're involved, darling." Helen's voice was obviously doing more than transferring acts.

"Have I missed anything significant?"

Everyone looked somewhat blank. Robin spoke up, "I guess the thing to say is, we have an idea of what the arrangement would be for whoever the situation works out for. What we had in mind was to provide the guest house without rental charge. The obligation would be to my mother-in-law and her needs."

"That sounds reasonable and acceptable in terms of compensation. What do you think, Sweetie, about providing the care?"

"I think from a couple of comments, it would be something I could do as long as Mrs. Bartlets' condition did not severely deteriorate."

Robin shifted back in her seat. "Chip and I hope you will take it," she said finalistically.

Helen felt her ears heat up. "What kind of time frame are you in, again?"

"No real rush. Why don't you two discuss it and then, if you are still interested, we can make sure the work that has to be done to the guest house is to your liking."

"Sounds fine, if you don't mind waiting a few days to finalize the decision," Stuart added.

"I would rather make the right decision than a hasty decision," Robin said as she stood. "Let's talk again in a few days. Meanwhile, we will not be considering anyone else."

After they left, Stuart couldn't wait to tell Helen his news.

"I met with the guy from Texas that Kevin brought to the table."

"You are going to love the guest house and I had no idea they would be fixing it up." Helen was on her feet now with her back to Stuart.

"He actually has a company in place to serve as the primary retention company." Stuart was pacing now.

"There's a little patio out back that is separate from the big house but has its own view of the lake," Helen ignored.

"I wonder if we can pay dividends to just a qualified portion of the policyholders without illegally discriminating against the others," Stuart pondered.

"What is the best time of the year to plant dogwoods?" she asked.

"Of course, if it is ours, we can make the call on that sort....What did you say?" He interrupted himself.

"I'm sorry. Have you been telling me about your meeting today?" Helen asked. The phone rang, cutting their conversation short.

"Well, tell me how it went," the voice demanded without explanation.

"Fine, thanks. How are you?"

"I'm sorry. I just wanted to know how it went with Ricky," Kevin asked.

"Really, better than I had hoped. Did you know Ricky has an offshore company in existence?" Stuart reported, rather than asked.

"No. What kind of company?"

"He said there wasn't much going on now, but it had been formed several years ago for shipping or something."

"What else did he say about it?" Kevin asked anxiously.

"He didn't tell me that until the latter part of our conversation, so I don't know really what he has in mind. I feel like the next step is to go to Philadelphia and crunch some numbers to see what the reinsurance is willing to do."

"When are we going?" Kevin asked.

"I'll call tomorrow and see if they agree. Then the meeting should take place pretty quickly."

"Do you look forward to going back to that city?" Kevin laughed.

"If the meeting is in the next couple of weeks, I won't be able to go."

Kevin's voice fell. "What?" The question was not for a repeat but for an explanation.

"Helen's in a threepoint stance to meet the stork and I don't even go to Atlanta every day right now. I can't leave."

"Not even for a day and a night?" Kevin pressed.

"No, not during this time."

CHAPTER 38

Kevin and Ricky climbed the old marble steps to the first floor of the massive downtown building. It put them in the lobby some five feet above the street. The architecture was heavy and Greek with polished marble interior columns and floors.

"Who are we meeting, exactly?" Ricky asked.

"Stuart and I spoke to him yesterday on a conference call. He is the one who ultimately makes the price call. The interest level is already high enough to do business. We just have to negotiate a price."

They stepped off the elevator when the doors opened on the designated floor. The receptionist's desk was like a mote to the castle entrance, but a small signboard welcomed them both by name so they approached with confidence. After being announced, they were given an escort to a conference room full of leather and walnut and served coffee.

"Kevin, Ricky, I'm Gordon Lee. Welcome to Philadelphia."

Once they got settled into their seats, Mr. Lee began.

"Well, gentlemen, I understand you fly out this afternoon and I want you to be our guests for lunch. So, I guess we should get started. We have assembled some numbers from the projections we have received and are now wondering how much retention you would like to discuss."

"We had hoped for something around $10,000 per claim," Kevin offered.

"That would require irrevocable or escrowed monies available in the range of $300,000."

Ricky inhaled deeply before he said, "Gordon, the way I see this thing, you have all the numbers. You have the public image of all the risk, but we are setting up a practical filter to keep the smaller ones out of your office. I can see where you would want us to profit. Kevin, here, and Stuart are going to sell this stuff and we'll pay somebody to handle claims for us. By the way, I think that should be you. That way if one goes from a two thousand dollar claim to a twenty thousand dollar claim, you'll have your hands on it from bottom to top."

"So far, I'm with you," Gordon acknowledged.

"The money is my department. If I don't get a decent return, I'll simply quit at the end of any year I can't justify it. So I suggest you come up with some numbers and claim handlers that make sense for all of us," Ricky pointed out.

"I think you've hit the nail on the head. We will be in a position to do that within a week. For now, I need to ask you for some housekeeping items. The primary insurance will be written through the company I understand you already have chartered."

"That's right. We are all three equal shareholders and I am capitalizing it myself," Ricky continued.

"Fine. Are there any other shareholders?"

"No. We held a directors meeting and noted the minutes to reflect our stock offering and distribution, our decision to be an insurance company and how we would declare dividends."

"That reminds me," began Gordon, "Stuart told me he was trying to develop an incentive plan that would reward the policyholders with refunds on a profit share basis. I think he's onto something and I am willing to put up our half of the money to test that idea. That way, the idea will benefit both of us and we are equally at risk."

"Would you make allowances for shock losses?" asked Kevin.

"No, I wouldn't advise it. I would keep it simple. The ones who are under a certain loss ratio get a dividend if the group as a whole is also under a certain loss ratio. That way, the insurance carriers have an accountability incentive back to the insureds. Stuart also said that all claims reports would be made available to the entire group if the insured involved gave his permission. I think that is a step toward cutting out some of the fraud factor."

Ricky leaned forward. "Will I get to meet anybody that swindles any of our money?"

"I'm not sure that would be wise," Gordon smiled.

"What's the next step?" asked Ricky.

"We need to draft an agreement, that is between your company and us to show that you are willing, as well as financially able, to provide the primary coverage for described exposures. It will spell out that you are purchasing reinsurance from us and also hiring us to handle all claims."

"Do you have attorneys that can do all that?"

"Sure," nodded Gordon.

"Then why don't you do that and we will let our attorney look it over when it's all put together?"

"Okay." He took a pen from his pocket. "What is the name of your company?"

"Cresent Indemnity."

"Fine. You'll have at least a rough draft in a few days.

★★★★★

Stuart paced anxiously. "Helen, I don't think we should wait if you think they are labor pains."

"I don't think they are anything else, but they are so far apart."

"Why press it to the last minute?" He poured a glass of milk and set the container on the table, left the refrigerator open and realized he had another glass on the coffee table that was still half full.

"I've got an idea," he said. "Let's call Dr. Richland's office and see if they think we should go to the hospital," she suggested.

"Okay. And if they don't, we can call around until we find someone that agrees with me."

Helen winced with pain. "That was a little stronger."

"I knew it. Come on, Sweetie. I'm leaving for the hospital."

"Do you mind if I get my stuff?"

"It's all in the car. I put it in while you went to the bathroom an hour ago."

They went arm in arm down the steps and out of the quadraplex building. The concrete steps that led down into the parking lot normally had a double space at the bottom that was clear of parked cars. Today, however, a Cutlass was backed into it like a starting block and the engine was running.

Stuart searched his pockets, first the left and then the right. Helen squeezed his arm. "If you are looking for the keys, the running engine suggests they would be near the ignition."

He reached for the door handle and confirmed his fear. He walked to the other side. It, too, was locked. "Where are your keys?" he asked.

She knitted her eyebrows. "In my purse....which I see in the back seat."

Stuart came back around and put his hand on her shoulder. "I think there's more good news. I'm sure I locked the door to our apartment."

"What are we going to do?" Helen was getting nervous.

"Don't worry, Sweetie. You sit here on the steps. I'll go to the Merrits and get a coathanger and a hammer. We'll be in the car and on our way in five minutes, one way or the other."

The car sputtered and stopped running. "Out of gas?" asked Helen and almost simultaneously winced again.

"Yes, I guess so," admitted Stuart. "I'm sorry."

"Stuart, this is not good."

As he was looking for an alternative car, a courier truck drove up. The driver got out in a hurry and was on his way up the wide set of steps when Stuart stopped him.

"Have you got any deliveries for the hospital?" Stuart asked.

"I think so. Why?"

"We need for you to deliver us to the hospital now or help me deliver twins where we sit. We have car problems."

"Get in, pal."

They hustled around to the passenger side and climbed in. The seating was a bit unusual, but they were able to make do okay.

The traffic snarled at Enota and again for someunknown reason at the Civic Center.

Stuart held Helen a little tighter. "You okay?"

The question was sincere, but the timing was off. Helen clinched his hand and squinted.

"Hold on, " hoped the driver outloud as he found a back street and wormed his way through the Brenau Campus. "Just two more minutes now."

"It feels like they are fighting to be the first born," she smiled.

The large square truck arrived at the emergency room entrance and Stuart jumped to the pavement well before it came to a stop. The driver reacted and was stopped by the time Stuart realized he needed to go back and get Helen.

"I'm fine," she assured him when he reached to get her from the high seat. She turned to the driver, "Thank you for the ride."

"You are very welcome. Good luck to all of you."

They were arm in arm through the automatic doors and the nurse at the desk was understanding and efficient. Both Stuart and Helen found themselves in a labor room in a very few minutes.

"I can't believe the check-in went that fast," Stuart marveled.

"It's time something today was a breeze....oh," her face grimaced. "They're getting closer....where's that epideral?'

(TEN YEARS LATER)
CHAPTER 39

Stuart walked up from the boathouse and stopped between the dock and the guest house. It was fall and he wanted to inspect the health of a dogwood limb that had been grafted. Helen walked up behind him and put her hand on his shoulder. He turned and kissed her lightly. "Where did you come from?"

"I just finished tying up a few loose ends and I watched from the porch as you brought the boat in. Is it running alright?"

"Fine. I don't know if the kids will want to take a ride, but I'll be ready if they do. You look relaxed. How many kids are coming?"

"About fifteen, I guess," she said casually.

Stuart took several steps toward the delivery truck driving up. The driver met him halfway.

The driver held out his parcel. "Chip Bartlett?"

"No," said Stuart. "We live here now. The Bartletts moved six or seven years ago to South Carolina. Can we get you a forwarding address?"

"No, thank you. We will just get it back to the sender."

Stuart and Helen walked on up to the house and went in.

"Sweetie, do you think your parents will ever come live with us?" Helen asked.

"Who knows? It's been discussed and there are several option available to them. Any particular reason you would ask that now?"

"I don't know. Today being the twins' birthday and your Mom sending the presents a couple of days ago and us standing down by the guest house that's vacant. I wish they were here, that's all."

They sat on the deck. "Ten years," Stuart pondered. "You've been great. Did you ever picture yourself giving them a ten year party?"

"I guess not."

"Do you remember when they were born what you first thought?"

"I don't guess I understand," Helen requested.

"I guess I mean Eric. Did the fact that his left arm was only half there frighten you?"

"I don't remember how long it was after their delivery before I actually was aware. One thing for sure, he doesn't treat it as a handicap," she stated.

"No doubt. I'm so glad you've been home with them. I can see the dividends those preschool years had almost daily."

"What time is Brooke getting here?"

"I'm sorry, I meant to tell you. She left a message on the answering machine. She got in last night so she could spend the night with her grandfather. You can pick her up any time."

"I think I'll go over and...."

The phone rang and he stopped. "Hello."

"Hey. Are you going to be around at three o'clock today?" asked the familiar voice.

"No, actually, I'll be out. The truth is I'll be around but who knows where. Today is Eric and Jennifer's birthday and we're having everybody but Barnum & Bailey over. Why?"

"I need for you to be in on a conference call with me and a guy Ricky wants us to talk to," Kevin explained.

"I don't think you can count on me until tonight or in the morning. We have horses for the kids and boat rides and everything."

"I'll postpone the call until seven o'clock tonight. Will you take it them?" His voice was accusing Stuart of unavailability.

"Okay, I'll be here." Stuart's voice showed his reluctance.

Helen shifted some things on the island and put out a batch of fresh oatmeal cookies. "Kevin?"

"Yeah."

"What is it?"

"I'm not sure. He wants me to be a part of a conference call with some guy that Ricky has been talking to."

Helen continued her slow pace around the work triangle of the large kitchen. "Do you have any idea what it is all about?"

"If I had to guess, I'd say it has something to do with taking Cresent public," he speculated.

"Why do you say that?"

"It's been mentioned and we are in a good position to do it. I guess.."

"You sound less than enthusiastic."

"It would represent a big change. I'm not sure I'm interested in that kind of change, even if it does mean more money."

Now Helen noticeably stopped her preparation. "How much more money do you want?"

He stood silently as she reminded him of the last several years with highlights.

"You have a corporate plane and a corporate beach condo. You hardly buy any reinsurance anymore for Cresent and you're doing a tremendous percentage of the work comp business in Georgia. I don't see the need for anything else."

"I don't know, Sweetie. The thought of taking a company public has its appeal. I don't want to create a lot of change. I am enjoying things the way they are. But by the same token, I don't want to let an opportunity go by."

"Then why not leave things alone?" Helen began her movement around the kitchen again.

"Standing still in business is harder than sitting on a parked unicycle. You almost always have to be moving in one direction or the other. I'm too young to move backwards. We are still in the productive years of our lives and we seem to have a good group to do business with."

"What does it take to go public?" Helen asked.

"You find a brokerage house to agree to sell the stock. But, before that, there are all kinds of financials to be done by the SEC and NASD. After that, you have to keep stockholders advised through regular reports of the vital signs of your business; which is not just your business anymore. We have all been pretty much in agreement the last few years about what risks to take and when to staff our own claims force. I'm not sure how I'll feel if I think our stock is a part of a mutual fund that is funding some blue-haired widow's fixed income."

"That's a lot of responsibility alright. I've seen how things like that affect you. You would want to call every shareholder if Cresent lost a point. And if it lost too much, you would want to guarantee their purchase value back to them as though you had borrowed their money."

"Well, in a sense, you have their money entrusted to you. I know they are supposed to have both eyes open when they buy the stock and there is some broker somewhere recommending it, but I would hate to see the money lost."

"How much time does it take to do something like this?"

"You mean how much effort on my part and time away from my family?" he clarified.

"After all, that is my most valuable investment."

"I don't see any room for additional commitments. We are doing a fair job of getting to Valdosta and Eric and Jennifer and becoming more and more involved in their extra-curriculars. I'll just have to see what this is all about, but right now I'm out of here. I get to pick up my Poco Pie without driving to the tropics. I'll be back in a few minutes."

"Pick up some water balloons on your way back home, please," she requested.

*****

"Hello."

"Kevin, it's Ricky."

"Hi. How are things."

"Fine. My man tells me he has a conference call with you and Stuart this afternoon."

"That's right, or sort of, anyway. Stuart has a conflict at three o'clock and wants to push it to tonight."

"That won't work. I happen to know he is leaving the country early evening and will be unreachable for several days. I really need for you to touch base with him today if possible."

Kevin switched ears with the phone. "I'll do what I can."

"Call me and let me know how it went."

"Will do."

Ricky hung up the phone and began dialing all in one motion.

"Hello?"

"Josh?"

"That's right. Who is this?"

"Ricky."

"Hello, old friend. What is the weather like in South Texas?"

"Better than in new York in November. I can promise you that much."

"I did not expect to talk to you today."

"I've changed my mind. I want to be on the line today when you make the conference call. I don't want anyone else to know it. I just want to be a fly on the wall."

"Do you suspect trouble?"

"I just want to insure that we don't have any," Ricky explained.

"Insurance is the business you're in, my friend."

"At least it has served me well."

CHAPTER 40

Stuart almost fell into his chair.

Helen came around the corner of the deck with a glass of tea. "Are you ok?" she asked.

"How do you do it?" he marveled as he took a swallow.

"I brought that for you, keep it," she smiled.

"Are you ok?" he asked.

"Is there some reason I wouldn't be?"

"Helen, that was not a normal birthday party, was it. Let's just reflect on a few things. That little Tad idiot tried to scale the boathouse and almost broke his neck before everybody was even here. Then, lets talk about Jennifer. Can you believe that?"

"Tell me exactly what happened again. I was on the phone."

"Eric was up on the deck...that end that is over the corner of the driveway. He threw the water balloon at Jennifer while she was on the horse and had actually dropped the reins. That's when the horse took off out of control. I don't know what would have happened if Red hadn't been at the end of the driveway with the trailer he brought all the horses in."

"Is she ok now?" Helen asked calmly.

"Then Brooke. What terrible luck that was. She's climbed that tree no less than a hundred times. Today the limb breaks and she had to hang by her fingers twenty feet up for over thirty seconds before one of the other children could get to her."

"Thankfully she didn't fall," Helen said.

"I wonder if they'll get over all that stuff."

"I think you're overreacting, Sweetie. Tell them the Brer Rabbit story and do one of your strength to weakness stories. Then you and I both can work with them. I don't think Brooke will have any effects. Jennifer, I noticed didn't ride anymore. You need to get her back in the saddle as soon as you can."

"I know. Maybe you're right...but still, how do you do it?"

The phone rang and Stuart stood. "I'll get it. I bet its Kevin with the rescheduled conference call."

"Stuart, I have Josh Stinson on the phone."

"Josh, nice to meet you."

"My pleasure. I've been reviewing some of the numbers Kevin sent up and I must say, things are happening better for you than most people who have tried to make it in that kind of insurance."

"We've been very fortunate," Stuart pointed out.

"I believe we make our own fortune, Stuart...good or bad."

"I guess our doctrine would differ on that point."

"Anyway, Kevin has contacted me regarding taking Cresent public and I think we've got something marketable. Is there anything in general you would like to discuss?"

"We would like to maintain ownership of twenty-five percent...that is, the three of us would hold equal shares of the twenty-five percent. As far as I am concerned, the rest could be sold. How do you feel, Kevin?"

"Fine by me. That is what we had discussed before. What are the steps, Josh?"

"We have to do a 'do diligence' and make filings and compile an audited financial and prospectus, as well as have complete personal financials on the three of you."

"Sounds like CPA and attorney stuff," observed Stuart. "I'm not much for details."

"I think it would be a good idea for you to come to New York and meet some of the players in our firm."

"What kind of time frame are we on?" Kevin asked.

"I would like to get you up here next week, if possible."

"That suits us fine...that is, it's okay with me."

"I should be fine, too, except for Thursday. I have a conflict that night."

"I'll see what I can do and let you know, gentlemen."

Two receivers were returned to their carriages and a couple of seconds passed. "Ricky?"

"I'm here."

"What do you think?" Josh asked.

"Simple as pie."

"Will you be coming up with them?"

"I think not."

"I understand, but don't you think you had better be involved in some of the preliminaries to avoid suspicion?"

"I've handled this situation for ten years, old friend. You leave the refinements to me."

"Anything you say, Boss."

CHAPTER 41

"Did everything at the party suit you?" Stuart looked over his orange juice as his oldest daughter came into the kitchen.

"It was great, Daddy, thanks," Brooke assured him.

"Where is everybody?"

"Ummm, mostly scrubbed and brushed. I was hoping it wouldn't be more than that." He pushed his chair back to address her first question. "Helen is watering plants or something. Jennifer and Eric are still asleep. In fact, I'd better get them moving if we're going to make Sunday School. Do me a favor, Poco. While I'm rousing the twins, would you fill the hummingbird feeder for me?"

"Sure. Just sugar water?"

"Yeah, somebody told Helen not to put red food coloring in the mixture anymore. It does something to the birds." He continued through the kitchen and on upstairs. Before going into the bedrooms, he went to the window in the upstairs hall that looked out on the back deck. Brooke slowed as she approached the feeder which hung from a tree limb a few feet from directly over the deck. She tested her reach and came up short. The portion of the deck nearest the feeder did not have a bench, but a rail with horizontal boards. Stuart could see her studying the possibility of standing on the lowest one. The 18" boost would have been adequate, but she decided against it. He left the bathroom when he saw Brooke call for Helen. In a few minutes, he was downstairs.

"Did you get the feeder filled okay?"

"I couldn't reach it. Helen got it for me."

"Thanks, anyway."

"What time are we heading out?"

"I thought you and I would leave from church. I need to be around, so I'll probably do a turn-around today."

"What time does that put you back here?"

"I guess about 8:30; not too bad."

"It would be nice if you could break up the trip."

"There's an old friend of mine in Macon. I've been telling myself for two years I'd stop and see him or spend the night with him, but it seems that every time I have a chance, I end up keeping on in whatever direction I'm driving. It really can be peaceful, believe it or not."

The room started to gather people as Helen shoved a sheet of bagel into the oven. "We're late," she warned, looking at the clock on the microwave. "Is Jennifer up?" she asked as Eric sat down at the island snack bar.

"She's in the shower." He sleepily uttered his first words of the day.

"We're okay," Stuart clamed. "We don't leave for over an hour."

"Brooke, Darling, your bag packed?"

"Yes, ma'am. All ready to go."

"You going to leave from church?" Helen asked Stuart.

"It's either that or listen to me preach." Stuart reminded them of the Sunday options they chose from on Valdosta Sundays. They had stopped several years earlier visiting a local church, but Stuart had always substituted with a sermon of his own. The net time gained was deemed worth the less-than-professional message.

"I've never said anything negative about our 'hotel church' experience," Helen protested his implication.

"You've never said anything to Mrs. Magrutter about bathtub cleaning either."

"She's legally blind and getting older. Besides, I can live with less-than-sparkling fixtures easier than I could less-than-acceptable homiletics for my children. You have always done a good job, and judging from the times we've all told you, I suspect you're on a fishing trip."

The sermon ended a couple of minutes before noon and Stuart went to the mens' room to put on sweat pants for his marathon. Brooke was standing next to the car in the parking lot when he came out. She caught his eye and hugged Helen and the twins goodbye.

"You ready?"

"All set." She buckled her seat belt and they drove down to Green Street and continued on to I-985.

CHAPTER 42

"Morning, everybody."

"Daddy, why are you in your bathrobe, cooking like it's Saturday or something?"

"You get the day off, why can't I?"

"You're not in school, for one thing."

"As my statement of support for education, I hereby declare a day off for everybody in this house."

"Daddy, that's an addition of one," Jennifer pointed out.

"Do you have any plans after breakfast?"

"No, sir."

"I think we'll be through by noon...that is if you want to spend a couple of hours with me."

"Sure. What did you have in mind?"

"I'd like to go over to Red's."

Jennifer's face dropped, but did not scowl. She remained silent as she pulled the stool under the snack bar of the island.

"Sparkle, it's not mandatory," Stuart assured her.

"You can stay with me?"

"Absolutely."

"I'd rather go on over before breakfast."

"That's fine with me. I'll give Red a call and change. You might want to put on some jeans...by the way, Darling, I appreciate your attitude."

The thought of choice entered her mind but she chose not to share it. "I'll be right down."

They walked across the area between the two houses. Red had already caught a horse and was putting the bridle on.

"Morning!" Stuart called.

"You decided to take early retirement?"

"I'm due. I've been at it for long enough. You may not know it, but I'll be forty in a few years. How much time could I have left? Say...where's Jessabel?"

"She's not herself this morning. I think you'll get just what you want from Briarpatch."

"Briarpatch?"

"That's a long story," Red said with a smirk.

"Well, I'm sure it will have the same happy ending. Okay, Jennifer, what I want you to do is the same exercise...."

"Stuart," Red's voice was instructional, "you might want to find some work to catch up on. Jennifer will be home in time for lunch."

Stuart went blank as he looked first at Red and then to Jennifer to see if she objected. She showed no opinion. "You're the doctor."

"We'll see you later."

"Bye, Daddy."

He wanted to ask if she was okay with this but resisted. "I'll be at home, Darling."

"Now, Missy," began Red, "you've rode enough to know that there ain't much going to happen to you that will end up tragic. So, what we're going to do now is get reacquainted with the idea that riding is fun. Do you know what this can do for you?"

Jennifer thought for a minute. "It's going to help my prayer life."

Red stretched the tobacco-filled lip into a wide grin. "That, too, but what your dad and I want you to realize is that fear is something that has to make sense. And being afraid of something that you used to get such a kick out of just don't make sense."

"So where's Jessabel?"

"This is going to be Briarpatch's assignment. Because when you get through with this, you'll be just like ole Brer Rabbit. When somebody invites you to ride horses, you'll be as cozy as he was in the briar patch."

"When you say 'through with this', what do you mean?"

"Oh, it won't take but a time or two for you to get back on your own again." Red's big smile was comforting.

"Will you lead him until I tell you to let go?"

"No surprises, honey. I promise. I just think it will only take a time or two. You'll have to set the pace."

182

CHAPTER 43

Helen stood at the end of the island in the kitchen. "I can't believe you specifically said not Thursday and here it is Thursday and you're leaving."

"I know, I'm sick. I don't like New York more than I don't like Atlanta, but this is one of those things. Has POC said anything to you about my not being here?"

"No, and I wish you would come up with another acronym for him."

"What?"

"Some how, 'Product of Conception' is not endearing."

"The people that talked to us about aborting the twins referred to them as that," Stuart reminded.

"You don't have to remind me of that. Anyway," she changed the focus, "what did he say when you told him you had to miss the game?"

"He was disappointed, but took it on himself to remind me that there would be a lot of other games."

"Can you believe he can play on the basketball team with his handicap?"

"It's all he's ever known. I don't think he can play many more years, but I think he can play soccer as long as he wants to, especially if he stays in a relatively small school."

Helen set a glass of orange juice in front of him. "What time is your flight?"

"Nine forty-eight."

"You better hit the road. Don't you wish you were flying up in the Commander?"

"Yes, it would be nice, but Ricky had it somewhere, and Kevin and I both are coming from different parts of the country. Besides, we are the guests of the guys in New York."

She leaned over and kissed him.

"Tell the kids I'll see them Saturday morning."

*****

The 727 taxied to the Le Guardia terminal and linked with the jetway. Stuart checked his watch and confirmed the time. The signs in the terminal directed him to baggage and he shouldered his carry-on bag and made the trek. The flight number was on the monitor when he got down and he scanned the luggage on the conveyor. After a dozen or so bags went by he spotted his and retrieved it. For the first time since he walked into the area, he now looked from side to side for his contact.

A tall young woman in a business suit with long auburn hair stepped almost into his space. She raised a posterboard sign that was at her side. The letter-size identification simply said "STUART—KEVIN". She smiled widely. "I was watching...and hoping you were one of mine."

"I'm Stuart," he smiled.

"Bridget." She stuck out her hand.

He shook the firm grip. "Nice to meet you."

She looked for a moment. "Why don't we see if we can locate your friend?"

"Fine. I don't think I've got anything showing his flight number or airline or anything. Do you have that information?"

"Yes," she said as she turned to the bank of monitors on the wall. She quickly moved her eyes to the corresponding date and rechecked her index card. "The flight is delayed," was the only explanation she offered for her quick disappearance.

Stuart watched as she confirmed the delay on a courtesy phone. "They say Kevin's flight is going to be a couple of hours."

Stuart looked at his watch. "What do you suggest?"

"I'm going to call someone at the office to keep a check on Kevin's flight. Meanwhile, I think you and I should continue on."

"What?"

"Why don't we get some lunch?"

"Okay."

They walked to the shortterm parking and Bridget indicated the Jaguar they would be driving. Stuart admired the hunter green, set off by the recent wax job. "Nice engineering."

"Why, thank you." Bridget looked down at herself, purposely misunderstanding. "Do you have any lunch preference?"

"No, breakfast was a little light so my appetite will be able to override my discriminating palate. You pick, it's your town."

They drove for a few minutes and Bridget paid the toll at a huge toll booth. "You know," she began, "you are staying at a condo that is several miles from the office. Why don't we do lunch close to your condo and then you can freshen up before your meeting this afternoon?"

"Suits me fine, but I don't usually make any major changes until after the end of the day."

"You may find things to be somewhat different up here. The afternoon meetings, for example, don't usually happen until after four o'clock and they go on into dinner. We can grab something a few blocks from the condo and then I'll show you to your quarters."

They parked in a garage and made their way to the elevator and down to the street level. "How long have you lived in New York?" he asked.

"All my life," she stated proudly.

"How fortunate," he remarked, hiding his sarcasm.

At the door of the restaurant the hostess greeted them and they were soon seated. Stuart turned his attention back to Bridget. "So, what exactly is your job description?"

"I work closely with Josh as his assistant. I usually end up doing a lot of this type of thing. It is so much more personal, when someone flies in like this, to meet and drive them rather than expect them to get themselves to the office and all. New York is a wonderful place but I wouldn't think it would be comforting to be a stranger here."

"No. I'd be as lost as an Easter egg," he confessed.

"Have you ever been here?"

"Once, two years ago. It was a convention on Long Island. I had a free day and decided to tour the town. I rode in on the train and then walked two dozen blocks to see the World Trade Center and Statue of Liberty and everything. I needed to be at my hotel by 5:00, so I decided to ride the subway. Well, I walked up to this lady who was waiting at a platform down in the bowels of the station I had wandered into. I asked her to tell me how to get to Long Island. She told me to wait on platform number twenty-seven and catch train number seventeen and ride it to Thirty Second Street. She then proceeded to make my way through the next two transitions of train to subway back to train. I didn't have so much as a crayon to write with and was retaining less than I would have from a violin lesson. Finally, I found some train or subway or something that started me in the right direction, but dumped me at Grand Central Station. I reasoned that not being able to see the sky was going to keep me lost, so I climbed out onto the street and got in a cab. I told the driver I'd give him a hundred dollars to take me to my hotel or I'd kill him if he didn't."

★★★★★

Eric leaned over and kissed his mother. "I'll be pretty late, Mom, but don't worry....Ashur's mother is going to take us all home."

"I wish I could see you play tonight, but I hope you understand."

"No problem, Mom. I'll see you in the morning. Don't wait up for me."

"Eric, I hope you don't take personal offense, but I do envision myself confirming your arrival prior to my going to bed."

He rolled his eyes, but felt the personal comfort of the boundaries he knew existed. "Okay," was the eloquent discourse of the preteen confirmation.

"Your daddy told me to give you one message."

"What?"

"Kick butt."

He smiled and looked away. "You're okay, Mom."

★★★★★

Stuart and Bridget walked into the corporate condo. Stuart had all the baggage including his briefcase. The townhouse floorplan was tastefully decorated from furniture to wall and window.

"I think you'll find most anything you need," she assured.

"Nice, very nice," Stuart complimented as he walked into the den, complete with fireplace.

"Let me check on the set-up." Bridget walked to the kitchenette and opened the refrigerator.

"I'll be fine, thanks," Stuart disclaimed.

"If you don't mind, I'm going to call the office again and check on the schedule."

She was picking up the phone as she was speaking. "Is Josh in, please?"

The silence that followed indicated the connection.

"Josh, have you heard anything from our other party, uh...Kevin?"

This hesitation was much less lengthy.

"He's with me, now. I thought I would bring him on to the condo and then just touch base with you."

Even less listening time.

"Okay, I'll let him know." She hung up and turned toward him. She looked at her watch. "Kevin's alternate flight does not get in for two hours, which puts him here in about three hours. Josh suggested that you make yourself comfortable and when Kevin gets here later, he will pick both of you up for dinner."

"That's fine. I'll just wait it out here. Do you want anything before you leave?"

She stood up and paced at a diagonal to his position. "You kill me," she remarked.

"Excuse me?"

"You haven't been here five minutes and your are acting like the host."

"I'm sorry, it's just where my hat is hanging; habit, I guess."

"Lunch. You also paid for lunch. You walked on calculated sides of me when we were on the sidewalk. Would you do all that if I were a man?"

"Probably not. Is it a problem? Stuart asked.

"I thought it would be....I mean, I always thought I would resent it until I saw you implement it. I must admit I find it rather intriguing."

He shifted his memory to the meeting. "I wonder what the story is on Kevin?" he asked thoughtfully.

She walked over to him and stepped well into his space. "Well, I'm sure he can take care of himself. You can still have dinner with Josh. And if he doesn't make it in tonight, I may get a chance to find out just how much of a gentleman you are in the morning."

Stuart rocked back on his heels. "You would have to ask Helen about that," he countered.

"If she is a true southern lady, she probably wouldn't object to me finding out on my own."

Stuart pinched his chin. Both feet were well under him now. "She's more of what I would call a mountain lady."

"What's that?" Bridget allowed him the space.

"She could host a debutante ball on the lawn and carry a sugar cube in her mouth all afternoon without melting it. But if she thought you were moving in on her husband, she'd kick your butt till your nose bled."

Bridget stepped back. "You don't know what you're missing."

"But I know what I've got. Can I show you to the door, Ma'am?"

CHAPTER 44

The van lumbered back down the highway and Eric reflected on the game's experience. He turned to his friend, "Ashur, tell me something."

"Ask it."

"Do you think you'll always go to a small Christian school?"

"I dunno, why?"

"It's different with us. I mean you and me. You've got real potential athletically. I'll max out pretty soon. It's fun, but let's face it, ten years old and playing with one hand is a bit different from hoping to play for the Hawks someday."

"You need to forget about what doesn't have a future and go for what does. You are a computer genius. Why don't you just do that?" Ashur encouraged.

"Maybe I will. I just think my dad would like to see me play sports. He's not much into computers and grades and stuff."

The van suddenly jolted and swerved to the shoulder of the road. "What was that?" Ashur's eyes were wide.

The van limped to a full stop. "Blowout," Eric answered flatly.

The lights came on inside the vehicle and the driver stood. "Gentlemen, we have had a blowout and we don't carry a spare on this thing."

"What are we going to do?" came a voice.

"We're only a mile from the school. Let's walk," was the first suggestion.

The driver cleared his throat. "I'm not sure where the car with the coach in it is. I suppose it would be fine if we walked on to the school."

Eric looked at his watch. "What time did you tell your mom to come get us?"

"Ten o'clock."

"It's just barely nine. I wonder why we are so far ahead of schedule?"

"I dunno. But we can call when we get to the school."

The group of seven filed off the van one by one and began the march over the small hill. The air was brisk and there was no moon. The school was five or six miles from town and they were surprised at how dark it was. Even the talking was squelched by the focus of their task and without meaning to, Eric and Ashur found themselves out front by several yards.

"Let's cut through the side and across the soccer field," Eric remembered.

"Okay," agreed Ashur. Looking back, he tried to signal the rest of the group to the short cut also.

The side of the campus was a wooded area that was buffered even more by a plum thicket on one edge of the soccer field. The soccer field was on ground higher than the school and as they walked from the trees, they could see the buildings silhouetted in front of them.

Suddenly, a form darted around the corner of the building, then another, and a third. Ashur checked his stride. "Did you see that?"

"Yeah. I had hoped you didn't." Eric was stopped. They backed up to the edge of the plum thicket. "Stop the others and let's see what happens."

"Okay." Ashur retraced the path through the plum trees. Eric watched intensely as two more figures slinked around to the front of the building. The angle of the building and his elevation gave him a view of the intruders. There was a large group of them forming around the flagpole in front. They began rocking it and then several got on the shoulders of some and they continued their objective until it began to sway in rhythm. Apparently, the base cracked, because they fell and jumped off in all directions and left it tilted.

Ashur came back to Eric's crouched position. "I stopped everybody. What's the deal?"

"Vandals, messing with our school."

"How many?"

"I can't count them, but it's a bunch."

"What are we going to do?"

"I've been thinking," Eric pinched his chin. "a bunch of bad guys and just a handful of good guys. Does that remind you of anything?"

They looked at each other and whispered simultaneously, "GIDEON."

"How?" Ashur asked.

"Can we get into the gym without being seen?"

"Sure. There's a chain on the double doors out back, but you can pull 'em as far as they'll open and climb in from the top," Ashur described.

"Okay. Here's what we'll do. you go back and tell the others to keep low and spread out around the back side of the campus. Tell them to get about ten yards apart and stay out of sight. Then all at once to come running down the hill, yelling for those guys to get out of here. Tell them to scream bloody murder."

"When do we do that?" Ashur asked.

"Wait for the signal. You won't have any trouble hearing it."

Eric crouched and ran to the gym while Ashur went his way. The door was just as Ashur had predicted and Eric was in over the opening in a flash. The inside of the vacant building echoed the click of the closing door and Eric instinctively lightened his step to a tiptoe. The lights of the exit signs were sufficient for his pre-adjusted eyes and he made his way to the supply closet. In one corner of the pitch dark room was a small console that he knew by heart. Closing the door securely behind him, he was safe to turn on the tiny stem-mounted light used to illuminate the control board. The cabinet underneath contained a library of tapes that he could now thumb through. He smiled when he found a suitable label. He now loaded the tape into the deck and located the four slide-activated volume controls marked OUTSIDE SPEAKERS. He pushed them to maximum output and took a deep breath and whispered the exhale, "Get 'em Lord," just as he pushed the play button.

Outside, the noise was a deafening, multidirectional terror. The half a dozen boys on the hillside avalanched, commanding the vandals to withdraw, in voices that were supported by an invisible army.

They obeyed with no regard for each other's well-being. Most ran and competed for hidden motor bikes across the road, while some would not trust the moment to anything mechanical and scrambled over fences. Eric made his way out of and around the building in time to see the retreat that was erupting in every direction. He was at the corner of the building snickering when one of the vagrants rounded the corner at a gallop and collided with him.

"What are you laughing at, Punk?" the burly twelve or thirteen-year-old snarled.

Eric gathered himself to a standing position and tried to swallow silently from a suddenly dry mouth. He stared and said nothing.

The adversary stepped closer and exaggerated his slight size advantage trying to establish more control. "I'm talking to you, Bubba." He jolted Eric backward with the palms of both hands to the shoulders. "Your name's Kerr, ain't it?" he said, glaring at the left arm.

Eric took one step backward in order to absorb the blow. He flexed his knees imperceivably and demanded, "Get away from my school."

"Or what?"

Thud. The punch from Eric's right fist splattered the bully's nose and sent a blinding flood from his tear ducts into his burning eyes. The pain surge was an anticipated, unavoidable instant after the impact and rendered him helpless. He fell over into a slump as the raid continued in loud shouts.

Eric looked and saw only allies on the lawn. He made his way back into the building and turned off the tape players and returned the controls to normal. He was climbing out when a police officer took hold of his arm.

The flashlight was pointed in such a way that he was seen and not seeing. "What's your name, son?"

"Eric Kerr."

"Your dad's name Stuart?"

"Yes, sir."

The light went down and he walked his small prisoner around to the front yard where one other officer and a small group of boys was assembled. "Are there any more of you?"

Eric looked around. "No, sir."

"Just what were you doing?"

"We were trying to stop a bunch of rednecks from wrecking our school," a voice explained and presented a spray paint can.

The officer holding Eric released his already relaxed grip on the arm. "We saw a lot of boys leaving as we pulled into the parking lot. Are you not part of that group?"

"No," chimed the boys with head shaking. "We were running them off," said Ashur.

The officer smiled. "We got a call from some lady across the road, and when we drove up and heard that awful racket, we didn't know what to think. What made that much noise?"

Everyone's eyes turned to Eric. He looked only at Ashur as he talked. "Do you remember in the spring when we were all giving the teachers fits wanting to go outside, and they decided to let us blow off some energy by putting on a skit about Joshua?"

"Yeah," said Ashur, "the whole school marched around in a big circle and then

189

they told us to scream and shout so we would feel what it was like at Jericho."

"That's right," said Eric. "I didn't know until later that somebody taped it and the tape was in the sound room in the gym. I remember it when we got here."

Ashur stuck up an open palm and Eric slapped it. The officers looked at each other in indecision. "Where are your parents?" one asked.

"We are back early," said Eric and looked at his watch. "They'll be here any minute."

"We're going to have a talk with them, boys. Taking matters into your own hands like this is not the route to take."

Ashur turned to Eric and smiled. "I think I will always go to a Christian school."

CHAPTER 45

The phone startled Stuart. He confirmed by the digital clock that it was 11:13. "Hello."

"Stuart, you've got to come home," the frantic voice proclaimed. "It's Eric. He's in trouble with the police."

"What...Helen, what on earth?"

"They just brought him home and it was awful. He's been in a fight at school with twenty boys."

"Sweetie, wait. I'm here and I can't be there this minute. Is Eric alright?"

"Yes, but he and...."

"Okay," Stuart interrupted, "Is he home?"

"Yes." Helen was no calmer but would agree to this line of questioning.

"What did the policeman tell you?"

"I didn't talk to him, exactly. I talked to Sara, who picked up Ashur and Eric after the ballgame."

"What did she say?"

"There were a bunch of vandals at the school and for some reason Eric and Ashur and the guys in their van got mixed up with them somehow. You've got to come home, Stuart."

"Okay, okay." His voice was calm. "Let me check with the airlines first thing in the morning and get a flight as soon as I can. Meanwhile, if Eric is home and in one piece, don't be too hard on him until we get the whole story. If he's been in a fight....chances are he's had enough for one night, anyway."

"I suppose you're right. That's why I waited until he was in bed to call. I didn't want you to have to get into it on the phone. I'd been waiting to call you and I guess I just blurted it out a little quick. Sorry if I startled you."

"No problem. I'm always glad to hear from you," he laughed.

"I wish I were there with you. Are you and Kevin in the same place?"

"Kevin's plane was delayed or something. The last word I got was that he's coming in early in the morning. In fact, I keep hearing it's pushed back."

"I'm sorry about this timing. It's just that Eric will be called to the principal's office tomorrow and I just hope you can get on home."

"I understand. Don't worry. I'll be in tomorrow."

Stuart turned off the alarm before it sounded and was on his way to a welcomed shower from the sleepless night, when he saw something different in the poor lighting. The small hallway to the other bedroom showed a suitcase on the floor. He peered through the crack to see enough to identify Kevin as the most likely of any circumstantial roommates. He walked back to his bed wondering how anyone had come in without his knowledge. Despite the risk of disturbing his partner, he quietly went back to the bathroom, closed the door and took as quick of a shower as he ever had. When he came out, Kevin's light was on and he was sitting on the bed.

"Sorry if I woke you up. What time did you get in?"

"Late. I guess it was about a quarter to twelve. But what a killer day. I waited in airports for what seemed like a week."

"What was the problem?"

"Beats me. I got to the airport and my ticket had been fouled up somehow, and they had record of me cancelling it and stopping the payment on my credit card. But since the tickets were bought for us, I just figured it was a mix up from Josh's office. So, I called and they did their deal and booked me on another flight. It went through Atlanta and over the river and through the woods and finally here. Did you get to meet with Josh?"

"Yeah, we had dinner, but decided not to talk much until we were all together."

"Well, I understand Ricky won't be in until tonight, so the meeting will be unusual."

"Now I've got a problem at home and need to get a flight out of here today." Kevin sighed. "What is it?"

"Eric. He's in some type of trouble and Helen's pretty upset."

"Well, I guess you and I can talk with Josh and then Ricky and I can finish up."

"I suppose. Anyway, let's get some breakfast and get our hands on Josh."

After breakfast, the two of them took a cab to the address on Josh's business card. The receptionist in the entrance to the ninth floor suite offered them a seat and soon Josh joined them with apologies for Kevin and invitations to the conference room. The three sat down amidst walnut wainscoting and original oils of someone's grandfathers. The heavy leather chairs and thick oriental rug gave the room large privacy.

Josh began, "We certainly are enthusiastic about this offering. In fact, we are in a position to take the whole block."

Stuart looked at Kevin and shifted in his seat. "Are you sure that is not just a bit premature to determine just now?"

"Not from our perspective. We are ready to proceed anytime you are."

Stuart looked again at Kevin. "Has it been pointed out that we as a threesome want to maintain a collective total of twenty-five percent of the outstanding shares?"

"Yes, Ricky told me it was something that would continue to be the minimum requirement unless you unanimously agreed to do otherwise."

"And has the opening price been discussed?" asked Kevin.

"Yes again," smiled Josh. "We thought we'd open at eleven dollars per share. That way we don't look like a penny stock."

"What about the prospectus and 'do diligence' and all that detail stuff?" Stuart wondered aloud.

"That is all being taken care of. Cresent's financials were in such good shape, that it should go rather quickly," Josh smiled pleasantly. "You have never taken a company public before, I understand."

"No," said Stuart, "but when I got my securities license, I remember a lot of SEC and NASD regulatory red tape that I can't believe has been this easy. I had more trouble getting a permit to renovate my house."

"That's what you hire us for." Josh's hand was palm up and his face relaxed.

Stuart snapped his fingers in spontaneous distraction. "I'm sorry. I forgot to call the airline. I'm going to have to get out of here today if possible. I'll be right back."

He excused himself and was directed to a phone. The call was made and he returned to the conference room. "I got a 2:30 flight," he announced.

"Nothing major, I hope," empathized Josh.

"I hope not, too. It's just one of those things we need to get to the bottom of as soon as possible; family matter."

"I understand. I have two sons myself," Josh consoled, then stood. "I'm going to suggest we take a moment to introduce you to a few members of our firm. It may be necessary for you to be in contact with them from time to time and I happen to think it's nice to put faces and names together."

As Josh walked out, a secretary walked in and asked, "Stuart?"

"Yes," he acknowledged.

"The airline just called and advised that you can get on a flight to Atlanta at 12:23."

He looked at his watch. "I would need to leave here in less than an hour to be able to get my luggage and make the flight."

Josh walked back in. "I couldn't help overhearing. Maybe I should get the contract and let you review it. If you feel comfortable signing, it will, of course, require Kevin and Ricky to be complete. That way we don't miss the opportunity of having you physically present." He walked out and was back in a matter of seconds.

"Thank you," Stuart accepted as Josh silently offered the thick booklet. He reviewed the pages containing prices and fees and found them all consistent with his prior understanding. He looked at Kevin. "Are you alright with this?"

"Sure, we've discussed it enough to have done it three times by now. Besides, we'll have more opportunity to dig through this after you've gone."

Stuart leaned forward. "I hope you can sell every share in one day, Josh." Then he signed his name.

*****

"Helen, sweetie, I'm home."

"Great. This is even earlier than I thought. Eric should be here any minute." She kissed him. "I'm sorry I sounded so spastic on the phone last night. It was just so unnerving how all this stuff was caving in, and you weren't here. I'm glad you don't travel much."

"Me, too." He stopped short. "Sounds like Eric's home."

"Hey, Dad."

"How 'bout it, POC?"

"Did you have a good trip?"

"Pretty good, I think. The results aren't all in yet. Son, I think we need to talk."

Come on into the study," said Stuart as he directed Eric into the room and shut the door.

"Did Mom tell you about last night?" Eric began.

"In very general terms. Why don't you start from the beginning?"

"We were coming back from the ballgame and had a flat tire just a half mile or so from the school. We decided to walk back, and when we got there we saw a bunch of guys tearing things up. We kind of cooked up something to run them off and it worked."

"Your mother said something about you being in a fight."

"Yes sir, I guess. This guy came around the corner of the gym and shoved me pretty hard and I told him to leave and he was kind of threatening me again, so I hit him."

"Did you use your prosthesis?"

"No, sir."

"You know I don't like the idea of fighting, but you also know I respect your judgment to defend yourself. Do you think you exercised good judgment?"

Eric looked away for an instant and then back again. "I think so, I mean he had shoved me and he was wanting to make trouble."

"It's not always clear, is it?"

"No, sir."

"Well, maybe in the next few days you might find an opportunity to find this guy and talk to him, that is if you know who he is."

"I never had seen him before, but he knew me."

"How do you know?"

"He knew my name. He looked at my arm and called my name."

Stuart sat back in his chair. "Your mom also mentioned police. Did you know any policemen?"

"Yes, sir. Samuel's dad was the one that took me to talk to Asher's mom."

"I know him fairly well. Listen, son. I'm going to talk to him. I hope you know I just want to hear his perspective. I have no doubt that what you've told me is the truth. We'll talk again, okay?"

"Sure," he said and stood up.

Stuart reached for his hand and shook it. "I love you, buddy."

"I love you, Daddy."

They walked out and Eric continued upstairs while Stuart went into the kitchen, where Helen was waiting.

"What did you do?"

"Nothing yet. I need more information."

"Well, he was involved in a fight and he took a matter into his own hands that he should not have."

"Sometimes a man has to do what a man has to do."

Helen rolled her eyes. "He's not a man."

Stuart smiled and raised his eyebrows. "And we must not prevent him from becoming one." He walked to the telephone. "Do you have a list of the parents at school and their phone numbers?"

"Middle shelf, toward the right. The folder is green. Why?"

"The policeman that Eric referred to is Terry Clay. "I'm going to give him a call."

The conference room door closed with a decided click. Josh turned and handed one of the two highball glasses to the man at the end of the table, then took the seat to his right. They each took a swallow, savored it and Ricky spoke first.

"Has everyone gone?"

"Not even the janitorial people will be in tonight," Josh answered.

"Kevin?"

"We had lunch after we put Stuart on the plane. We conveniently allowed Bridget to give him the office tour and take him home."

Ricky smiled and took another pull from the amber glass. "That will be a night for him to remember." He cocked his head sideways. "I almost forgot our little wager. Did Bridget find Stuart alright?"

Josh reached into his pocket and took out a money clip. He selected a crisp one-hundred-dollar bill and flipped it to Ricky. "That's the first time I've heard of anything like that happening. I told her specifically...."

"No problem. I knew not to count on it."

"He's not normal." Josh said of Stuart.

"No matter. We have his signature now and the rest of this will be a cakewalk...a beautiful ten year cake walk."

CHAPTER 46

"Have you got two pillows of identical weight and value?" Stuart asked as he closed the brimming trunk.

"We are going to have to get the van fixed. This car is just not made for a family of four to travel in," Helen evaluated.

"Can we get started, please?"

"I didn't get a chance to put gas in the car, I'm sorry," she confessed.

"No problem. I didn't get cash either. Maybe we'll be on the road by dark," He muttered.

Jennifer snatched the device in Eric's hand. "You've already broken yours. I have a tape I have to listen to for school."

Helen turned around and at the same time gripped Stuart's arm, "Stop the car, Stuart."

It was only a hundred feet down the drive and he could tell from her tone she was not suggesting an option. He obeyed without hesitation.

"Now," she began, as if anyone doubted the next point to be made, "we have made this trip a dozen times a year for as long as the two of you have been alive. I will not tolerate the attitude either of you has demonstrated so far. The tape player will not be used by either of you unless you can work out a way to share it. One more outburst or somebody is going to ride in the trunk."

"Ninety-nine bottles of beer on...."

"Stuart, please," she said, exasperated.

"Okay, gang. We'll be on 365 or 985 or whatever they call it, in ten or fifteen minutes. I would suggest that Jennifer put in her tape that she needs to do first and since Eric was out till 10:30 last night, I think you, son, should sit back and see if a nap happens. Meanwhile, your mom and I are going to actually finish some sentences."

Everyone took their assignments and pretty soon the car was moving at a southwesterly direction toward Atlanta.

"Sweetie, you haven't really told me all about the stock deal since you got the word from Kevin that it had all gone down," Helen requested.

"Well, that is kind of the story. It is a done deal and Josh's firm has taken all of the offering to be sold."

"I know, but it seems, I guess like there should have been more conversation about it....even from you."

"It was somewhat anti–climatic, I guess....at least from what I thought it would be like when I was a junior in college. I had always hoped I would be in some power suit in a power setting in some admirable group that would have made some journalist evoke envy from the rest of society. What happened for me was crammed between soccer and ballet and unsung by any choir."

"I'm sorry." She moved closer to him in the car. "And now you're hauling everyone to maintain family relationships. I guess it's a little unusual for an economics major to be in such pursuit of family development.

"It's not that. I, above most people, understand the significance of family development. I just wish it wasn't such a high-maintenance activity. Sometimes, I guess I would like to be in the center of the stage on certain days. It seems that all we do, we do with family development at the center of the agenda. I'm not sure I can compete in the world around me when I am focusing on remaining conversant with Big Bird and some mutant sewer turtles while my adversaries are juggling the fire batons of capitalism."

"I guess that depends on what you are trying to build." Her voice begged the question and he bit.

"What do you mean?"

"Are you trying to develop future parents and interacting human beings or teach your children to conquer some temporal corner of some ambiguous segment of corporate America?"

"Again, help me on the qualifiers," Stuart requested with raised eyebrows.

Just then, Eric arched his back and kicked, instead of stretched, toward Jennifer. She responded with an abrupt squeal, and returned the kick. Verbal exchanges ping-ponged and were accelerating before Helen could get a handle on it.

"Settle down, you two," she instructed. She turned her attention back to Stuart. "I mean it has always been your objective to be a daddy and a husband first, and only a secondary desire to be a businessman. Now, it sounds like you resent the obligations of your primary job."

He scratched his head and looked out of the driver side window. "Sweetie, I don't resent it at all. I would just like....I don't know, I guess I wanted somebody to jump out of a cake or something."

She reached over and squeezed his hand. "I'm sorry I don't say it enough, but you are my hero.

They drove another couple of hours in unusually uninterrupted conversation.

"What's the car doing?" Helen reacted, suddenly.

"Lurching, sputtering and coughing," Stuart announced flatly.

"Obviously. I was hoping to learn the cause and cure of it." Helen needlessly explained.

The car hesitated drastically, then lunged and accelerated up to fifty miles an hour.

"It's a fuel supply problem," Stuart remarked as he checked the gauge. "We have plenty of gas but it's not getting to the engine somehow."

"What would cause that?"

"Could be some kind of obstruction in the fuel line like a clogged fuel filter. It's sporadic so I don't think it's actually in the firing inside the engine."

"So what do we do?"

198

"Let's limp ten more miles into Macon and find a real service station that has somebody working there with grease on his hands."

"What if it doesn't make it?"

"Then we'll all have a nice stroll."

The miles passed slowly and everyone's anxiety lessened when the exit ramp was halfway behind them. They drove into the station and Stuart was relieved to see a hydraulic lift with a capable looking mechanic walking out of the bay.

After a few minutes under the car the mechanic said, "This is the trouble." He sat up on the creeper and held out the car's mechanical heart.

"Are you sure?" Stuart wondered how it could be diagnosed without a test.

"If it ain't, you don't owe me nothing."

Helen and Jennifer came around the corner. "What's the news?" Helen asked.

"Fuel pump, or so it seems."

"How long to fix it?"

"Labor will apparently be no time at all, judging from what it took to get it off. The part is another matter. We'll have to see what he says."

"Well, folks," the mechanic began, "you got any kin in Macon?"

"I'm afraid not. Why?"

"I called the parts house and the dealership. The closest fuel pump is in Atlanta and they asked if we wanted it put on the bus. I told 'em to go ahead. It will be in tonight and I can pick it up in the morning. You can be on your way about nine o'clock. Now, if there's any of that you don't care for, better let me know quick."

"If that's the deal, then we'll make arrangements to get a room," Stuart accepted.

"Good luck. That new fairground thing in Perry is having some kind of shindig. I been hearing about it on the radio for a month," the mechanic advised.

"You know what, Sweetie? There's an old friend of mine in town that I haven't talked to in several years. I think I'll see if I can find him. Why don't you walk the kids over to that restaurant and get them a coke or something. If Eddie is available, I'll see if he'll let us take his family to dinner."

In a moment, Stuart joined them. "We have lodging for the night. I'm glad we didn't tell Brooke to expect us until tomorrow. So we haven't fouled her plans up too badly. We'll need to call her tonight and tell her the problem."

"Where are we staying?"

"This guy is a friend of mine from college. We lived together for a while with two or three other guys. He left school a couple of quarters before I did to move back to Macon."

"What is the story on his family?" Helen asked.

"I know he's married, at least he was the last time I talked to him several years ago. I don't know about kids, though."

"Daddy, I'm hungry. Can we get something to eat?" Eric asked.

"Why don't we sort of roll with the punches, POC and see what happens? We are going to have a host and I'm sure we won't run the risk of starving."

Stuart's face caused everyone to look to the parking lot. "That was quick." He got up and picked up the ticket for the drinks. "Let's go," he said, after dropping a five dollar bill on the table. "Our ride is here."

"FAST!"

"STU-BALL!" he returned the enthusiastic handshake.

"Meet my family....wife, Helen....Jennifer and Eric."

"Welcome to middle Georgia. Come on and let's get you accommodated for the night.

"Sweetie," Helen interjected, "you ride with...with Eddie, I think I heard his name in another conversation, and we will follow."

"Sorry, I guess I was a bit informal in my introduction." He turned to Eddie, "Is your house tough to find?"

"Not at all."

They separated and processed through the neighborhood streets until they pulled into the level pea gravel drive that stopped outside the brick and lattice carport.

"Up the stairs, first door on the left. You'll be the only ones using the bath at the end of the hall."

"Thank you," Stuart acknowledged.

"Glad to have you folks here. If you don't see it, ask for it. We have a mission for hospitality living on the gnat line."

"I'm not going to put everything we own into the room, Sweetie. Can you get by on just a couple of these steamer trunks?" Stuart teased as he handled the luggage.

"Sure." She cut her eyes. "You are welcome to sleep in either one of them."

They shuffled and arranged and Helen stayed upstairs to freshen up while Stuart, Eddie and the twins found themselves in the den.

"Did your dad ever tell you about when he explored the possibilities of a career with the railroad?" Eddie asked the twins.

"No," Eric prodded with enthusiastic inflection.

Stuart's face showed his admission of disadvantage.

"We had been in the library for five hours," Eddie settled back into his wingback and took the floor. "In case you didn't know it, your dad and libraries don't get along real well. Anyway, five hours was too much for him. It was after dark when we left and we hadn't said much to each other as we drove the first couple of blocks toward home. We stopped at a railroad crossing to wait for a train. 'I wonder where it's going?' I asked 'East' was your dad's one-word answer. We looked at each other. 'You ready for that midterm?' I asked. 'I'm so shell-shocked after sitting in that concentration camp, I couldn't spell my name,' he agreed. Well, we looked one more time at the train and back at each other, then I pulled up to a vacant building, we locked the car and jumped on the train.

Eric's eyes dilated, "While it was going?"

"That's right, with no money and no idea where we would end up."

"Where did you sleep?" Jennifer wondered.

"That was a funny thing. The train torqued up to about fifty miles an hour once we went out of town and it got cold on top of the boxcar we were sitting on. We finally got the hang of jumping from car to car and were looking for a way to get out of the cold. We happened on a shipment of cars that was probably from the GM plant in Doraville. Anyway, we climbed into this brand new Cutlass. I guess they figured that nobody would steal it the way it was chained down, so they had left the keys in it. We cranked it up, turned on the heater and radio and rode in chauffeured style like we were somebody."

"Is that legal, Daddy?"

"Listen, Fast," the voice tone was obviously running interference, "I want to get us a steak. Take me to the best place. I'll even let you cook it."

Eddie smiled at Helen as she came down the steps. "We're going out for a few minutes. I called Carol at her mother's and told her what to expect so don't worry about getting shot when she comes in."

200

"Dad, how did you get home and all that stuff?"

"Come on with us, Eric," Eddie gestured, "I'll tell you the rest of the story."

They pulled out of the driveway. "you see this ring?" Eddie held up his hand and displayed the onyx and gold with the Greek letters SAE.

"Yes, sir," Eric participated.

"When we came to a stop at about sunup the next morning, we were in a freight yard. Our train began switching and unhooking and we were not real comfortable with where we were in life. So, we dismounted and ran around the old freight depot, out of the yard and onto a back street. The sign on the depot said Abbyville, so we knew we had crossed into South Carolina. We were without money and only partially convinced of how far from Athens we were. We asked for directions to the bus station and found we were close enough to walk. The lady at the ticket counter seemed friendly enough, but she was not interested in advancing us tickets or unsecured credit. The only thing we had was the ring on my finger. She agreed to give us the tickets out of her pocket and hold my ring until we mailed her the money for the tickets. We got home that afternoon and had to get some guys at the fraternity house to take us back to my car."

"Is that legal, I mean, to ride a train?" Eric asked again.

"So, Fast, tell me exactly what you're doing nowadays," Stuart slipped the question.

Stock jocky, for several years now. In fact, if you don't mind, I'd like to run by the office while we're out. It will only take a second."

"Sure."

"What about you?"

"Insurance. It's funny you mention stock. We just took our company public."

"Really? Who's selling it for you?" Eddie turned into the office parking lot.

"A guy in New York that one of my partners knows. We put a workers compensation company together about ten years ago and its done fairly well since."

"What's the guy's name....in New York, I mean?"

"Josh Stinson."

"Sounds familiar, but I don't know why." Eddie turned off the car and opened the door. "Come on in."

"This is nice," Stuart admired.

"Thanks. I've enjoyed it for the most part...you know," his hand was in his pocket and he took out a small key. "If you don't mind, I'd like to access your stock and make it available to some of my clientele."

"Suits me fine. We have set the amount we want to sell, and as far as I'm concerned, the sooner, the better," Stuart agreed.

"We have an office in New York, like everybody else in this business. I'll give the Josh guy a call and see if he'll let me sell some to some of my people. In fact," Eddie tapped the computer with his pencil, "this blink box is supposed to be able to tell me things I need to know...but the market is closed."

"I've got one of his cards, if you want to try him now."

"Okay. Can't hurt."

"Let me introduce you." Stuart took the phone and dialed from the card he had pulled from his wallet. He soon had Josh on the line.

"Afternoon, Stuart. How are you?"

"Fine. I won't tie you up but a minute. I have a friend that is a broker here in Georgia and I want you to talk with him. He seems to have some idea that you two might have some common ground on this stock offering."

"I'll be glad to speak with him."

"Hello, Josh. My name is Eddie Finell. I was hoping to work with you if it's appropriate in distributing some stock."

"That would be fine, Eddie. I'll need to send you some prospectus and so forth."

"Great. I'll fax you my stuff Monday and we can talk more next week. I really appreciate your willingness to work with me."

"Any friend of Stuart's is a friend of mine. I'll look forward to hearing from you next week."

"That was easy enough."

Josh pushed the button to call a programmed number.

"Hello."

"Ricky, I'm glad I caught you. I just got an unusual phone call."

"Oh?"

"Stuart and some friend of his that is a broker wanted to talk to me about distribution of Cresent. The friend wants to sell to some of his clients."

"What did you tell him?"

"I told him fine."

"Good. Just slow-walk him," Ricky advised.

"He'll be sending some preliminary information to me Monday."

"Let everything move smoothly up to the point of transferring any stock. Keep me posted."

"Sure thing," Josh accounted.

CHAPTER 47

Stuart settled in and looked around his field of vision. "You've got a great place here, Fast. How long have you lived here?"

"Three years, I guess. Thanks, we enjoy it."

"How long have you been in the investment business?"

"Same three years."

"I never would have figured you for a stock broker, somehow. Do you like it?"

"Yes. It's what I do and I've been fortunate to be in a firm that's well respected. I've got a sort of partnership with another broker inside the firm and we've had good response to some specialized pension work we're doing." Eddie took a swallow of Coca Cola and changed the focus. "Tell me about you."

"It's been unusual for several years. You and I haven't talked through much of it. After Helen and I were first married, I was unemployed for several months. It was actually the result of doing something for the right reasons. I left a relationship with a dishonest man."

"Stuart, I want to ask you something personal...and I have a reason. Did you get angry...at God during that time?" Eddie ventured.

Stuart could tell the question sought more than superficial information. "Yes, I guess...I know I did. I really probably expected some type of reward for my heroic walkout. Instead I had a pregnant wife and no job."

"We lost a fifteen month old to some weird pneumonia. I was not able to deal with it very well at all." Eddie informed with a sigh.

"What changed?" Stuart asked. "I guess that was the reason you had for asking what you did."

"Yes it was, and as for the change, it was real. I finally realized God is God and He has no debt to me. No matter what I do, He is not obligated to reward me, regardless of how good I think I've been."

"That's it, allright. The trouble is, we think we are able to lift ourselves to some level of acceptability...when it's only grace that affords us anything."

"So, how did the unemployment go?" Eddie asked.

"You avoid parties and places where people are going to ask you what you do. Our whole...culture is so hung up about what we do for a living; as if that's the sum and substance of who we are."

"Did Helen work?"

"During the time up until the twins were about here. She pulled our fat out of the fire...and continues to," Stuart honored.

"You mean even now?"

"No, no. Not if you still mean financially. She would, and could, but the need hasn't existed for sometime. I mean the important stuff, like when I can't tell the difference between what's important and what's just phantom worry."

"I learned a lot about Carol when Amy died, too. She's good stock and I'm blessed to have her. I probably wouldn't have had the insight to appreciate her otherwise."

"Gentlemen, I've had it. The twins are down and you two have actually out-talked Carol and me. I'm going to bed."

"Me too," Stuart agreed as he stood. "See you in the morning, Fast."

"Goodnight."

★★★★★

The large chair swiveled slowly back toward the desk and a cigar was removed from its apparitional position to make way for the receiver.

"Hello."

"Ricky?"

"Yeah?"

"You're at the office late."

"Waiting for your call. Where's the plane?"

"El Paso, why?"

"I need a favor. Do you remember our little...resort back east?"

"Why?"

"Tell you later. Do you know the spot?" Ricky inserted.

"Not much chance of forgetting that," he laughed.

★★★★★

The next morning after breakfast, Stuart loaded the car and Eddie ferried everyone back to the service station.

Stuart closed the trunk and turned to grip Eddie's hand. He got a hug instead. "Thanks for the traveler's rest."

"Mi Casa, Su Casa."

With everyone belted in and the car equipped with a new fuel pump, they took their place in the sparse Saturday morning traffic of I-475. Before the perimeter had taken them two miles, Stuart braked rather sharply and checked his rearview mirror.

"What are you doing?" Helen demanded.

"Hang on a second." He veered into the median and came to a controlled stop behind a dual one-ton pickup. "I'll be just a second." He jumped out leaving his passengers speechless.

"KIRK!" Stuart purposely barked in the large man's window.

"OH!....For the love of Pete. You took ten years off my life. What are you doing?"

"Sales call." Stuart walked around the front of the truck and let himself in the passenger side. "Nice ride. Did you buy it new?"

"No other way to do it."

"I didn't know you were up this way. What brings you to middle Georgia?"

"It's not me. I mean I don't even like money. It's those narrow-minded people I owe," Kirk laughed.

"That your rig?" Stuart pointed to the autograder.

"Naw...I'm leasing it. I don't know much about this kind of work, but you've got to dance to the tune that's playing. Just a minute...sit tight, that fool things' under-cutting the grade again." Kirk was on the ground in a flash and left the door open.

The two-way radio static popped and the voice on it cleared "Unit 4 to 1." The static popped again and the radio fell silent. In a moment it spoke again. "Unit 1, come in, Kirk."

Stuart's suspicion was confirmed and he picked up the microphone and pressed the key button with his thumb. "Kirk's on the autograder. I'll tell him to call you when he gets back in the truck."

"There's no rush," the mechanical voice replied.

Stuart hung the microphone in the bracket on the dash. The static popped again, but this time the voice quality was distorted and distant.

"It's me but I'm not coming to the office right now. I've got to go down to Perry first thing. What are you doing in on Saturday, anyway?"

"Well, what are you doing calling if you didn't think I would be?" the unidentified female challenged.

Stuart adjusted the squelch and turned the volume to maximum.

The conversation continued. "I was hoping to catch the old man in. Is he around?"

"Are you kidding?" she teased.

The pause made Stuart wonder if he would hear anymore...even though he was actually eavesdropping.

"Glad to see you working, young man. What can I do for you?" A new, older male voice entered this strange media.

"Check a name. Josh Stinson."

"I know the name. What of it?"

Stuart's ears perked. He scrambled to close the open door and squelch the equipment noise from outside.

"Friend of mine needs to know whatever you can tell us."

"He has been a maverick for a lot of years. Last I heard, he was working for a small brokerage house in the city, I can't remember the name of it, but the owner was some guy in Texas."

"Oil man?" the voice asked. Stuart now realized it belonged to Eddie.

The driver door opened abruptly and Stuart jumped. Kirk quickly cranked the engine and stuck out his hand. "I've got to make tracks to the parts house. You're welcome to hang around till I get back."

Stuart stared at the silent radio. "Uh...no, I'd better get back in the saddle. Thanks."

"Good to see ya, Bubba." Kirk said.

"You too."

Stuart made the way back to his car filled with a family wanting explanation for the median parking job. "Sorry ya'll, I had to stop. That was Kirk that you've heard me talk about. I was going to ask him to come say hello, but it didn't work out that way.

★★★★★

"I specifically don't want to use it, that's all I have to say. Make the necessary arrangements."

"You're the boss, Ricky. I can pull a couple of strings and see what's available."

"No, I'll pull the strings. This is a private matter. It's not exactly what I planned, but no long-term harm can come of it. I am going to reconsider my first objection. Go ahead as you had planned and use it."

"I'll talk to you in a couple of days."

★★★★★

Stuart slowed as he found himself in a bumper-to-bumper line into the Valdosta airport property. They could see the dozens of teams in various stages of unrolling, fanning, buckling and firing big hot-air balloons. A sign pointed to parking up ahead and another one confirmed a question Brooke had already asked.

"Dad, what does tethered mean?" Brooke asked.

"You can ride up in a balloon that is roped to the ground."

"Look at all the different color schemes," Helen pointed out.

"What's the point of all of it...I mean, is it a race or something?" asked Jennifer.

"The point is hobby or fun. I think I remember something about the goal being a set of car keys hanging on a flag pole over at the mall in the big open area where they were landing a couple of years ago."

They found their way to a parking area and began to walk around among the ant hill of activity all independently organized into what would soon be a bouffant ballet a thousand feet high.

Across the same grounds, an impatient pair paced, rather than strolled.

The middle-aged Latin American snapped the toothpick in half and spit the stub out emphatically. "Who would have thought all this nonsense would trap us here?" he complained to his companion.

"It looks crazy now, but once these balloons get up, the patch will be open again. Besides, the more hectic things are, the more difficult it will be to single this plane out. The thing that concerns me is how we are going to nab this guy while he is at large in a town of thirty-thousand with his whole family."

"You just fly the plane. Leave the rest to me. I've got the address of the daughter and description of the car along with pictures of the whole miserable little clan."

"Then lets take a walk, and when the traffic clears, we'll rent a car and move on with the rest of the program."

"Whatever. We can't get in or out now."

They made their way into the crowd and walked from team to team, watching as equipment was assembled and ordered into the magic of lighter-than-air flight. After a half hour or so of wandering, nature called and the dark-skinned pair decided to seek the perimeter of the surrounding trees. Their return trip led them through a large area of parked cars.

"Look at this, man." He was standing dead still with a notepad in his hand.

"What is it?"

"Our man is here."

"Are you sure? That's a pretty common car."

"Hall County tags won't be pretty common here today."

"So, what do we do?"

"First thing is to disable the car in case we can't find him. Then we find him."

"How do we disable the car?"

"You crawl under the front end and snatch the lead off the starter. I'll keep an eye out."

"As a pilot, my twenty/twenty probably qualifies me for that job."

"Just do it."

Once the assignment was completed, the pilot reappeared. His watchman was casually looking at a photograph while he leaned on the fender of Stuart's car. "Take a look at this picture and let's split up. We'll meet here....no, over by that live oak with all the Spanish moss, in exactly thirty minutes."

They dispersed in opposite directions.

★★★★★

"Mom, can we run over there and get a snow cone?"

"I want you to stay with us, Darling." Helen required.

Stuart touched her lightly and no verbal communication was necessary. She looked at him and mildly objected with her eyes, but ultimately consented. "Okay, but be back here in ten minutes."

The trio bolted and raced to the small stand. Helen took the opportunity to be verbal. "I don't like crowds and separated kids. I heard of a family in a theme park that had a two-year-old snatched. They notified the security people and each parent took a gate. The remaining gates were locked. The mother finally spotted the little girl two hours later. Her hair was cut and she was wearing a totally different outfit. The man who had snatched her had also given her something to put her to sleep. She was draped across his shoulder and he was almost out."

Stuart did not roll his eyes, but it was only out of respect for his wife that he didn't.

★★★★★

"I've got 'em picked out," announced the pilot.

"Are you positive?"

"No doubt. The boy has one arm and the wife is a dish, just like the picture. What now?"

"How long before we can take off?"

"No more than an hour."

"Okay, you walk me to our group and then you keep going to the plane. Make whatever arrangements you need to so we can leave as soon as I get my job done."

"It's none of my business, but killing anyone would be insane in this setting. We wouldn't be able to leave if any commotion started."

"You're right, it's none of your business."

★★★★★

"Stuart, I'm going over to that food stand. I don't see all of them."

"Fine. I'm going to stay here. This big one is going to lift off any minute.

Helen walked directly to the end of the stand and found only Jennifer still there. "Where are Eric and Brooke?" she demanded.

"They went over to the guy that is giving rides."

"Where?"

"I'm not sure, but it's in that direction," Jennifer pointed.

"Come on." She grabbed Jennifer's hand and headed for the ride. When she reached the line for the ride, she did not recognize anyone.

"Are you sure they came here?' She glared into Jennifer's eyes.

"That's what they said they were doing."

"Well, where are they?" Helen snapped in her anxiousness.

"Look." Jennifer pointed to the balloon. It was just touching down. Eric was in the basket.

Helen bulldozed the line and grabbed Eric. "Where's Brooke?"

"I dunno, Mom. She was here when we went up. Man, you can see all the way to...."

"Come with me, both of you. Maybe she went back to your father."

Now with a twin by each hand, Helen briskly straight-lined them to Stuart. "Have you seen Brooke?"

"No. Why?"

"Why...why?" Helen echoed herself, "you don't get it, do you?"

"Sweetie, she's fifteen years old. In some cultures, she's an old maid. I'm sure she bumped into a friend from school and they are trying to get up the nerve to talk to some boy who...."

"Stop, stop, stop. Here's the deal. You and I and the twins are going to walk hand in hand to the building they run this airport out of and talk to someone about helping us find Brooke."

He thought she was over-reacting, but did not dare offer anything other than compliance.

The foursome walked into the small office and were greeted by a friendly smile. The middle-aged Latin American stood and beckoned them in.

Helen was the first to speak. "We need to speak to someone about a teenage girl, our daughter. We don't know that she's missing, but we haven't seen her in half an hour."

"Very well. Do you have a picture of her?"

Stuart produced his wallet. "This is less than a year old," he explained as he presented the school picture.

"I know this girl. I mean I just saw her with some young people right out here." He offered them the door and then led them to a line of airplanes. The party came to a stop beside an aero commander of unfamiliar paint and markings. Stuart instinctively looked at the registration number. He turned to the stranger. "I don't see how...."

The plane door opened and he turned to see the pilot. "We can leave any time."

Jennifer gasped and Stuart snatched his head around to see her hand in her captor's grasp. He was holding a serrated four-inch blade across her wrist. Brooke was inside the plane.

"Now, dear Kerrs, you will be my guests on a little trip to a resort you will be sure to enjoy. Now...get in before I bleed this one like a hog at slaughter."

The whole family looked at Stuart. He looked into Brooke's frightened eyes.

"Let's go," he instructed the others reluctantly.

They filed in and took seats. The two captors went into the cockpit and closed the door behind them.

Helen looked at the door and then at Stuart. He leaned toward her and shook his head. "The master switch engages a safety device that makes it impossible to open."

She grasped his wrist. "What is happening to us?"

"I don't have a clue," he admitted.

"I'm scared."

He put his hand on her thigh. "Frankly, I am too, but we should take this time we have in private to consider the situation."

"I don't know what to consider besides the fact we are being kidnapped in a plane that looks like the company's."

The engine whirred and fired and the plane began to taxi.

"Listen," said Stuart. "Let's learn as much as we can. Eric, do you have your pocket knife?"

"Yes, sir."

"Helen, hand me a pen."

She opened her purse. "Here."

He passed it over to Eric. "Is there a magazine or something in here?"

They all scrambled to search seat pockets and under seats.

"I've got one," announced Brooke.

"Find as blank of a page as you can. Jennifer, you and Eric swap seats. I want him to be in the seat with the full window exposure.

"Here's a page with just a one-word advertisement on it."

"Good." Stuart took the magazine and folded it back to put the selected page face up. He handed it to Eric. "Draw a circle about five inches in diameter."

Eric laid his prosthesis on the page and pivoted with the pen like a compass. The circle was almost perfect.

"Now, put the number 0 at the top. Put the number 90 on the right and 180 at the bottom...."

"And the number 270 on the left," Eric interrupted.

"Exactly. Now take your pocket knife and stick the blade through the center from underneath until it extends the full length of the blade."

Eric followed the instructions and held out the finished product. "Now what?"

"Someone give him a sheet of paper to write on."

"Here's an envelope," offered Helen. "It's a birthday card to my dad." Her mouth clinched.

"Don't write on the front, Eric. We'll need to mail that in a couple of days." His eyes reassured Helen. "Okay, do you have on the watch with the 'stop watch' timer?"

"Yes, sir."

"Hold your 'compass' so the sun can hit it."

The shadow of the blade fell across the circle.

"Now, orient it such that the shadow falls on the 270 mark."

"Okay, done."

"I want you to keep the shadow on that mark when we get airborne and out of this field's pattern. You will be recording the time and direction by your stop watch and noting the compass degree heading that would be an imaginary line from your naval through the nose of the plane."

"I got it," Eric assured.

"Now, we can learn within reason where we will be. Let's all discuss why we are going."

Helen shifted so she could see Stuart as the plane left the ground.

"What unusual has happened lately?" Stuart asked.

"That weird night Eric got in trouble at school with those motorcycle guys," remember Jennifer.

"Getting kidnapped today," said Brooke.

"Your whole trip to New York," reminded Helen.

"When do you want me to start timing?" asked Eric.

Stuart looked out of the window. "We're about five thousand and climbing," he observed. "Can anybody still see the airport?"

"No."

"No."

"Then it should be exactly behind us. Start timing now, Eric, and you can make a note when we stop climbing. What is our heading?"

Eric held the magazine level and slightly turned it until the shadow was across the 270 mark. He held it in his right hand and with his hook, placed the pen pointing out from his naval. "The imaginary line would be between 0 and 90."

"Okay, put a point halfway between 0 and 90 and label it 45. Then put a little letter A on the point of the circle that represents our current heading. I will want to know how long we fly heading A."

"Gotcha." He made sure his stop watch was running.

"Now, Sweetie, what do you mean my trip to New York was unusual?" Stuart asked.

"Well, you made a public offering of a company for one thing and it seemed like it took less trouble than you had getting a tag for your car."

"I won't argue that. Now, Jennifer, what was weird about the night Eric had his trouble at school?"

"Those guys were from out of town and that creepy one even knew Eric's name. Don't you think that's odd?"

"Yes, I do, and it caused me to come home a day early from New York."

"And it's weird that this should happen here, in Valdosta," said Brooke. "I mean, who knew we were all going to be together today?"

"have you got another sheet of paper and a pen?"

"I've got a pen and here's a shopping list."

"Write down the names of who knew we were here."

"Kevin, my dad. Eddie found out last night."

"That reminds me. He called Josh from his office and that's not all. Talk about unusual, this morning when I pulled into the median to speak to Kirk, I heard Eddie make a call on his car phone to some older guy in his office. I was actually picking up the signal on Kirk's two way radio somehow."

"Could you hear what was said?"

"Yes, but I'm not sure of the accuracy of it. The older guy told Eddie that Josh's firm was owned by a man in Texas."

"Ricky?" asked Helen.

"He didn't say." Stuart turned. "Note that we've leveled off, Eric."

"Did Ricky know we were coming here?"

"I think so, but I'm not sure. I usually tell a lot of people. Let's speed it up and try to blame Ricky. How does it fit?"

"A lot of 'hard to explain money'," Helen accused.

"I don't think it's that hard to explain. He made it in the shipping business."

"What about this plane?" asked Helen. "How much did you have to do with picking out the company plane?"

"Very little, actually. Ricky did most of the negotiating."

"Don't you think it's unusual that this is identical to the company plane?" she added.

"Yes, I even found myself glancing at the 'N' number."

"What was it?"

"476CS, why?"

"Because ya'll selected the number of the company plane," she reminded.

"You're right, and it is 819CI....which is our street address and CI for Cresent Indemnity."

"Do you think we could be guests of Cresent Shipping?" she wondered.

"Okay, there's enough information to hypothesize Ricky. Now, why and what's next?"

"What does he have to gain?" Helen asked.

"Assuming that the guy talking to Eddie is right, Ricky, at this moment owns seventy-five percent plus one-third of twenty-five percent of Cresent Indemnity, so he can do anything he pleases."

"So long as it's legal," Helen qualified.

"What?" Stuart asked.

"Well, you pose no threat to him as a shareholder, since you are in a minority, but what about the knowledge you have of the business. You would know anything that looked like monkey business right away," she explained.

"I can't imagine him being foolish enough to try something outright illegal."

"Last time I checked, kidnapping was not a merit badge. But, let's think of what he could do that would be hardest to detect."

"In an insurance company, there's nothing lying around but money in different categories," Stuart considered.

"Categories?"

"Same ole stuff...retained earnings and reserves...that's it—reserves. He could siphon the reserves to nothing without much problem if he didn't do it all at once. He knows I would not have supported that. It's needed for claims of the policyholders," Stuart diagnosed.

"But what could you do?"

"I don't know. We are speculating too much."

"Dad, we're turning."

"Okay, get the new heading and stop time on heading A. I think our first move is to escape. I'm not sure who has us, but I have to think anyone desperate enough to kidnap us is not above doing great harm to us," Stuart said looking out the window.

"What else could be done in a company like that to put money in Ricky's pocket?"

"Well it's a stock company, obviously. Stock companies pay profit-driven dividends. If someone owned a tremendous amount of stock, he could do some smoke and mirror tricks with the dividends." He turned to Jennifer. "You said that one of those guys knew Eric's name and they were all or a lot of them from out of town."

"Out of state," she corrected.

"I wonder what in the world anyone could have done to set up a thing like that at school?"

"I, for one, always wondered why our team came up to an empty parking lot a full hour early, even after having a blowout," Helen remembered.

"I hadn't thought of it before, but you're right. The parents should have been waiting on them." He turned to Helen. "I know you were not picking up that night, but where did the information about the game time come from?"

"I can't remember exactly, but how on earth could some bad guy get so involved as to tamper with a school schedule and the game times?"

"Like I said, I'm lost. If we stick to what we know, we still have enough information to run any time we get the chance. So, since we probably will not have a lot of private talk time when we hit the ground, let's set some guidelines. As many as we are, we might be separated, so the first thing we need is a meeting place. It is logical to assume if we are flying in, flying out might be our best bet, so as soon as we land, let's try to identify a safe place to meet that's near the airport."

"How do you know they won't take us to a city or something, miles from the airport?" Helen asked.

"The one that did all the talking said we were going to what he called a resort," Stuart answered.

CHAPTER 48

"Grass strip," Stuart remarked as the wheels touched. "We must be in the boonies."

"Any idea?"

"From Eric's numbers, I'd say West Virginia. Hang on to the envelope, son, we need to get a chance to put it against a sectional chart. Listen, quick. If we get separated and get free, meet at this end of the runway in the trees."

The cabin door opened. "Hope you folks didn't mind flying without a flight attendant."

They all silently began to unbuckle their seatbelts. Eric's knife was in his pocket and the page of the magazine was removed. The plane door opened and the bearded man waited for the prop to stop turning before stepping out. He greeted two other men who were in a jeep. A third led a beautiful black horse. The three were in green camo fatigues and their faces were all business. The Kerr family was instructed to get into the jeep, and "Badger" as he was called by the jeep driver, was handed the reins to the horse. He swung his leg over and situated himself in the saddle.

"Let's move!" Badger instructed.

Stuart watched as the third man walked back to a small hut with a sod roof. He thought of how invisible everything would be from the air. Even the wind-sock by the hut was dull green. The jeep climbed a slight grade and the plane taxied down the strip itself to the downwind end. There it pivoted and headed into the wind before taking off.

The driver smiled with tobacco stained teeth and winked his scarred left eye. "Looks like you folks will be in camp awhile."

"In camp?" Stuart asked.

"Shut up," growled Badger from his horse.

The grade steepened and the meadow like area was tapering toward the dense woods. It looked as though a small roadway went through the trees, but it was still some two hundred yards ahead and difficult to make out. They rode in silence, crouched with pointed knees in the back of the small open air vehicle. A noise from overhead caused everyone to scan the sky.

Badger looked at his watch. "He's not due for two hours. He'll just have to wait."

The plane was a loud, twin engine and Stuart could not tell much about it without turning around on his wheelwell seat in the small space behind the seats. It disappeared behind the hill that now separated them from the small landing strip.

The driver snorted, "This stuff is like glass. What is it anyway?"

"It's been here since they moved the camp here. I don't know what it is," the other man responded.

Stuart kept his knowledge that it was slate to himself. It began to be apparent that this was probably an old mining camp designed to harvest coal from man-size shafts, probably most active around the late 1920's.

Suddenly a loud hissing sound claimed everyone's attention. "I called it; tire's been cut." The driver struck the steering wheel with his clenched fist and nearly cussed the bark off a nearby hemlock.

They began to unbolt the spare from the back in its upright bracket. Stuart stretched his back and stood. "I've got to find a men's room."

"Three minutes. Every minute past that is a finger from the little princess here," Badger said and nodded at Brooke.

Stuart acknowledged with his own nod. He climbed down and walked up to the woods, stepping toward the sound of water running. A few yards into the trees, he came to an old, iron, foot bridge. He walked out a few feet. The hand cables were still in place and all seemed solid. The span was between two sheer bluffs and, barely visible on the other side, was the outline of two gray cabins. His eyes went to the bottom of the tight ravine. A pipe snaked down on the cabin side to a large blue hole. The remains of a ram pump were distinguishable on the bank. Hand drill marks in the rock suggested the miners had dynamited the hole for bathing and water reclamation. He guessed the height from the foot bridge to the water to be twenty feet.

"Four minutes," called the voice.

Stuart walked back with his head high and noticeable inhaled deeply. "Man, I love the mountains."

Badger's face was the testimony of his disgust. "What have you been smoking, Fool. For all you know, we're going to kill you this very day." He turned his attention. "What about the tire?"

"Ready in a minute."

"I don't know," began Stuart. "I'm sure you have your orders. But I'm not dead so I have a lot to be thankful for. Even the little things have gone okay."

"What little things?" the bearded adversary demanded.

"Well, we're riding in this jeep for one thing. Few people are scared of a jeep...but my youngest daughter had a brush with real trouble on a horse sometime back. It terrified her. And, we could have been made to walk across that old bridge to the cabin. My other daughter took a fall that made her scared of heights...the way I see it, things could be worse." He climbed back in and sat down.

"Tire's ready, Badger. We just need to put the flat in the bracket."

"Leave it, Roy." He got off the horse. "Hey, you...Pedro!"

"Me?" the right seat rider pointed to himself.

"Yeah. Get the blonde kid and take a walk. Short cut to the secure cabin."

"Come on, man, this is not necessary," Stuart protested.

"It is necessary for me, Mr. Kerr. You see it is impossible for me to enjoy my day if you are enjoying yours. And you, kid with the bandana, come here." He pointed to Jennifer.

By now, Brooke's arm was in the tight grip of her captor and he was leading her toward the footbridge. "So what in the world will we do with the time when we get to the cabin?" he hissed in her ear. "They will be a half hour behind us," he laughed loudly with his mouth close.

Stuart spoke in Brooke's direction as he watched his daughter being dragged away. "Come on, Badger, that bridge is nearly twenty feet high, and over water." He looked back to see Jennifer being shoved onto the nervous back of the confused horse. Badger laughed, "Now, let's see if we can give you a little riding lesson."

Stuart caught Jennifer's eye and found only question there. "I'm sorry I ran my mouth, little Sparkle. Just remember, timing is everything when you decide to play your trump card."

Jennifer confirmed her suspicions with a knowing look to him and quickly to Brooke on the foot bridge, whose slight nod lit the fuse. She felt her shoulder blades strain to touch each other at her spine. The horse tensed at her thighs' grip, then bolted violently at the instant her heels dug into his sides. Jennifer's confident hands negotiated the reins.

"Stop!" shouted Badger. "Get her!" he ordered.

The man on the bridge released Brooke and started toward the jeep. Realizing the mistake, he turned back to his charge in time to see her vault over the handrail, dive into the air, snap parallel then rotate in time to rip the water's surface.

"Come on, now, Fool," Badger tried to coordinate when he saw his second prisoner vaporize.

The two ran toward the jeep which the driver started. Just as they crossed in front, Eric's hook tore the flesh of the driver's left leg. His reflex jerked his foot from the clutch and the iron green frog jumped into the hips of the startled men. Stuart had a gun in Badger's face in an instant. He scarcely remembered his fist knocking the driver out of the vehicle first.

"I thought you said they were...scared," Badger complained.

"They seemed to have gotten over it," Helen put in with a proud smile.

Stuart turned to her, "Shall we kill all of them?"

"No, just the ones with impure motives."

"Give me your boots...one at a time," Stuart decided.

"Our boots?" Badger questioned.

"If you act now, you can hand them to me without the feet still in them."

They began to pull at the laces and one at a time, tossed the boots to an area beside Stuart's feet.

"Now, take a barefoot stroll across the foot-bridge," he directed with the gun he had acquired. "Wait a minute...those heavy clothes might provide moccasins to devious minds." He turned to Helen. "Sweetie, turn the jeep around and keep your head pointed South. Now, the rest of you, shuck down to your shorts and pile your clothes up right here. When that's done, get across the bridge."

They did as the gun directed and Stuart loaded every article into the jeep. He motioned them on across the foot-bridge and directed Helen to back up close enough to hook the wench cable to one end. When she pulled forward, the opposite end of the I-beam slid free and swung for an instant before its massive load pulled the frayed wench cable from its own hook assembly.

"That ought to create an obstacle," he concluded satisfactorily and the jeep made its way down the rutted roadway. "I guess we better stop down stream a hundred yards or so and see if we can pick up Brooke."

Helen slowed and Stuart jumped. "Stay in with your mother, son," he told Eric.

The bank at this point on their side was only half the height and Stuart stepped into the clearing at the same moment Brooke had decided to climb from the water and make her way by land to their prearranged meeting place. "Hey, Poco," Stuart almost whispered, "how about a ride?"

"Sounds great. Is everybody together?"

"We're missing Jennifer for the moment."

They walked to the jeep and Helen continued backtracking slowly toward the airstrip. "How close?" she asked the question on everyone's mind.

"That's about as close as we dare. The next quarter of a mile should be on foot and close to the trees. See if you can get this thing into those trees before we get out."

"Now," began Helen, "let's pray Jennifer is where we said we'd meet."

"And there is some kind of transportation for us besides this jeep," Brooke added.

"Amen."

They picked a way through the woods that looked to be an old game trail. The bed of evergreen needles carpeted the damp ground and silenced their footfalls. Stuart held up his palm and they all stopped. The sight in front of them caused Helen to gasp aloud, bringing nonverbal admonishment on her by everyone. Closer than they realized was a large airplane and the loose horse grazing about thirty yards out in the open. Three men were unloading the plane onto a utility truck. Further scanning revealed Jennifer lying down at the base of the tree they had pointed out earlier. A bridle hung in the fallen-down fence ten feet behind her. The men seemed unconcerned about the horse.

"What now?" Helen had to know.

"Let's let the crowd thin out some," Stuart delayed.

They watched as the men began walking toward a building.

"Is that all of them?" Helen asked.

Stuart nodded yes.

Stuart's voice was almost reverent, "DC3."

"Can you fly it?"

"I'm supposed to be able to fly the box it came in," he said, his eyes never leaving the old plane. He motioned for Jennifer to join them. "Nice ride, Sparkle."

"Sorry the horse broke loose."

Stuart watched as the truck stopped outside the building. "No problem, Darling. Now," he turned his attention to Eric, "you come with me. The rest of you wait here." When the men in the distance had all disappeared into the building, the father and son team crouched and ran to the plane. Stuart had signaled for Eric to remain on the ground as he lightly vaulted to the trailing edge and on to the walk area of the giant left wing. With his right hand on the fuselage and barely above a crawl height, he made his way to the first porthole sized window. He muttered a simple prayer before peering in. One glance told the whole story. The cavernous body was empty.

He looked over the leading edge and through the great feathered prop to confirm no activity outside the small building. He then turned to Helen's waiting stare and motioned for her to bring the girls as he crabwalked down the wing and jumped to the ground a few feet forward of the double cargo doors. The handle showed frequent use. Helen and the girls were now at his side and he pulled the latch and reached in to push the step assembly out of the way. Dropping to one knee provided a step for first Helen, then the remainder of the group. The door was pulled and latched closed.

"Why are there no seats, Daddy?" Brooke wanted to know.

"Stripped for cargo...I shudder to think what kind," he answered without letting up in his focus to get in the left seat and scan the black instrument panel.

"What is this thing, Sweetie?" Helen looked all around.

"Douglas Commercial 3...Gooney Bird...DC-3. One of the most versatile and serviceable birds to ever fly."

"You sound like you would like to have one," she observed.

"I'd like to BE one," he said quickly as he looked again at the building. "Now, we are not detectable in here, but the minute we crank those Wright SGR-1820-G radials, business is going to pick up fast. The problem is," he said, looking now at the windsock, "we are at the wrong end of the runway."

"Why?"

"This field will be tough enough to handle as short as it is...but with the wind doing ten knots at our back, it puts this into the risky zone. Normally, you would taxi down to the other end and turn around so you could take off into the wind, but I'm afraid we don't have that luxury. They would take that truck and stop us for sure if we just went strolling by."

"So, we wait for the wind to change?"

"Again, we lack the luxury. We will just have to get all we can out of her...."

Helen squeezed his hand. "It's worth a try."

He checked the panel and flipped the master switch to "on". The electronic hum began and he watched as the instruments came to life. "Fuel is perfect...not too full for weight, plenty for a good long ride. This is it," he announced.

First, the right engine, then the left began to spin until the props were invisible and the coughing had stopped. "I'm going to try some flap," he declared as he pushed the throttles to their limits. "Here we go."

The brakes' release gave a gentle lunge and they started up the runway. In just a few yards, he popped the yoke forward and coaxed the tail wheel from the turf. "Good sign," he pointed out as the plane was now level and bearing its full weight on the main gear. The feel of the grass strip was still too detectable to hope the wings were developing any lift. Now two men ran out of the building and looked at each other in confusion.

"Need more," he shook his head.

"Lord, help us," Helen partitioned.

"Dad, could you drop that thing under the belly to lighten the load?"

"What thing?" Stuart's voice was anxious and his eyes searched the panel.

"It looked like a fire extinguisher the size of Jena."

Just then Stuart's eyes locked on the small handwritten letters JATO at the left corner of the panel. "Nice going, POC," he smiled and flipped the switch.

A new and sudden noise was followed by a sharp shove, and the speed began to lightly bounce the plane across the less-than-perfect terrain.

CHAPTER 49

The huge frame rotated and Stuart began an immediate slight left hand bank to work away from the mountains. He breathed out slowly as the stall light flickered, then stayed off. The nose responded to his gentle tug on the yoke and they climbed easily above the trees.

"What was that last switch?" Helen now settled into her seat.

"JATO is what some of these things were fitted with to deal with short runways. It means 'jet assisted take off' and it is actually a bottle under the fuselage."

"Well, I'm for it," she sighed. "Now, where to?"

"I'm not sure what kind of mileage we can get out of this thing but I think we have some unfinished business."

"I was afraid you'd been thinking again. What have you got in mind?"

"I think we have about concluded that Ricky is at the bottom of all this and if he is, there's no way we can stay in bed with him. I don't know what he's planning, but he has been at it long enough to have all his ducks in a row."

"What do you plan to do?"

"I don't know. For now, we have to get back out of here and into more familiar air space. I'm not overly concerned with the way we left things back there. We probably have several hours' advantage on whatever we do, if we do it in a straight line."

★★★★★

"How do you plan to get to Macon without contacting someone?" said Helen.

"I'm hoping to recognize something on the ground. We should have come up over Lake Hartwell. If we can identify that, we could take I-85 to Jefferson and then 129 to Athens. From there, we just go down old Augusta Highway southwest till we get to the first big town that smells like rotten eggs."

"All that road following sounds like cheating."

"Wait, look." He pointed out the windshield. "That small town in those hills. Does it look familiar to you?"

She craned her neck and began to check references. "It could be Brevard, but if it is, where is Ashville?"

"Good point." He looked around for a road out of the small town to see if he could pick up the city. No luck. "We can't be sure, but if this is Brevard, that mountain is Ceasar's Head and I know we'll be able to pick out the lake in a few minutes." He moved the nose slightly right and pinpointed a new heading of 190. "Just a guess," he admitted.

"Why Macon?"

"I'm not sure, Sweetie. I'm afraid we're in a mess that is going to change our lives dramatically. If we can't continue in this relationship, we have to find some way to get out of it without getting shot, going broke, or leaving the policyholders high and dry."

"We've been broke before," she reminded with an assuring smile.

"Are you going for two out of three?" He didn't wait for an answer. "I don't know...I feel like I went to sleep at the switch. It's hard to believe something like this took place right under my nose."

She put her hand on his arm. "Would you rather wake up and realize your children were grown and you didn't know them?" "You've seen all of Brooke's Nutcracker performances. Eric has been camping with you more than he's been to a mall, and just the other day, Jennifer said she hoped she could marry a man just like you. In the game that counts...husband and father, you win."

"Thanks."

Eric leaned forward. "Where are we?"

"Fine thing for you to ask. You're the navigator." Stuart looked at his watch. "We've missed Hartwell by now. Keep your eyes peeled for anything that might help."

"Chicken houses," announced Jennifer.

"Good girl, Sparkle, but I'm afraid that's a bit general even if it does make you feel closer to home."

"Does missing the lake mean that wasn't Brevard?" Helen wanted to know.

"Not necessarily. We aren't sure of the heading from Brevard to the lake and the wind is a factor.

"Look, Daddy. There's a racetrack," pointed Brooke.

Helen leaned out of her seat. "Road Atlanta?"

"No, it's a small oval. That may be Jefferson. The road leading out of it looks good...I think I see Arcade." They flew in anticipation for five long minutes. "Yep, those are the railroad grain elevators and there's the country club coming into Athens. We'll be in Macon in no time."

"Dad, I've got to go to the bathroom," Eric admitted.

"Go to the back of the plane...but wait until we've passed Sanford Stadium."

★★★★★

"What do you mean 'got away'?"

The sheepish look now had the blood drained from it also. "There was a plane here...an empty plane and they stole it. None of us knows where they were going."

"We can't very well call the FAA and report our plane missing." Ricky's hand clinched. "I will hold you, Badger, personally responsible if this ten-year plan sours. The numbers here make me a very anxious man. I will make arrangements for the plane you were in earlier to be there by the time he gets there. Then, you go to Gainesville. The plane he's in will be easy to learn about the minute it hits the ground. Call me the minute you land in Gainesville."

CHAPTER 50

Everyone braced instinctively. The huge tires bounced and resettled to the pavement. Stuart applied the brakes and then throttled the engines to zero. "I was moving faster than I thought."

"Good landing, Sweetie," Helen congratulated.

"Which one? I think I gave you two to choose from."

"We're on the ground. That was the first step. Any idea of step number two?"

"Let's get to a phone."

They taxied to the tiedown line and shut the engines down. Stuart hoped he had not attracted a lot of attention from the airport personnel. Everyone got out and they all walked to the fixed base operator's main building.

"Could I borrow your phone?"

He got Eddie on the phone and requested that he come quickly to pick them up from the airport.

"I'll be there in twenty minutes," Eddie replied.

They hung up and Stuart joined his family in a sitting area. A young man came in and asked for someone to top off his plane. "Who's DC3 is that on the apron?"

Eric started to speak and Stuart caught his eye. They all sat silently. The clerk shrugged his shoulders and the young pilot went out to personally oversee the refueling of his single engine.

"Why didn't you say something, Dad?" Eric asked as the door closed.

"The sooner we can be disassociated from that plane, the better."

Helen leaned over and in a low voice said, "I don't mean to question you, but why are we in Macon?"

"I don't know if they will try to follow us or not, but whatever the reason was for them to kidnap us, it may be sufficient reason for them to do something worse. I want to get away from that plane and on to higher ground. Meanwhile, I'd like a minute to try to figure out what's going on. I don't think they'll look for us here...not right at first, anyway."

"TAXI."

They turned to see Eddie.

He smiled. "Years without so much as a card. Now daily visits. Is it some old guilt you're trying to purge?"

"Thanks, Fast. Let's go."

"You look serious...worse, you look scared."

They all got into the car. Luckily, no one was at the counter when they walked out, so no explanations were necessary about a plane that was lined up but not tied down.

Eddie looked back over his left shoulder to clear the traffic. "So, what's the story?"

"Do you mind going around 475?"

"It's not really on the way, but today is the day for negotiations and not rules. Sure."

"We've had a bad day, Eddie, and we don't know all the whys."

"What are the whats?"

"We were kidnapped and flown from Valdosta to somewhere in the mountains. I think it was West Virginia. We were going to be held there for awhile and I think it has something to do with this recent public offering of our company."

"What makes you say that?"

"This morning, we were on our way to Valdosta, and I saw a friend and policyholder on 475 with his construction crew. I stopped to speak, and while I was in his truck, he had to jump out for a minute. Then something very strange happened. I heard you call your office on your car phone. Fast, I need to meet the man you spoke to this morning. And if my friend is still on his job site, I need to get him to follow us to that meeting. Can you call to see if your man is still there?"

Eddie was already reaching for the phone. In a moment his friend was on the line.

"If it's okay, I'd like to know all he knows about Josh Stinson without telling him anything about my day just yet," said Stuart.

"And the 475 part?" Eddie reminded as they merged into the right line of traffic at the end of the acceleration lane.

"Yes. Do you know where on the bypass all the construction is going on?"

"About three miles ahead."

"When you get there, pull into the median."

"Okay." Eddie's voice showed his open compliance with sarcasm.

The equipment was parked and no sign of activity was evident. Pull in anyway, please," Stuart countered the silent objection.

He got out of the passenger side and walked up to the parked truck. He put one hand on the hood to ceremoniously check the temperature.

A head and shoulder popped out at his feet. "Can I help you, Stu?"

He jumped. Hearing and seeing the unexpected simultaneously, caused him to stumble back. "Kirk, you scared me out of five years."

The large, over-alled contractor stood up beside Stuart. "This old truck's alright I guess." he defended. "I just wrung off the u-joint on the four wheel. The one I got to put in ain't fitting."

"Can you drive it in two-wheel or is the shaft hanging there like a loose tooth?"

"I tied it up with bailing wire to do just that. What's on your mind?"

"I've got a problem, Kirk, and I may be up to my ears in alligators. You might even have a stake in it."

"Okay, what do we do to drain the swamp?"

"Can you follow us a couple of miles to my friend's office?"

"On my way."

The drive to Eddie's office was silent. Stuart was preoccupied with not knowing what he was going to hear or say. They were in the empty parking lot in five minutes.

"Can just the two of us go in for now...I mean to talk to the guy you called?"

"Sure. We can all go into the conference room." Eddie closed his car door behind him. "Come on in," he beckoned everyone. "There are cokes and snacks in the room adjoining the conference room. Please make yourselves at home."

Stuart took Helen by the arm. "You remember Kirk from the convention in Atlanta." They were now at Kirk's truck door.

"Sure. Good to see you."

"You, too, Helen. Hi, kids."

"Hi, Mr. Mayes," the individual voices greeted.

Eddie was holding the open door as they all filed past. "If you don't see it, ask for it," he reminded. "Come this way, Stuart."

Stuart turned to Helen and Kirk. "Fill him in Sweetie, on everything. I'll join you all in a few minutes. Kirk, I'd appreciate your ideas on what Helen is about to tell you."

Eddie and Stuart walked to the end of the building by way of the long hall that seemed too narrow for modern fire codes. Eddie opened the door and led the way into the heavy, richly colored room. The smell of pipe smoke was evident. Stuart locked eyes with the older gentleman as he rose and walked around his desk to greet them. They looked into each other's eyes comfortably waiting to be introduced.

"Stuart Kerr, meet Malcolm MacCauley."

"Sir."

"My pleasure."

Eddie continued, "Malcolm has managed this office since the early fifties."

"Stuart needs your help, Malcolm. When I called you this morning and asked you about Josh Stinson, it was for him. Things have become more serious and I would consider it a favor if you could tell us what you know of him."

Malcolm looked at Eddie while he was speaking. "I made a call or two after you phoned me from your car phone this morning," he began. "I wanted to know who your friend was or might be. The only connection I could make between you and Stinson was an old college roomie from Middle Tennessee who has recently taken an insurance company public. A regional company that just writes workers compensation coverage...mainly for contractors."

Eddie and Stuart smiled at each other. "Think of what he'd be like if he believed in computers," Eddie mocked.

"Anyway, it is just as I thought with Stinson. He is a yes man to the guy in Texas who owns the Broker dealer."

"What guy?" Eddie asked.

"Stuart already knows that by now." Malcolm was looking straight at Stuart.

"I should have known much earlier," he said as his eyes dropped.

"So what's the deal?" Eddie asked Stuart.

"What are my options?" Stuart said ignoring Eddie.

"What are your objectives?" Malcolm countered.

"To keep my family safe and to act in the interest of my policyholders."

Malcolm stood. "Excuse us please, Eddie."

Stuart held up one index finger to Eddie. "Call my office and have my buy/sell agreement faxed. Helen will give you the weekend number and talk to Jo Ann."

The young, tired aviator in his leather flight jacket walked into the small sitting area of the Gainesville airport. "Top off the 172 for me, please. And, could I get you to sign my log book?"

"Sure thing. Headed out right away?"

"Last leg. I started in Augusta, then Macon, now here, and if everything goes well, I'll be sleeping in my own bed in Augusta tonight. This is my last cross-country before my check-ride."

"Anything happening with the weather system around Macon?"

"No, at least not while I was there. In fact, there wasn't much going on around there this evening at all...except for the DC3 which I haven't seen many of."

A dark, closely barbered man of forty came to the counter. "Excuse me, did you say you saw a DC3 today?"

The young pilot smiled as he faced his interviewer. "That's right. In Macon a couple of hours ago."

"Those are rare. Ironically, I represent a restoration effort that has that plane on the list to purchase this year. I would consider it well worth my trip to see it. I wonder if you could answer a few questions about it?"

"I'll tell you what I can."

★★★★★

"Now," Malcolm said, "what do you know for sure?"

"I know for sure that we put a work comp company together a few years ago. The three of us were the only shareholders. The company took on a lot of premium early because of the dissatisfactory situation in the market. Fortunately, we profited to a more than projected degree and were able to almost annually retain a higher risk and therefore, purchasing less and less reinsurance. Before long, we discussed making an offering but could not all agree on it."

Malcolm broke in, "Why could you not agree?"

"I was adverse to risking policyholder claims and shareholders equity all at once. We were not together on the reserves."

"Then what?"

"Recently, it began to seem logical. We had proven solvent and we all wanted to try another state or two and maybe even pick up another line or two. The stock sale would capitalize that and not load us with pure debt. Anyway, several unusual things have occurred in the past couple of weeks, the climax of which is today's kidnapping."

"I presume you suspect Ricky?" Malcolm specified.

"Yes, sir. I do."

"Let's say you're right. What are his objectives now?"

"I need help on that, but control of the company gives him several blank checks. He and I have had disagreements in the past about settlements of claims and distribution of money I felt should be left in reserve. The profit share dividends were another issue, too. This would eliminate any need of those deadlocks that Kevin would not swing vote. Anyway, I don't know the issue of timing, but I would imagine that, too, is key."

Malcolm now walked across the heavy oriental rug and poured a short tier of liquid from the decanter. He reached under the antique sideboard and exposed a small ice maker. After he had dropped several cubes into the glass, he returned to his seat in front of the massive desk. "The new trade agreement with Mexico," he announced flatly, then savored his first mouthful. "NAFTA."

"Of course. The old shipping company," Stuart exhaled. "He can interchange money with no tax liability now that the walls are down."

"He's beaten you, I'm afraid. What about your policyholders?"

"They should have their interest represented."

"How are you going to trap him into that?"

"I'll need to find a lot of cheese to trap a rat like that."

Malcolm stood and said, "Good luck, Stuart."

"Thank you, sir," he accepted uncomfortably and moved toward the door.

"Let me know how things work out."

"Somehow, I feel as though you'll find out yourself," he smiled. Stuart made his way down the hall and into the conference room. The buzz of conversation stopped when he walked in.

"Well?" Helen was the first to speak.

"Where do you want to stay tonight?" Stuart asked calmly.

Eddie cocked his head. "I didn't think it was a good idea to stay with me, so I called and got you a hotel room."

"Thanks. That's probably smart."

"So," Kirk boomed, "What's the story?"

Stuart sat down at the conference table. "I'm afraid we've been had. It seems that one man now controls well over fifty-one percent of the stock in Cresent Indemnity."

"I take it you don't trust this man," Kirk continued.

"Lately...no."

"Write me with another company and I'll cancel my Cresent policy. And, I'll put out a letter to the Association to go with another company."

"The reason we formed Cresent is because the market was in such a mess for work comp. I don't see it any better now."

"So, how can we force this guy to do right?"

"Kirk, can you form a group of about a dozen contractors that you can trust with anything?"

"Probably."

"How would you like to own, as a group, one third of twenty-five percent of Cresent? That's our, Helen and I...our present ownership."

"I don't know about raising the money to pay for it."

Stuart turned his attention to the faxed pages on the table. "I see Jo Ann faxed the buy-sell agreement. Let's see...yeah, here it is. 'The stock held by each share holder is agreed to be unrestricted and...blah, blah' more legalcase. So, I remembered, I did not have to offer this to Ricky or even Kevin. The fact is, I can sell it to you for any price I set, and I choose to sell it to you for...." he looked at Helen and she nodded consent, "one dollar."

Kirk sat for a moment. "I give you my word if it is ever sold, the money will go to you or your family; full price."

Helen cleared her throat. "How will that help?"

"I'll write a letter for Kirk to the Securities Exchange Commission and one to the Insurance Commissioner, putting them on notice of concerning activities of the company. Even Ricky will have his hands full dealing with a dozen contractors who are his policyholders as well as his shareholders. Hopefully, we can get the regulatory people to keep him under a microscope." Stuart said, standing, "Let's adjourn."

Kirk shook his hand. "How will you come out of all this?"

"I don't know. I think I just want to disappear for a few days."

Eddie walked beside him to the door. "This is the name of the hotel. I think you'll like it. Is your Series 7 still valid?"

"Yeah," he answered without thinking.

They got into the car and drove to the hotel.

"Without luggage, this check-in stuff is a breeze," Stuart said in an upbeat voice as they got on the elevator.

"So now what?" asked Helen.

"I think, in order to be safe, we should fall out of existence for a while. As for the house, and cars and everything, we can be thankful there is no debt on anything. I think I would like to consider another line of work." They were at their room now.

"Like what?" Helen asked calmly.

He sat on the edge of the bed closest to the wall. "I don't know... you remember when we thought about seminary?"

"Yes. The money held us back as I recall."

"Hard to tell how broke we are now. But, at least, we have time as an ally and not as an enemy. We could liquidate and probably live in a lesser situation for a couple of years without income if need be."

"I know it sounds strange, but I feel...."

The phone rang and Stuart slid down to answer it. "Hello. Oh hi, Eddie."

As soon as he hung up with Eddie, Stuart asked for everyone's attention.

"Do you remember when I got my broker's license?"

"Sure," Helen said.

"Eddie just informed me that what I did today was a broker transacted sale and fully commissionable. He further has cleared with his manager to pass all the commission to us."

"Do I have to ask the amount?"

"Two hundred and twenty-seven thousand dollars," Stuart said in disbelief.

Helen looked down at the key in her hand and laughed at it.

"What?" he asked.

She held up the key for him to see.

"So? Room number 828."

"No, look closer," she now pointed. "RM828. That is the abbreviation for Romans 8:28."

Brooke walked between them and recited, "All things work together for good for those who love the Lord and are called according to His purpose."